More praise for
UNNATURAL SELECTION

"No one does it better than Aaron Elkins . . . Elkins has assembled most of the elements of the classic whodunit: an isolated locale, a panoply of suspects, an unlikely criminal, and a quirky detective. Add to these a glimpse into the world of forensic anthropology, and you have a novel that . . . will satisfy your craving for genteel entertainment." —*The San Diego Union-Tribune*

"The forensic accuracy is admirable, and the plotting compelling." —*Booklist*

"Aaron Elkins triumphs again . . . Elkins draws his characters with a fine brush, taking ample time to create texture and depth, doing so with an extremely dry sense of humor . . . A book about a character and a subject readers will long remember." —*The Mystery Reader*

"As always, a new Gideon Oliver mystery is worth celebrating . . . Watching Gideon solve the case using his unique methods is always entertaining. I can't wait for the next in the series." —*The Romance Reader's Connection*

"[A] neat mystery." —*Kirkus Reviews*

"A well thought-out mystery and the killer is the last person anyone would expect." —*The Best Reviews*

continued . . .

WHERE THERE'S A WILL

"Elkins's writing skills are superb, his research impeccable, and his plots intriguing. [He] has established himself as a master craftsman."
—*Booklist*

"The whole world is Gideon Oliver's playing field in Aaron Elkins's stylish mysteries about a globe-trotting forensic anthropologist." —*The New York Times Book Review*

"[Elkins's] science is for real and his writing is brisk and entertaining. Oliver is one of the best characters in all of contemporary mystery fiction." —*Oregon Statesman Journal*

"Fabulous . . . [a] first-rate who-done-it . . . a fine tropical mystery."
—*Midwest Book Review*

GOOD BLOOD

"First rate! Elegant, ingenious, and beautifully crafted."
—Sue Grafton

"Elkins has long been a top-rank writer and it's always a pure delight when he brings out another book."
—Earl Emerson

"Elkins's eleventh mystery shows the forensic anthropologist in fine form . . . The forensic facts Elkins chooses to include and the brisk pace of the plot make for a total success." —*Publishers Weekly*

"Aaron Elkins's 'skeleton detective,' Gideon Oliver, can't even take a vacation without bumping into bones. Thank goodness. Otherwise we would not have *Good Blood* . . . Mr. Elkins never fails to enlighten and entertain . . . His only failing is that he makes us wait too long between books." —*The Washington Times*

UNNATURAL SELECTION

AARON ELKINS

BERKLEY PRIME CRIME, NEW YORK

THE BERKLEY PUBLISHING GROUP
Published by the Penguin Group
Penguin Group (USA) Inc.
375 Hudson Street, New York, New York 10014, USA

Penguin Group (Canada), 90 Eglinton Avenue East, Suite 700, Toronto, Ontario M4P 2Y3, Canada
(a division of Pearson Penguin Canada Inc.)
Penguin Books Ltd., 80 Strand, London WC2R 0RL, England
Penguin Group Ireland, 25 St. Stephen's Green, Dublin 2, Ireland (a division of Penguin Books Ltd.)
Penguin Group (Australia), 250 Camberwell Road, Camberwell, Victoria 3124, Australia
(a division of Pearson Australia Group Pty. Ltd.)
Penguin Books India Pvt. Ltd., 11 Community Centre, Panchsheel Park, New Delhi—110 017, India
Penguin Group (NZ), 67 Apollo Drive, Rosedale, North Shore 0745, Auckland, New Zealand
(a division of Pearson New Zealand Ltd.)
Penguin Books (South Africa) (Pty.) Ltd., 24 Sturdee Avenue, Rosebank, Johannesburg 2196,
South Africa

Penguin Books Ltd., Registered Offices: 80 Strand, London WC2R 0RL, England

This is a work of fiction. Names, characters, places, and incidents either are the product of the author's imagination or are used fictitiously, and any resemblance to actual persons, living or dead, business establishments, events, or locales is entirely coincidental. The publisher does not have any control over and does not assume any responsiblity for author or third-party websites or their content.

UNNATURAL SELECTION

A Berkley Prime Crime Book / published by arrangement with the author

PRINTING HISTORY
Berkley Prime Crime hardcover edition / June 2006
Berkley Prime Crime mass-market edition / July 2007

Copyright © 2006 by Aaron Elkins
The Edgar® name is a registered service mark of the Mystery Writers of America, Inc.
Cover art by Dan Craig.
Cover design by Steve Ferlauto.

ISBN: 978-0-425-21605-7

BERKLEY® PRIME CRIME
Berkley Prime Crime Books are published by The Berkley Publishing Group,
a division of Penguin Group (USA) Inc.,
375 Hudson Street, New York, New York 10014.
The name BERKLEY PRIME CRIME and the BERKLEY PRIME CRIME design
are trademarks belonging to Penguin Group (USA) Inc.

PRINTED IN THE UNITED STATES OF AMERICA

10 9 8 7 6 5 4 3 2 1

Acknowledgments

As usual with my books, there is plenty of blame to go around, primarily to my old friends, the eminent scientists of the Mountain, Desert, and Coastal Forensic Anthropologists Association, who continue to permit me to attend their annual "bone bashes," even though they know full well that I'm there with theft expressly in mind. For *Unnatural Selection*, I owe thanks in particular to Walt Birkby and Stan Rhine for their patient management of my continuing education in forensic anthropology; to Krista Latham for answering my questions on DNA and making the technology almost comprehensible; and to Bruce Parks for keeping me honest on autopsy procedure.

It was a landmark paper by Curtis Wienker of the University of South Florida, Tampa that served as the kernel from which *Unnatural Selection* grew, and Dr. Wienker then provided counsel to make sure I got it straight. Adela Morris of the Institute for Canine Forensics and her dog Rhea were my enthusiastic guides on all matters canine. My fellow writer, fellow anthropologist, and friend Brian Fagan kindly read the manuscript to help me eliminate the more egregious awkwardisms in my rendition of Britspeak.

In England, Sergeant Alan Mobbs and Sergeant Tom Holmes, both of the Devon and Cornwall Constabulary, were my consultants on local law enforcement, and Amanda Martin of the Isles of Scilly Museum was also generous with her help.

The Star Castle that is owned in the book by Vasily Kozlov is really there, but Kozlov isn't. The sixteenth-century fortified structure continues its existence nowadays as St. Mary's premier restaurant-hotel, and I wish to thank Robert Francis, its managing director, for his hospitality and his ready agreement to permit murder on the premises—with the provision that I didn't kill anybody via restaurant-induced food poisoning.

ONE

The Selway-Bitterroot Wilderness, Montana
August 28, 2002

FOR six days and nights she had roamed, feverish and disoriented, drinking little and eating next to nothing. A few fibrous tree mushrooms, some ants and cutworms she had slashed from rotting logs, a wilting patch of skunk cabbage, the already scavenged corpse of a baby elk she had stumbled across. But where were the berries she depended on, the sweet, juicy, nutrition-rich blackberries and huckleberries that would sustain her through her long winter sleep? Always before there had been berries. She would gorge on them for weeks on end through the long, warm, sunny fall afternoons. This year, what few there were were shriveled and hard.

And the trails and the markers, what had happened to them? Where were the trees whose bark she had clawed to mark her territory? Where were the worn, well-known paths she had trodden her whole life, back to the time when she and her brothers had wrestled and play-growled on them at their mother's side? They had been there forever, and then one day she had awakened from a nap and every-thing had changed. Smells, sights, sounds, places—all new and frightening. Nothing was familiar. How could that be?

These were not thoughts and questions in her mind, for her mind could not form thoughts or questions, but in some dim recess of her brain she was aware that things were not as they were supposed to be, as they had always been. She knew too, if "knew" was the right word, that she was in pain, but she had forgotten the fall down the cliffside that had splintered her humerus and driven its jagged ends into her flesh, and she understood nothing of the fever and the raging infection that had spread through her bloodstream from it.

What she knew—all she knew—was: hunger; thirst; pain; confusion.

On the seventh morning, dazed and starving, following smells she had never encountered before, she limped heav-ily into a clearing and sensed at once the utter alienness of the place. In it were objects she had never seen, never imagined. She stood perfectly still, at the very edge of the forest wall, into the protection of which she could escape if she had to, her snout lifted, sniffing the alluring, alarming odors.

On the far side of the space, beyond the jumble of unfa-miliar things in the center, an amazing creature appeared; the only being she had ever seen, other than her own kind, that could stand on its hind legs. The creature made tenta-tive sounds.

"Oh, wow. Hey, you. Shoo."

The bear too reared nervously onto her hind legs to see the strange thing better, to sniff better at its scent. Was this a threat, an enemy? Was it food? She threw back her head and loosed the fierce, long, huffing roar that was half-uncertainty, half-belligerence.

The smaller creature shrank back, made more sounds. "Oh, my God! Doug . . . *Doug*! Where's the—"

It was food, the she-bear decided. She dropped onto her three uninjured legs and loped painfully, purposefully toward it.

The Missoula Messenger, August 31, 2002

CANADIAN COUPLE KILLED, PARTIALLY EATEN BY GRIZZLY

Bill Giles
The Associated Press

Selway-Bitterroot Wilderness, MT—In a horrific incident at Lost Horse Creek campground, on the Idaho–Montana border about forty miles southwest of Missoula, two campers were attacked and killed Wednesday morning by a marauding grizzly bear.

The dead are Douglas Edward Borba and his wife, Mary Walker Borba, both twenty-six-year-old graduate students in environmental sciences at McGill University in Montreal. In an ironic twist of fate, the Borbas were in the Wilderness as part of a preliminary study to assess the ecological impact of the recent restoration of grizzlies to the area. Accompanying them was the director of the study, J. Leonard Kazin, 50, an associate professor at the university, and two other students, Edward K. Jekyll and Elise Martineau. Mr. Kazin was unharmed, as were Mr. Jekyll and Ms. Martineau, who had both gone to Darby for supplies at the time of the incident.

The attack occurred shortly after dawn on August 28, said Selway-Bitterroot Wilderness spokesperson Dawn Grisi in a prepared statement. "The bear apparently attacked without provocation. To our knowledge, this is the first time that a grizzly bear has fatally attacked humans in the Wilderness."

Kazin, sleeping in a separate tent, was awakened by the sounds of screams and scuffling and emerged to find Mr. Borba frantically punching at the bear, which was hunched over the prostrate form of his wife. Kazin saw the bear slap at Borba, sending him several feet through the air and apparently fracturing his skull and shoulder blade.

"I ran back into my tent and got the pepper spray," said a distraught Kazin, clad in a borrowed ranger uniform, "but by then the bear was gnawing at Mary's body and you could see that she was beyond help by then. I was able to drag Doug a few yards away, but I think he was already dead, too. There was just nothing I could do. I tried calling 911 but the damn cell phone wouldn't work. I'm telling you, there was absolutely nothing I could do to help them. I feel terrible. But all I could do was grab my shoes and trek on out to the pickup and drive back up to Darby, to the West Fork Ranger Station, to tell them what happened. I was in my underwear. I still don't have my own clothes."

When rangers arrived at the scene they found both bodies partially eaten. They were able to track the radio-collared bear for a quarter of a mile, then shoot it.

"Doug and Mary were the cream of the crop of our grad students," Kazin told this reporter. "Mary was on her way to becoming a topflight ecologist, following in her father's footsteps, and Doug had already been offered a lecturer slot on the faculty for next year. It's not only an awful personal tragedy, it's a terrible loss to science."

The incident is sure to inflame the ongoing controversy over the federal plan to gradually restore the Selway-Bitterroot Wilderness's grizzly bear population. An earlier proposal by the Fish and Wildlife Service was scrapped in 2001 in the face of opposition from the governors of Idaho and Montana, and from citizens' groups citing danger to humans and domestic animals.

However, a modified version of the plan was reintroduced and partially implemented earlier this year, largely due to the campaign spearheaded by prominent wildlife advocate and author Edgar Villarreal (*Wild No More: America's Vanishing Wilderness Heritage*), who twice appeared before committees of Congress in support of the program. The dead bear's collar identifies it as one of the initial group of five taken from the North Cascades in Washington State and resettled in Selway-Bitterroot earlier this month.

"Grizzly bears, like other bears, generally avoid humans," spokesperson Grisi said in a prepared statement. "Attacks on human beings are extremely rare. Since 1970, they have averaged only one a year in the entire United States, mostly to hunters, and mostly nonfatal. We are assuming that this particular animal may have been maddened with pain as the result of a recently broken and infected leg, and also may have been starving due to this year's extremely dry local conditions, which have virtually destroyed the area's berry crop. The National Park Service offers its sincere condolences to the families and will do everything possible to ensure that no such incident occurs in the future."

Villarreal, contacted at his home in Alaska, said that the incident was "unfortunate" and declined further comment.

T W O

Penzance, Cornwall, England
Three Years Later: June 10, 2005

YOU'D have to go a long way to find another town with the historical appeal of Penzance. Not that there's much to see that's over a couple of hundred years old, but most of what there is, is to be found in its charming and atmospheric old inns and pubs. Julie and Gideon Oliver, being eager students of history and keen trenchermen as well, had spent a large and enjoyable portion of their day immersed in historical-culinary research. Fish-and-chips lunch at the tiny, crooked Turk's Head on Chapel Street ("the oldest building in Penzance, circa 1231"); pre-dinner pints at the Union Hotel up the block ("Here was news of Admiral Nelson's great victory at Trafalgar, and of his tragic death, first received in England"); and dinner down at the waterfront, at the salty old Dolphin Inn ("Where tobacco was smoked in England for the first time").

They were in the Dolphin now, or rather outside it, at

one of the wooden trestle tables in the front courtyard, overlooking the docks, where work-stained commercial fishing vessels bobbed side by side in the oily water, and rusting, mysterious machinery stood as if abandoned along the stone quay. Their meal of beef-and-mushroom pie had gone down well, and the after-dinner coffee was doing the same. Relaxed and full, getting sleepy in the slanting evening sunlight, Gideon was contentedly watching the ferry *Scillonian III* disgorge its load of tired foot passengers from the Isles of Scilly, forty miles off the coast. Tomorrow he and Julie would be taking the same ferry the other way, for a weeklong stay on St. Mary's, the largest and most settled of the little-known archipelago.

Julie, in the meantime, was absently browsing in the *International Herald Tribune*, occasionally citing something that she thought might catch Gideon's interest.

"Oh, look," she said, "they found Edgar Villarreal."

"Found him? He's not dead after all?"

"No, he's dead, all right," she said, continuing to read. "I mean they finally found his remains. He—" She suddenly sat up straight. "Oh, my God, he was eaten by a grizzly bear! Can you believe that? Isn't that bizarre?"

"Not much of a way to go."

"No, I mean . . . a *bear*? Remember, when that couple was killed in Montana—"

"The Borbas."

"And Edgar just . . . What did you say?"

"The Borbas. That was their name."

"Amazing." She lowered the paper. "Now why would you remember something like that? It was three years ago."

"It's a gift, I suppose. An infallible memory. Comes in handy in my line of work."

"Yes, well, I wish your gift would kick in once in a while when I ask you stop for milk or veggies on your way home."

"Well, you know, it comes and goes," he said, smiling. "What were you saying about Villarreal?"

"Well, when those people, the Borbas, were killed, people pretty much blamed him for bringing the grizzlies back—didn't one of the families sue him?—and he just shrugged it off." She mimed a mock yawn. "*C'est la vie*, one of those things."

"I remember, yes. It did seem a little cold-blooded."

"A *little*! Brr. And now the same thing's happened to him. It's almost like . . . fate. Just desserts."

"I see what you mean. And some people say there's no such thing as poetic justice."

"But it's not only that, it's just that fatal grizzly bear attacks are practically nonexistent these days. They just don't happen anymore."

Gideon nodded. Julie was a supervising park ranger at Olympic National Park, back home in Port Angeles, Washington, and she knew whereof she spoke. "I may be wrong," she said, "but I'm pretty sure the last people killed by grizzlies in North America—outside of Alaska, anyway—were those same two people in Bitterroot. And maybe a couple of deaths in Alaska since then, no more. And now Edgar. It's—I don't know, it's almost too much of a coincidence."

"That is weird, all right," Gideon agreed. "How do they know that's what happened to him?"

"Well, there isn't much here . . ." She folded the paper back and read aloud: " 'The remains of the American author and activist, who had not been seen since failing to return from his remote bear-research base camp ninety miles east of Anchorage in August 2003, were discovered in a bear den less than a mile from the camp. They were identified as human by Dr. Leslie Roach, consulting police surgeon for the Alaska State Police post at Talkeetna, who determined that the fragments were approximately two to three years old and had been through the digestive system of a bear.' " She shuddered. "Can you really tell that from the bones?"

"Oh, yes," Gideon said, "if you know what you're doing."

She continued reading. " 'There is little doubt that they are the remains of Mr. Villarreal," said state police sergeant Monte Franks. "There's no one else it could conceivably be.' "

"Hm," Gideon said.

"Hm, what?"

"Hm, nothing, just 'hm.' "

"No, when you say 'hm,' it must mean something. What is it?"

"Julie, I'm a professor. I'm supposed to go around saying 'hm.' It's expected of me."

She looked at him, her dark, pretty, close-cropped head tilted to one side. "Hmmm," she said doubtfully.

Gideon laughed. "Anything else in the article?"

She went back to reading aloud. " 'Mr. Villarreal, a resident of Willow, Alaska, was often cited as a modern American success story, the son of Cuban migrant citrus workers in Florida. He worked alongside them from the time he was five years old. Contacted today, his agent, Marcus Stein, said: "At seventeen this guy was still picking oranges down in Dade County, barely speaking English. At forty he was one of America's most respected and best-known environmentalists. He was one hell of a guy." Mr. Villarreal was, however, also a controversial figure whose vigorous, blunt defense of the wilderness and of wilderness animals had embroiled him in controversy many times over the years. He leaves no immediate relatives.' "

She folded the paper. "That's it."

The check had come while she had been talking, and Gideon laid the amount on the table. "So," he said. "Can I interest you in a sunset walk along the Promenade?"

"Does it come with a Cornish clotted-cream ice cream cone?"

"But of course."

"I know it's awful of me to say it," she said soberly as they arose, "but this year's meeting will be a lot more . . .

well, civil, relaxed . . . without Edgar's being there, if you know what I mean."

"Mm," Gideon said.

" 'Mm'? Is that different than 'hm'?"

"A minor dialectical variant."

THE meeting of which they spoke, and the reason for their being in this remote corner of England, was the Consortium of the Scillies, the wonderfully inaptly named brainchild of American multimillionaire and noted eccentric Vasily Kozlov. Kozlov, who had come to the United States from the Soviet Union as a non-English-speaking twenty-eight-year-old, had struggled his way through evening high school and community college in only five years, and then gotten a job as a low-level laboratory technician in the research division of a soap and detergent company in New Jersey, where he'd worked for nearly five years. In his spare time, the brilliant, inquisitive Kozlov had come up with a revolutionary way of determining the surface tension of liquids by measuring the reflected variance of light intensity at different points on the surface. When he had offered to sell his method to the company, the chemists who were his superiors had laughed off the skinny guy with the wild hair, the two-year degree, the mad-Russian accent, and the grandiose ideas. Kozlov had quit his job, moved back in with his parents in Brooklyn at the age of thirty-eight, and spent the next several years refining his technique and trying to sell it to other companies and to the United States government. But he had been baffled and frustrated by bureaucratic red tape and scientific indifference.

An uncle who owned a Russian bakery chain had come to his rescue, offering to back him in return for a share of the profits, if any. Kozlov had jumped at the chance, and within a year he had turned out his first prototype. Two years after that the company he'd originally worked for came back, hat in hand, to apply for a license for its use. And in another ten years every major detergent maker and toothpaste producer in Europe and the United States was using the Kozlov method in their research and production departments. Not long after, this gifted foreigner of little formal education, working in his own laboratory, developed a new, non-petroleum-based surfactant that had the detergent-makers lining up on his doorstep all over again.

By the age of fifty-five, Kozlov was an extremely rich man. He was also a confirmed iconoclast, with a ferocious disdain for the scientific and bureaucratic establishments. A three-time divorcé, but still a romantic through and through, he sold out to his uncle, bought a dry-moated, sixteenth-century castle high on a hill on St. Mary's Island, and retired to live out his days in brooding, baronial splendor. This lasted the restless and intellectually curious Kozlov all of two months, by which time he had developed an interest in natural history, devoting himself with typical Kozlovian intensity to the particular study of the abundant mosses and liverworts to be found in the unusually temperate climate of the Scillies.

In a year he'd learned all there was to know, or all he wanted to know, about the habits of *Telaranea murphyae* and *Lophocolea bispinosa* and their kind. Restless and bored, feeling himself getting old before his time, he cast about for a way to marry his newly awakened interest in the natural environment and his old anger at and contempt for bureaucracy and academia. What he came up with was the funding of an ongoing forum for the practical, realistic consideration of conservation and biodiversity issues—something that would be completely outside the obstructiveness and foot-dragging of government and academic scientists. Thus was born the Consortium of the Scillies. (When his attorney had delicately suggested that the name was perhaps not all it might be, Kozlov had scratched his head and replied in his mangled

English: "Is better—Scilly Consortium?" The attorney had let it go.)

The consortium was to consist of five to seven Fellows, personally chosen by Kozlov from applications submitted to him, with a decided preference toward people that he recognized as blood-brothers: mavericks, firebrands, and, most important, "self-made" men and women. They would also be expected to be capable of "civilized discourse with those who might disagree with them." (He had made it clear that he meant this at the very first convocation in 1995, when two Fellows got into a shouting match over the role that cow flatulence played or didn't play in global warming. The disgusted Kozlov had thrown them both out.)

Participants would meet twice, two years apart. The first weeklong meeting would be to review current issues and refine subjects for subsequent monographs by individual members. Two years later, they would formally present their papers, with discussion following. The papers, along with the discussions, would then be published as the *Transactions of the Consortium of the Scillies*. A new group of Fellows would be chosen for the following two-year cycle, and so on.

The sessions would be at Kozlov's castle on St. Mary's, where participants would also live and dine. All expenses would be covered, and there would be a $50,000 stipend out of Kozlov's own pocket, to be presented when their papers were delivered and accepted at the second meeting. With stipulations like these, there was no shortage of applicants. Right from the start, the biannual *Transactions*, with their offbeat, unorthodox views and conclusions, had created a stir in the media that gladdened Kozlov's heart, despite their being received with amused derision in mainstream conservation circles.

Having begun in 1995, the consortium was now in its fourth incarnation, and had changed little, except that Kozlov, responding reluctantly to mainstream criticism, now included one or two token "establishment" participants in the mix. The current consortium had two such members. One was Liz Petra, an archaeologist with the State of New York, who had years ago taken a couple of courses with Gideon and whose specialty was "garbology," the study of populations through analysis of their waste products and refuse. The other, amazingly enough, was Julie. She had sent in her application mostly as a lark—it was understood that her $50,000 stipend would go to the National Park Service in any case—but the paper she proposed to research and write, an assessment of changing wildfire management policies, had caught Kozlov's interest. And so here she was, with Gideon along for the ride.

The first of the two meetings, two years earlier, had come during finals week at the University of Washington, making it impossible for him to come with her. This time the quarter was over, and so here he was too, proud of his wife and quite content to be playing the unaccustomed role of accompanying spouse.

THE Penzance Promenade is actually the top of the nineteenth-century, block-cut-stone seawall, with a wide shingle beach on one side and the old town sloping up away from it on the other. They had walked its length, from Battery Rocks, past the Victorian-era Jubilee Swimming Pool and the public gardens, and down the long row of seaside hotels, guest houses, and restaurants, to the curve in Mount's Bay, where town, seawall, and promenade all peter out. It's a nice walk at sunset, when the massive granite blocks underfoot look golden and the air itself has a burnished, Victorian feel to it, and it tends to make walkers reflective.

"It's not that Edgar didn't have something valuable to add," Julie mused as they sat on the last of the benches, finishing their ice cream cones, "but, well, he was one of those people who just sucked the oxygen out of the room. I remember, at dinner sometimes, when he'd leave early, it was as if this glowering black cloud had lifted."

"I know. I've seen him on TV panels once or twice," Gideon said. "Kind of a bully, I thought."

"I'd say most people who had anything to do with him would agree with that."

"Also very taken with himself—the handsome, brooding defender of the wilds."

"That, too. Definitely."

"Come on, let's head back," Gideon said.

Strolling eastward on the promenade brings with it the famous view of St. Michael's Mount, the great, castle-topped medieval stone pile sitting in isolated glory far out in Mount's Bay, and for a few minutes they walked toward it in silence, watching it turn from amber, to pale straw, to flaming orange as dusk settled in.

"Gideon," Julie said after a while, "are you going to sit in on any of the sessions? Vasily would love for you to participate. He told me so in the last e-mail. He really respects you."

"If I sit in, would he stop charging me twenty bucks a day?"

They both laughed, but it was a fact. Kozlov, generous as he might be in some respects, was a penny-pincher in others. Fellows were welcome to bring partners to the meetings, but additional food and lodging charges of twenty dollars a day ("to pay for extra work-staff peoples") would be applied.

"He just might," Julie said.

"Even so, I think I'll pass. I have some work with me, and I also want to get over to the outer islands to see the Bronze and Iron Age sites, and then—"

"No, really, why won't you?"

Gideon hesitated and shrugged. "I just don't think I'd be comfortable getting involved. It doesn't sound like my kind of thing." He was treading carefully. Julie was naturally delighted to be a Fellow, and Gideon was delighted for her; the last thing in the world he wanted to do was to rain on her parade.

"I don't understand why not. 'Issues in Biodiversity and Conservation Biology.' I'd think it would be just your cup of tea."

"Well, the thing is . . . you know, I looked at the participants' bios, and frankly, I wasn't exactly bowled over by them."

"These are pretty capable people, Gideon. Vasily's a little eccentric, yes, but he's a certified genius, and he didn't pick a bunch of wackos."

"I know that. But except for Liz, there's not a single Ph.D. in the crowd, and her degree's in archaeology, with a specialty in garbage."

"What about Rudy Walker, your old buddy from the University of Wisconsin? You said he was smart."

Rudy Walker was the one other member of the consortium that Gideon knew personally, although it had been many years since they'd been in touch. The two of them had been research assistants at Wisconsin when they were working on their doctorates. Rudy was seven or eight years the elder—he had gotten a medical discharge from the Army after shattering both wrists during the invasion of Grenada, and he'd had a wife and a five-year-old daughter. He had taken the younger, greener Gideon under his wing. They had worked together, with Rudy as the senior assistant, on an important but grisly project for their major professor: injecting dyes into the soft, developing bones of aborted fetuses of varying known ages to determine the exact progression of skeletal formation. Despite the morbid hours in the lab (windowless and underground, to avoid offending the sensitive or the delicate-stomached), Gideon remembered his years at Wisconsin as a happy time of much laughter and much learning. This was thanks largely to Rudy. There had been so many late-night pizzas at the Student Union, so many pitchers of beer, so many abstruse, hilarious, academic arguments with Rudy and his equally vibrant young wife Fran, another anthropology grad student. A great time, looked back upon with pleasure.

And yes, Rudy was smart, all right.

"He got his Master's—with honors—but never did get his doctorate," Gideon maintained. "I went on to Arizona for mine, and Rudy went to Penn State, but he quit before he finished—never took his comps, never did a dissertation—to take a job with some private college up in Toronto, and there he stayed. Apparently never finished up. No Ph.D. on his bio."

"Oho, now we're getting down to brass tacks. Only Ph.D.'s meet your high standards of discourse, is that it?"

"If the subject is as complex as biodiversity and the people talking about it expect to be taken seriously—yes."

"Gideon, has anyone ever told you you're an intellectual snob?"

He laughed. "Not since last Friday. Look, let me put it this way. As smart as some of these people might be—and I grant you, Kozlov himself is a bona fide genius—they don't have the advantage of a thorough, rigorous, scientific education. Okay, they know a lot, but, like anybody who's 'self-made,' they're also bound to have gaps—misapprehensions, misconceptions—that they don't even know they have because they've never been tested, they've never been required to learn material they don't feel like learning, and they've never had to put together a dissertation to the satisfaction of a highly critical committee."

"So?"

"So you know me; if I'm sitting there and I hear some typical misunderstandings, say about the mechanics of evolution or natural selection, getting thrown around as if they were good science, I'm not sure I could control myself."

"You might go into lecture mode, you mean."

"Exactly, the dreaded lecture mode. I wouldn't be able to help myself. I'd bore the hell out of everybody. And this isn't my show, Julie. Nobody's there to hear me."

There was more to it than that, but he wasn't about to give voice to it. Simply put, this was one of Julie's rare chances to shine outside the world of the National Park Service. She had put a lot of time and a lot of work into her paper, and he wasn't about to take even a remote chance of upstaging her.

She gave it some thought. "You know, I'm beginning to see the wisdom of your position," she said.

"Good, I'm glad that's settled."

For a few minutes they walked along amicably enough, hand in hand, and then Julie suddenly stopped and turned to face him.

"Wait a minute, all I have is an M.A. Therefore I can't be taken seriously?"

"Well, in your case—"

She held up a warning finger. "Consider your reply carefully."

"In your case," he continued smoothly, "you're not pretending to be an authority on biodiversity. You're here as a wildfire management expert—which you certainly are."

"Uh-huh, and what about my paper? Is it full of 'misapprehensions' and 'misconceptions'?"

"I think," he said, unblinking, "that your paper is absolutely brilliant."

Their eyes remained locked for a second more. "Good answer," she said as they began walking again.

"Whew," he said softly.

"FROM this vantage point," intoned the sonorous voice from the loudspeakers, "we look back at the whole of Land's End, the rugged promontory that marks the south-easternmost point of the mainland of England. And we are lulled by our first sense of the gentle Atlantic swell, which has traveled three thousand miles, only to impotently expend its energy against these stark and ancient cliffs."

"Gentle swells!" somebody called out. "Try lookin' out the bloody window, mate!"

The ripple of laughter that greeted this was a trifle apprehensive, but after a few anxious minutes during which people's eyes roamed in search of a quick exit to the open air of the deck, should one become necessary, the surge grew calm and the ferry settled into a slow heave that most of the passengers found more relaxing than discomforting. The minority who felt otherwise gratefully followed the posted directions to the windowless lowest deck, where ranks of permanently set-up cots were waiting.

The soothing narrative continued: "And now, in the far distance we can see the Isles of Scilly themselves, the fabled Fortunate Islands, thought by many to be the mountain peaks of the sunken, lost land of Lyonesse. There are five inhabited islands, forty uninhabited ones, and a hundred-and-fifty—"

"Am I wrong," Gideon asked Julie, "or is that Liz Petra in the snack bar line?" He pointed at a small, plump figure in a shawl, a flowing peasant skirt, and sandals.

Julie turned to look. "It sure is. Liz! Over here!"

The pixie-faced blonde's eyes lit up. "Julene! Hello! Be there in a sec." She went back to paying for the bag of Cadbury's Chocolate Fingers she was buying.

Gideon looked at Julie, eyebrows raised. "'*Julene*'?"

Julie mumbled something.

"What?"

"Oh, heck, it just seemed more professional," she muttered.

"Ah. Well, I suppose it is, at that." He was happier than ever with his decision not to horn in on the meetings.

"Well, hi there, Julene!" Liz chirped as Julie jumped up to embrace her. "My favorite fellow Fellow! And I see you've brought the famous, or should I say infamous, Skeleton Detective along with you." She stuck out her hand. "Long time no see, prof."

It had been more than five years since she'd sat in on his nonhuman primate social behavior seminar as a graduate student in archaeology, but she seemed to have changed not a bit: still the same soft, dimply, unfailingly jolly dumpling of a person she was back then, grandmotherly (despite her pretty face) and chuckling, nurturing even at the age of thirty-five, and still apparently favoring the same vintage-clothing-store wardrobe, which had been passé even then. Only now she was a figure of note in the unlikely but burgeoning discipline of refuse archaeology.

"It's great to see you again, Liz," he said, grasping her hand and moving over to make room for her in their booth. "What's new in the world of garbage?"

"Things have been pretty trashy, actually," she said, plopping down. "So how's the bone business?"

"Oh, kind of dry, to tell the truth."

Julie rolled her eyes at this show of what passed for academic humor. "Liz, they found Edgar's remains, did you hear? He was eaten by a *bear*!"

Liz's clear blue eyes sparkled even more. "Yes, Joey just told me. Is that creepy, or what?"

"Joey Dillard? Is he on this ferry too?"

"Well, he was a minute ago. Back there near the Coke machine."

Julie looked over Liz's shoulder and waved. "Joey! Come join us!"

Joey Dillard, if Gideon remembered correctly, had been an investigative reporter for a paper somewhere in the Midwest—Gary, or Des Moines. He had been assigned to do a series on a new meat-packing operation and had come away so revolted that he became a vegetarian on the spot. He then joined PETA—People for the Ethical Treatment of Animals—and several lesser-known groups, had since become an officer in some of them, and was now a fairly well-known writer for various animal-rights, vegetarian, and ecology magazines and Web publications.

Knowing his background, Gideon had anticipated an investigative reporter–type: assertive, belligerent, and pushy. Instead, a toothy, bespectacled, generally alarmed-looking young man with fine, pale, almost colorless hair trimmed in a crew-cut acknowledged Liz's wave and made his way toward them. A faint tic jumped below his right eye. He earnestly clasped a couple of dog-eared magazines to his narrow chest and wore two large, worded buttons on his shirt.

"Oh, Lord" Gideon muttered, "save me from people who walk around with buttons."

Julie smiled. "Oh, Joey's not so bad—"

"As long as you don't take him too seriously," Liz said kindly. "He means well."

"I know," Julie said. "He's sweet, really."

Dillard made his hellos, shook hands with Gideon (a cold, damp palm), and sat down next to Julie. The button below his left collar-point said *People who abuse animals rarely stop there.* The bigger one on his right, less ominous but more comprehensible, said *Animals are not fabric. Wear your own damn skin.*

Dillard saw Gideon reading them and nervously drew himself up a little straighter, ready to do battle, the tic beneath his eye speeding up. But Gideon, determined not to make waves, simply said, "Glad to meet you, Joey. We were just talking about Edgar Villarreal."

Joey immediately lowered his guns, reset the safeties, and relaxed. "You mean the bear? God, that was just so terrible. I'm really going to miss his contributions this year." As far as Gideon could tell, Joey meant it, but he noted that Liz and Julie declined to commiserate.

Joey noticed too. "I mean, sure, he may have had a few problems personalitywise," he mumbled, "but he really added something valuable, you have to give him that." When no one seemed willing to give him that, Joey turned it up a notch. "Personally, I *liked* the guy."

Another long beat passed before Liz finally responded, the corners of her mouth turned down. "Well, it's not as if he would have been here anyway. He did quit, you know."

"He did?" said Julie.

"He did?" said Joey.

"Didn't you know? I heard it from Vasily months ago."

"But why?" Joey asked.

"Well"—she offered the bag of milk-chocolate-covered biscuits around. Joey was the only taker—"remember when he gave that talk in town and, what was his name, Pete Williams got all over his case?"

"Who's Pete Williams?" Gideon asked, but they were too absorbed to hear him.

"How could I forget?" Joey asked. "It was awful. Edgar was really, really upset. We all went over to the Bishop and Wolf for a drink afterward, and he was muttering in his beer, remember?"

Liz nodded and put on an overblown version of Villarreal's mild Spanish accent. "'I keel 'im, dat bastar', dat leedle peepsqueak.' Anyway, apparently it was enough to make him never want to come back. That and a few million other reasons, but that had to be the last straw. Anyway, when he got back to the States he faxed Vasily a letter resigning from the consortium. I don't think Vasily was too upset to hear it. Frankly, I wasn't too upset myself."

"I guess he didn't need the fifty thousand," Joey said. "I sure wish I could say that." He removed a thin, tar-black cellophane-wrapped cigar from a shirt pocket and held it up. "Do you mind?"

"Yes," said Liz.

"Yes," said Julie.

"Oh," Joey said meekly and put it back in his pocket. "Sorry."

"You can save it for the catwalk," Liz said, and then explained to Gideon: "There's a kind of catwalk around the roof of the castle. He prowls it after dark, like the Phantom of the Opera, smoking his foul weed."

"It's the only place they let me," Joey said with a sigh.

"What do you mean, 'they'? Those are Kozlov's house rules. Don't blame us. Not that I'm objecting to them."

"I didn't go to that talk of Edgar's," Julie said. "It was the final night, and I suppose I'd had more than enough of Edgar Villarreal by then. I heard it didn't go well, but what exactly happened?"

Between them, Liz and Joey explained. Villarreal, as the best-known of the consortium fellows, had been approached by the local tourist office and asked to make a public presentation in Hugh Town, St. Mary's main village. He had agreed, and on their final night on St. Mary's, he had given a talk at Methodist Hall. Not many had come: two dozen curious locals; six or eight tourists who'd happened to be on St. Mary's and were starved for something—anything—to do in the evening; all of the consortium attendees other than Julie; and three reporters, one from as far away as Plymouth—plus Pete Williams, who had been hanging around all week, having come all the way from London.

Williams was an English writer who was researching a book (*Movers and Shakers of the Earth*) on personalities in the environmental movement. He had originally applied to be a consortium fellow himself but had been turned down by Kozlov as having no original contribution to offer. He had shown up anyway, staying at a B&B in town, and had interviewed some of the attendees for his book. Villarreal had denied his request for an interview with rather nasty condescension.

But Williams had gotten his own back at the Methodist Hall session, pretty much commandeering the question-and-answer session. He had fired hard questions at Villarreal, at first about his sense of responsibility and regret for

the deaths of the two students in the Bitterroot Wilderness
Area. Villarreal had put him off with pro forma regrets—
"these things happen," "restoring the wilderness comes with
a price," "they obviously didn't take proper precautions,"
and so on. Many had been shocked at his indifference.

Then it had turned personal. There was apparently a history of enmity between the two men, and an increasingly
agitated Williams had made it clear that Villarreal was going to be "exposed" in the book he was writing.

"Isn't it true," he'd demanded at one point, "that you
never finished your Ph.D. at Cornell, even though you ad-
vertise yourself as *Doctor* Villarreal?"

"That's so," Villarreal had responded, "but I do have a
doctorate from Stanford."

"An *honorary* doctorate!" Williams had shrieked triumphantly. "And isn't it true—"

Villarreal had gotten contemptuously to his feet and
outshouted him. "Isn't it true that you've been playing second fiddle to me for years and just can't stand it? Isn't it
true that you applied to this consortium and didn't get in,
while I did? Isn't it true that you applied for the Cambridge
research fellowship and didn't get it because I did? And
isn't it true . . ."

In the end, Kozlov had stepped in and asked Williams to
leave, although it took a constable who was in attendance
to make it happen.

Villarreal had waited until Williams had been escorted
out before getting in the last word. "And if anybody wants
to know what I'm really sorry about," he'd declared bru-
tally, "what I really regret—it's that they killed that bear in
Montana. There was no need for that. What was the point?
Human stupidity is not an excuse for murdering a rare,
beautiful wild animal."

"A cold fish, all right," Gideon said now.

"It so happens I agree with him," Joey declared, or
rather blurted. "Intellectually speaking."

"Oh, pish-tush," Liz said with a flap of her hand. "You do not."

"Yes, I do."

"No, you don't," said Julie.

"Yes, I *do!*" Joey's voice went up half an octave, coming perilously close to a screech. "All right, sure, Edgar was no prize as a human being, but that doesn't mean that what he said wasn't right. I'll trade a human life for a grizzly's life any day of the week. There's no difference between Edgar and me on that score." He glared at the three of them, his tic going full blast.

"Sure, there is," Liz said, using her thumb to flip another chocolate-covered cookie to him, which he deftly snatched out of the air. "That sonofabitch really believed that shit. You don't."

Joey started to reply, then grinned and hung his head. "Maybe not every word."

"Look who's here," Julie said glancing up. "Victor."

Gideon followed her gaze with a mixture of curiosity and dread. If there *was* one certified wacko in the group, he thought, it had to be Victor Waldo, editor of the *Journal of Spiritual and Sacred Ecology* and founder of the Crystal Butte Earth/Body Center, located in the White Mountains of New Hampshire. ("Effortlessly absorb timeless shamanistic techniques for healing, growth, and homeostasis in our authentic Kirghiz mountain yurts.")

Once again, however, Gideon was surprised at what he saw. He'd half-expected a bearded dropout in a tie-dyed sweatshirt, or maybe fringed buckskin, or with a ratty Afghan thrown over his shoulders, but Victor Waldo's long chin was clean-shaven and his lean body was neatly attired in a tweed sport coat and well-pressed trousers. With his short, steel-gray hair, his proboscis of a nose—lifted slightly as if searching for an elusive scent—his pale, cold, intelligent eyes, and an all-around dryness of manner, he could have passed with ease for a professor of microeconomics. It was very hard indeed to imagine him thumping ceremonial drums, or whatever it was they did in an authentic Kirghiz mountain yurt.

"Hey, Victor, how you doing?" Liz yelled. "Come join us. Is Kathie with you?"

Waldo waited until he came within normal speaking range to reply. "No, she isn't. As a matter of fact, Kathie and I are no longer . . . No, she isn't. We've separated."

That prompted a knowing, embarrassed glance between Liz and Julie, and they quickly moved on to another subject. "Pull up a chair, Victor," Liz said. "Have you heard about Edgar?"

He had not, and after the bear story had been told once again and Waldo had expressed the requisite astonishment and a distinctly cool minimum of sorrow at his loss, Gideon, in the interest of furthering his own knowledge, apologized for never having read the *Journal*, and asked if Waldo would be kind enough to give him some idea of what exactly the province of spiritual and sacred ecology comprised. Out of the corner of his eye he saw Liz wince.

Like any expert asked to talk about his field, Waldo obliged with an enthusiasm that brought a stony glitter to his washed-out blue eyes. "Certainly. In a nutshell, it provides an alternative paradigm to the non-relational ways of being in the world that have traditionally dominated Western thought. It relies on a model that aims for a synergistic relationship with other species and ecosystems. It explores the dialectic between . . ."

Good gosh, Gideon thought, he even talks like a professor of microeconomics.

". . . indigenous world views, earth-connected spirituality—"

The disembodied voice from the loudspeakers came to the rescue by resuming its tranquil monologue: "And now, as the beautiful Isle of St. Mary's comes into our near view, its rocks reveal the ravages of time and tide, against which—".

Everyone took this as a signal to gather up belongings and move toward the exits. After quick handshakes all around, Julie and Gideon found themselves out on deck in the disembarkation line as the ferry slid sidewise up to the Hugh Town quay.

"What did you think of Victor?" a smiling Julie asked.

"Interesting. Not that I had a clue to what he was talking about."

"No, nobody does. But he *is* interesting."

"Why did Kozlov choose him? Is it just one more way of annoying the establishment?

"No, I don't think so. I think Vasily is simply a genuinely open-minded person who doesn't write off people because they don't happen to agree with his own views on science." She paused for a beat. "Not like some people I know."

"Hey . . ." Gideon said, laughing.

Julie pointed to a green promontory topped by a low, gray, undeniably Elizabethan castle that was surrounded by a walled, star-shaped keep.

"That's Garrison Hill," she said, "and that's Kozlov's place on top of it. Star Castle."

"Looks nice."

"It is. There'll be a van on the dock to pick up our bags for us, and we're early, so what do you say we stretch our legs a little and walk up to the castle? I'll give you a tour of Hugh Town on the way. It won't take long."

"Love to."

Hugh Town was more village than town, a narrow, quarter-mile-long neck of land connecting Garrison Hill to the rest of the island, bordered by Town Beach on one side and the brilliant white sand of Porthcressa Beach on the other. Only three streets wide, it had a couple of banks, a chemist, three or four pubs and hotels, as many restaurants, a not so super "supermarket," and a few guest houses and craft shops. All in all, a quiet, pleasant, prosperous, not overly quaint British village of the sort that had once been typical of England but was rarely to be found now, certainly not within fifty miles of London.

Its particular glory was in the rock gardens and in the cascading masses of flowers that were everywhere, sustained by a subtropical climate that felt more like Bermuda than Britain. Even with stopping often to admire the plantings, in less than an hour they had covered every foot of Hugh Street, the Strand, and the Parade, had walked up Garrison Hill Lane, and had entered the castle grounds through a massive stone gateway with ER 1593 carved deeply into the lintel.

Seen from inside the thick walls, Star Castle was not quite as impressive as it had seemed from the dock. A squat three stories high, with little in the way of ornamentation, it had been built with fortification in mind, not high living. It had stood without apparent decline for over four hundred years now and looked good for another four hundred at least.

Kozlov was not there to greet them. They were met in a tiny office-reception area by his secretary, a pale, soft man—like some delicate, vulnerable crustacean that had come into the light without its shell—who presented a quiet but distinctly starchy mien. ("I am Mr. Kozlov's majordomo. My name is Mr. Moreton.") He showed them to the guest rooms on the second floor, and opened a door on which there was a marble plaque: THE DUKE OF HAMILTON ROOM. Inside it was sparely but comfortably furnished: a big four-poster bed, two chairs, an ancient armoire, and a folding writing desk.

"And who was the Duke of Hamilton?" Gideon asked. "Was he a guest here?"

"He was a prisoner in this room in the year 1643. The rooms, you see, are named for the many notables who have been imprisoned here."

"Ah. And what did the duke do?"

"I understand his loyalty to the monarchy was held in question. He was believed to be a supporter of Cromwell, although there is room for doubt on the matter."

"Last year," Julie said, "I was next door in the Sir John Wildman Room. *He* was imprisoned for being disloyal to Cromwell and supporting the monarchy."

"Times change," Gideon observed.

Mr. Moreton's hand swept the surroundings. "I'm told the duke found his lodgings here quite comfortable."

"And I know we will too," said Julie.

Pleased, Mr. Moreton brushed a finger along either side of an immaculately trimmed, pencil-thin mustache. "The reception is at six," he told them. "A number of local dignitaries have been invited."

"Thank you, Mr. Moreton," Gideon said.

"Dinner will be at seven-thirty, in the dungeon. Madam. Sir." He closed the door soundlessly behind him.

"Now there's a line that hasn't been heard since *The Addams Family*," Gideon remarked when he'd left. "Dinner in the dungeon. What do we get, gruel?"

"I doubt it," Julie said, laughing. "As dungeons go, it's pretty nice. You'll see, you'll be impressed."

"I'm already impressed. I never met a real majordomo before."

A few minutes later, with their bags open on the beds, she paused in her arranging of the bags' contents in the armoire. (This was a task that always fell to Julie. The alternative was chaos, bewilderment, and wrinkled clothes.)

"Gideon?"

"Mm?" He was wandering absently around the room, testing out the window seat that was cut into the three-foot-thick walls, running his hand over the rough-plastered walls themselves, the age-darkened wood of the eighteenth-century armoire, and the smooth round columns of the bed, and taking in the primitively carved, dark-painted beams that supported the low ceilings. "Those are real adze marks on them," he mused, his head tipped back. He was able to reach them with his hand and feel the delicate scoring from the individual adze blows. "Probably the original sixteenth-century beams."

"Gideon, tonight's reception—you *will* be there for that, won't you?"

"Uh-huh."

"And you'll be nice to everyone?"

He looked at her, surprised. "When am I not nice to everyone? I was nice to Joey Dillard, wasn't I? And he was wearing buttons."

"Well, I was just thinking . . . if it's like last time, Vasily will be making a sort of speech to set the agenda, and he does have some, uh, odd ideas about evolution and things that even I can spot. If he should say something that isn't exactly accurate, you won't jump all over him, will you?"

Gideon sighed. "I can't win, can I? Last night you were upset because I didn't want to participate. Today all you want is for me to keep my lip buttoned."

"I just want . . . Oh, come on, you know perfectly well what I mean."

"Julie," he said, as they closed the door to their room behind them, "you can count on me. I will be the very model of decorum and restraint; the perfect spouse."

THREE

AND at first, he was.

With the weather as mild as it was, the reception was held outdoors on the castle ramparts. Eighteen feet wide and bordered by sturdy, four-foot-high stone parapets, these earth-filled, star-shaped walls (with cannon ports, some empty, some with rusted seventeenth-century cannons in the points of the stars) surrounded the castle itself, creating a deep, narrow passageway that circled the building on the inside. On the outside, the ramparts overlooked a dry moat, with a wonderful view over Hugh Town harbor, the bright, blue-green sea beyond, and the low, mounded green silhouettes of the nearby islands. Kozlov or a previous owner had sodded the top of the thick walls so that there was now a rich, green lawn underfoot, with a few old picnic tables scattered about, and a well-stocked bar that had been set up for the occasion.

Vasily Kozlov, dressed in a bright yellow T-shirt, Bermudas, and sandals, was there to greet them—and to exuberantly embrace Julie—when they arrived at the top of the stone steps that led to the ramparts. Striking in appearance, with a short, bouncing, bullet-shaped body and an amazing head of corkscrewed white hair (he looked like Pablo Picasso in a fright wig, a magazine article had once said), he pumped Gideon's hand—an energetic, two-handed grip—and beamed up at him.

"So, comes to my house famous Mr. Skeleton Detective! Welcome, welcome!"

"Thanks for having me, Mr. Kozlov. I'm glad to be here."

"Please, please, is 'Vasily.' You come sit in consortium, yes? Any time, any time. Talk all you want. What you say?"

"If I do, do I get a discount on lodging costs?" It had made Julie laugh. He thought it might do the same for Kozlov.

It did. "Harr, harr," Kozlov rumbled, reaching up to thump Gideon on the shoulder and turning to welcome the next of his guests, still chuckling. "Is funny."

"Looks as if you'll just have to resign yourself to that twenty bucks a day," Julie said. "Come on, let me introduce you to some of the others." She took his arm and led him toward a group milling near the bar. As they approached, a tall, gaunt man, with a gold chain around his neck and overdue for a haircut, shifted his highball to his left hand and stuck out his right. "Hello, Gideon, I'd heard you were coming. It's been a while."

Gideon stopped, puzzled. He freely admitted to being more generally absentminded than most, but not when it came to people. People, he remembered. But this cadaverous, round-shouldered guy with the lined face and the sour twist to his mouth, and the gold chain . . .

"Uh—it's nice to—" he began.

Julie rescued him. "Why, hello, Rudy. How are you?"

Gideon's heart contracted. This grim, walking ghost was Rudy Walker, the friend of his youth, the man he'd been so looking forward to seeing again? Where was the easy, open-faced smile, the lively, cocky tilt of the head,

the suggestion of good fun just around the corner? He recognized him now, but the changes were very great. It was
as if he were looking at a faded monochrome photograph
of the full-color Rudy he'd known. It had been more than
twenty years, of course, and Rudy, older than Gideon,
would be pushing fifty now, but still . . .

"—to see you again, Rudy," he finished, taking the proffered hand. It was clammy, possibly from the drink he'd
been holding. "How's Fran, is she here?"

"Fran died," Rudy said without expression. "She got
cancer."

Ah, was that it, then? They had been extravagantly, almost embarrassingly, in love, Rudy and Fran. Was it her
death that had changed him so? It wasn't so hard to imagine. Gideon too had lost his much-loved first wife some
eight years ago, in an automobile accident. Nora had been
the center of his life, his anchor, the reason that he drew
breath, and her death had undone him. For one long, terrible year he was drowning in grief, unable to come to terms
with it. But then, as more time passed, the extremity of his
sorrow—of all his emotions—diminished, and he felt himself dwindling into a husk, without aims, or interests, or
passions, isolated from everything and interacting with
others by rote. He looked on the outside world as a sort of
television set; the power was on but it was permanently
tuned between channels, so that there was life in there
somewhere, but it was just static and fuzz, unimportant and
without meaning. He couldn't remember—literally could
not remember—how it was that one smiled, and when he
tried, it hurt his face.

And then, astonishingly, wondrously, along had come
the funny, pretty park ranger Julie Tendler, and he had
thawed, fallen in love once more, and come thankfully to
life again. But his meeting her at all had been so random, so
unlikely—she had been peripherally involved in the finding of some remains he'd been asked to examine in

Olympic National Park—it would have been frighteningly easy to have missed each other. What would have happened then? Without Julie, would he have turned into Rudy?

Very probably, yes. Well, without the gold chain, but he'd certainly been well on the way. Julie's hand was still warm in the crook of his elbow. Gently, he covered it with his own.

"I'm so sorry, Rudy, I didn't know. She was a terrific person."

"Yes," Rudy said, managing a small, pinched grimace of a smile. He shrugged and took a double-slug from his drink. "Well, you've certainly come a long way since Madison, Gideon. I've followed your career."

Gideon jumped at the chance to change the subject. "And I yours, Rudy," he said, not entirely honestly. "You've made quite a name for yourself too."

The truth was he'd pretty much forgotten about Rudy Walker until Julie told him that he was one of the consortium participants. Then he'd looked him up and found an impressive string of articles and monographs that he'd contributed to ecology journals, popular magazines, and conference proceedings. Rudy had indeed made a name for himself, first as an articulate defender of America's remaining pristine wilderness, and then, in a famous, or infamous, *Atlantic* magazine piece, he'd reversed course and come out in favor of opening up the wilds to roads, cars, and even— talk about anathema to environmentalists—snowmobiles.

"If snowmobiles are the only way to see our great national parks in winter (and mostly, they are)," he'd written, "then I say let's have the snowmobiles. Sure they're noisy, sure they pollute, but so do cars in the summer. So do people, wherever they go. If the more extreme environmentalists had their way, human beings would be prohibited from our national parks altogether, so that no one annoyed the deer, or the bears, or the moose, or the titmice. But what's the point of preserving a wilderness no one can see?

Whose enjoyment are we preserving it for? The titmice's? I don't think so. In my book, people come before titmice."

It had turned him into a pariah overnight.

"Quite a name is right," he said now. "I'm the man they love to hate. The whole damn ecology crowd sees me as a traitor to the cause. Yea, I am an abomination to mine own kind. Ever since Black February."

"Black February?"

"The date of the piece in the *Atlantic*. February 2003. Before then, they loved me, couldn't get enough of me. But now . . ." He trailed off, darkly shaking his head.

"I know the way it can be," Gideon said. "We gentle academics can get pretty brutal when you step on our pet theories."

"They actually hiss me at the meetings, did you know that? Can you imagine? At what are supposed to be scholarly conferences? Sometimes they walk out on my presentations." Rudy had a rigid, skeletal grin on his face. "They wait until I get to the lectern, then get up and leave, all together, just in case I might miss the point."

Gideon lifted his shoulders in sympathy. Over time, that kind of treatment alone would have been enough to sour Rudy, never mind losing Fran. "That sounds rough, Rudy. I don't know if I agree altogether with your position, but I give you credit for sticking to it."

"They're in love with the notion of biodiversity," Rudy said bitterly, mostly to himself. "It's thought diversity they can't stand."

"Well . . ." Gideon said, searching for something to drop into the awkward pause, ". . . how's your little girl doing?" He struggled to come up with her name. "Little Mary, although I suppose she's not so little any more. She was only five or six the last time I saw her. I bet—"

But Rudy, festering over his treatment in academia, was jiggling the ice in his otherwise empty glass and looking longingly toward the bar.

"Well, look," Gideon said, "why don't we have a pint in town one of these days and catch up, just the two of us?"

"Sure, that'd be good," Rudy said absently. "Well, then . . ." He smiled that lame, pathetic smile again and stalked off to the bar.

"Sad," Gideon said. "Was he like that at the last meeting?"

"Oh, he lightened up about once every three days, but most of the time, yes. Not easy to get to know. I learned more about him these last five minutes than I did in a whole week last time. I never knew he had any children. I never even knew he'd been married."

"Oh, yes, he and Fran were . . . well, the way you and I are. I envied them." He shook his head and sighed. "Come on, I could use a drink myself."

At the bar, drinks were being poured by two young women in decorous Ye Olde Tea Shoppe uniforms—shiny, black, mid-calf-length dresses with scalloped white collars, white buttons down the front, short sleeves with pointy, turned-up white cuffs, and little white headpieces to match. Julie took a glass of red wine from the row that had already been poured. Gideon asked for a Glenlivet single-malt Scotch served neat. At twenty dollars a day, he felt entitled to splurge. As they clinked glasses, Liz came up.

"I have to borrow your wife for a minute," she said, drawing Julie off. "I need some advice. Girl stuff."

Gideon raised his glass in acquiescence and took a sip, relishing the velvety, peaty flow that warmed him from gullet to stomach. "You like poker?" a voice said into his ear, Vasily Kozlov having sidled up to his elbow.

"Poker? Sure, sometimes."

"Is old tradition here. Ten o'clock, in dining hall, every night. Last hand midnight, penny-ante, ten pence limit, three raises, just for fun, you know? Mens only. Shall you come?"

"I don't know about every night, Vasily, but you bet, I'll come by tonight. Thanks for asking me."

"Bring plenty money," Kozlov said with a twinkling leer as he threaded off through the crowd.

"I got invited to the poker game," Gideon told Julie when she got back from whatever advice-giving Liz had needed.

"Ah, I thought he'd ask you. Are you going?"

"Tonight, anyway. I haven't played poker in a long time; should be fun."

"Are you good at it?"

"As a matter of fact, I am. I'm figuring on getting that twenty bucks back."

"Good luck. They tell me Vasily turns into a shark when he gets behind a handful of cards."

"So do I. Wait and see. I'll buy you lunch tomorrow with my winnings."

"I'll look forward to it," Julie said neutrally. "Oh, and here's the last of our Fellows. Donald Pinckney, this is my husband, Gideon."

"Happy to meet you, Donald." Gideon stuck out his hand and smiled, but his heart sank: another guy wearing a button.

But this bright yellow one made him laugh. *If we're not supposed to eat animals, why are they made of meat?*

Donald Pinckney, he remembered, was the pro-hunting voice at the consortium, but he looked about as much like Gideon's idea of a hunter as Joey Dillard looked like an investigative reporter. A tall, balding, bookish man in a crisp blue linen sport coat and bow tie, with mild, seemingly myopic eyes behind wire-rimmed glasses, he seemed like the last person in the world who would willingly be found crouching in a cold, wet duck blind at dawn, with a shotgun to his shoulder.

"And I you, Gideon," he said. "I'm afraid I haven't read any of your books, but—"

"What? You haven't read *A Structuro-Functional Approach to Pleistocene Hominid Phylogeny*? I can hardly believe what I'm hearing."

"I need hardly say, however, that it is quite naturally on my must-read list at present," Pinckney said without missing a beat. "But what I was going to say was that I saw you on The Learning Channel not long ago and was extremely impressed by what you're able to deduce from a few skeletal fragments."

"Only if they're the right fragments," Gideon said modestly. "Fortunately, the TV people had the right fragments. I've read a few of *your* pieces, Donald, and I have to say you make a heck of a good case for hunting as a positive conservation measure; I'm almost convinced myself."

"I'm gratified to hear it."

"What's your favorite game?"

"I beg your pardon?"

"I was asking what kind of animals you like to hunt— deer, ducks, um . . ." What else did hunters go after? ". . . elk, geese, um . . ."

"What kind of—" Pinckney blinked at him, pained. "Are you serious? Do I look to you to be the sort of man who'd go around with a gun, shooting ducks and geese? Let alone *gutting* them and all the rest of it?" He gave a small shudder. "No, thank you."

"But I thought—I mean, don't you—"

"Donald is an advocate of ethical, environmentally sensitive hunting," Julie said, enjoying this. "It doesn't mean that he likes doing it himself."

"Any more than I would enjoy electrocuting people, which I wouldn't," Pinckney explained, "just because I support capital punishment, which I do."

"I guess that makes sense," Gideon said, with enough doubt in his voice that Pinckney felt it necessary to expand.

"I was an administrator with the Pennsylvania Department of Fish and Wildlife for twenty-one years, Gideon, and in that time I moderated a good many meetings with various lobbying and pressure groups. Against my own instincts, I eventually concluded that, motives aside, the pro-hunting lobby had an extremely sound approach to wildlife conservation; a good deal sounder—and considerably less shrill—than the anti-hunting groups." He directed a disparaging flick of his head in the direction of Joey Dillard, who was busy proselytizing a small, captive audience a few yards away. "I've been saying so ever since, that's all."

He looked again toward where Joey was holding forth. "Would you mind excusing me? I feel a strong need to go and correct whatever distortions of reality our earnest young friend is inflicting on those unfortunate people. I'm very happy to know you, Gideon." He nodded briskly at Julie. "Julene."

There was the delicate sound of a musical triangle being rung for attention, and they turned to see the pale, stately Mr. Moreton standing in front of one of the gun ports, delicately striking it with a metal rod that he held with pinky extended. *Tink. Tink. Tink.*

Kozlov, who had clambered onto the two stone steps leading up to the port, waved happily to his guests, arms high, like a feisty bantamweight entering the ring. The sun, setting directly behind him, turned his wild hair into a halo of steel wool.

"Here comes the speech," Julie said. "Remember, you promised."

But Kozlov uttered only four words, thoroughly garbled, but full of good cheer.

"Hawkay, evwerybawdyss . . . lat's *itt!*"

"*What* did the man say?" someone next to Gideon asked. "Was he speaking Russian?"

"No, English," Gideon said. "He said, 'Okay, everybody, let's eat.' " And to Julie: "And I'm certainly not going to argue with that."

THE dungeon was indeed "pretty nice," as dungeons went, with coves and niches that roughly corresponded to the castle's star-shaped exterior, and a paramecium-shaped bar in the small, open central area. The rough-finished stone walls bore a clean coat of white paint and were adorned with eighteenth-century weaponry and navigational equipment. At one end of the bar, a bronze plate screwed to the top said: "African hardwood from the wreck of HMS *Retort*, sunk by French gunfire off the Stones in 1799."

Because there was no single space large enough to hold all the guests at one table, people were seated in groups of three and four in the various niches. Gideon's place was at a table also apparently made from the remains of the unfortunate *Retort*, along with Rudy Walker and Madeleine Goodfellow, the director of the Isles of Scilly Museum in Hugh Town. Earlier, Madeleine had announced that on Wednesday, the consortium's midpoint, the museum would be pleased to host a picnic-dinner for the participants on Holgate's Green, the pleasant little park at the other end of the village. Kozlov had graciously accepted on behalf of all.

The other person at the table, according to the place cards, was Cheryl Pinckney, Donald's wife, to whom Gideon had been introduced at the reception. But her chair was empty.

Madeleine, a buxom, amiable woman in her fifties who wore her glasses on a lanyard and several rounds of jangling jewelry on her wrist, and who was given to knowledgeable if somewhat disjointed prattling, made conversation easy—or rather, unnecessary—at first by talking at some length about the history of the castle while the roasted-vegetable salads were served and eaten. Star Castle had been built in 1593 by order of Queen Elizabeth, as a defensive response to the "Spanish Menace," and had often seen action through the centuries. As for the dungeon in which they presently sat, yes, it had been used as a prison for enemy sailors and soldiers early in the seventeenth century. Later, when the Scillies had become a sort of in-country exile for aristocrats who had gotten themselves in trouble of one kind or another with the crown, Star Castle had once again served as a prison. But this time its inhabitants, being of a higher class, were usually transferred directly from the Tower of London and lodged—often with their servants in attendance—in the "apartments" in which the consortium participants were now staying. In 1646, the future Charles II, on the run from the Roundheads, had taken refuge at the castle; and in 1847 Queen Victoria had taken tea in what had then been, and still was, the lounge on the second floor. In 1921, the Prince of Wales, later to become the Duke of Windsor, had lunched . . .

After a while, this subject, extensive as it was, petered out, and conversation slowed to a crawl, what with Cheryl's being absent and Rudy as good as absent. He sat in silence, drawn in on himself like a bird in a pelting rain, moodily nursing his drink and no doubt brooding upon the vindictive consequences visited upon free thinkers who had the temerity to challenge the established orthodoxies of their field.

"And what is your field, Gideon?" Madeleine asked with a well-bred show of interest as the salads were cleared away. She had a fluty, mezzo-soprano voice that would have gone perfectly with a lorgnette, Gideon thought with a smile, suddenly realizing who it was she reminded him of. She could have doubled in looks, and even in manner, for Margaret Dumont, that *grande-dame* of the silver screen whom Groucho Marx had persecuted and punctured with such relentless glee in movie after movie. ("Captain, this leaves me speechless." "Well, see that you remain that way." "Mr. Hammer, you must leave my room. We must have regard for certain conventions." "One guy isn't enough, she's gotta have a convention.")

"I'm a physical anthropologist," Gideon said. "I teach at the University of Washington."

"No!" She put down her wineglass. "Do you mean you know about *bones*?"

Rudy surfaced. "Does he know about bones!" he muttered with a laugh. "Lady, you're talking to the Skeleton Detective himself."

"The, er, Skeleton . . ."

"I do a fair amount of forensic consulting," Gideon explained. Not for the first time did he wish to hell the reporter who'd pasted that nickname—as impossible to peel off as a stuck-on label from a tomato—on him all those years ago. "Mostly on skeletal remains."

"How totally fascinating." Her interest now was genuine enough. She pulled her chair closer to the table and closer to Gideon. He caught a strong whiff of talcum powder. "I wonder—were you planning on visiting the museum?"

"Of course. I'm looking forward to it."

Julie had told him about the place. "It's your kind of museum," she'd said. "Small, simple but thorough, nicely done. Nothing fancy. You'd like it."

"Any skeletal material?" he'd asked Julie hopefully.

The answer had been no, not that she recalled, but still there'd seemed enough of interest to occupy him for an enjoyable hour or two sometime during the week.

Madeleine moved her wineglass over the table in coy, tentative circles. "Well, while you're there, I wonder if you might . . . that is, I can't help *but* wonder . . . Well, you see, we have some human skeletal remains in storage. There's one set in particular that I was hoping might be of interest to you—a leftover casualty from the Civil War, one of Cromwell's soldiers. They found it sixty years ago, all scrunched up at the bottom of a dried-up well here on Garrison Hill, near the outer walls, costume and all. Well, the costume's been on display ever since the museum opened, but the bones have been stored in the basement all this time."

"Are you asking me to look at them for you?" Gideon asked.

"Yes, if you'd be interested."

Bless you, he thought. What he'd told Julie about visiting the local Bronze and Iron Age sites was certainly true—as an anthropologist specializing in prehistory, he couldn't help but be interested in them. But the Scillies had hundreds of such sites, and, frankly, one visit to a "village" consisting of a few scars in the ground and two or three hearth or grinding stones still in place went a long way. If he were down in the dirt with a brush and trowel in his hands, digging away, uncovering the past himself, that would have been one thing; but seeing them as a tourist— just wandering around pretending to make sense of the plaques—would get old pretty fast, and he'd been wondering just what it was he was really going to do with his time.

"I'm interested, all right," he said.

"There isn't much left, of course; just some arm and leg bones. Still, I'd love to exhibit them with the costume, don't you see, but what could I say about them? I don't know enough about them to say anything interesting—you know, how old he was, or . . . or whatever it is that a person like you could deduce. I asked my doctor to tell us what he could about them, but he just took one look at them and laughed. They're probably human and probably male; that was as far as he was willing to put himself out."

Gideon smiled. "Pretty safe guess, considering that they were wearing a seventeenth-century soldier's uniform."

"Oh, and he also said one of the bones looked diseased, but bones weren't his specialty. You'd think doctors would know more about skeletons, wouldn't you?"

"They do, really. It's just that they know more about them in living people. It's the opposite with me. I'll be able to tell you a lot about a bone found out in the desert some-where, but don't ask me to set a green-stick fracture in some kid who fell off a fence."

"I see." She hesitated. "Then may I take it that you might be inclined to stop by for a few minutes and sort through them some time during the week?"

"I'd love to," he said sincerely. "How about tomorrow

morning? And for more than a few minutes—for as long as it takes, if you like."

There were, in fact, few prospects that pleased him more than having an entire morning—an entire day, if possible—sitting by himself in some dusty lab or store-room with a pot of coffee cooling beside him, surrounded by anonymous fragments of human bone; patiently using Elmer's glue to piece together the skeletons; equally patiently using his education and intellect to piece together the lives of these now-forgotten people who had come before. There was a near-mystical contentment in it, a sense that he was speaking on their behalf, telling the world for them: *Here I am, I did exist; this is who I was, this is what I did, this is how I died.*

"Oh, you dear man, that's super!" Madeleine shrilled. "We have a few other old bones in our storage room as well—odds and ends, mostly, I suppose you'd say—but if you'd care to see them as well—"

"These are what—Iron Age? Bronze Age?"

"Oh, dear, no," Madeleine said. "Any human remains that come out of a prehistoric site go straight to the BM—the British Museum. No, these are simply the odd ulna or tibia that pops up on the beach from time to time. Old shipwrecks and such, don't you know. Not all that unusual, really. People don't know what to do about them, so they get turned in to the museum. We keep them a year or two for appearances' sake, and then we quietly dispose of them."

"Ah." Gideon was disappointed, but not very. The older the better, as far as he was concerned, but bones were bones. There was always something of interest.

"We'd keep them longer, I suppose," she rattled on, "if there were any hope of having them looked at by an expert, but we've never been able to lure one out here to go through them. No context, no skeletal populations of any size at all, do you see, so there isn't much to be learned in any broad sense."

"I understand their point, but I can't agree with that. There's always something to be learned."

"My dear man, I'm *thrilled* to hear you say that." She had puffed up with pleasure like a pouter pigeon. "Are there any tools you'd like me to have there for you?"

"Sure, a metal tape measure and a magnifying glass would be good." He shrugged, thinking. "Oh, and some glue, in case there's any repair to be done—Duco or Elmer's would be good, but whatever you use for pottery would do."

She nodded. "I'll have them there for you. And is that all you need?" She seemed surprised. "Don't you people use calipers and such? We have both kinds, spreading and sliding."

"Well, yes," he said a little defensively, "if I were doing a really exhaustive analysis. But all I'll be trying to do here is to give you some general idea of who the guy was. I don't think there's much reason to—"

"No, no, of course not," she said quickly, "a general idea is precisely what I want, and I appreciate it enormously." She chewed tentatively on her lower lip. "And, er, Gideon, I suppose I should have mentioned this earlier, but—"

"Hello, everyone, sorry to be late." Cheryl Pinckney, Donald's wife, had arrived in a cloud of musky perfume and slipped into her seat beside Gideon as the main course of Chicken Kiev and rice pilaf was being set out.

Madeleine smiled coolly at her. Rudy gave her a surly, vaguely lustful nod.

"Just the rice for me," she told the waitress, turning her head away from the Chicken Kiev as if it smelled bad. "And some salad, no dressing, oil and vinegar on the side. Pardon me, Gideon," she said huskily as her forearm grazed his.

A moment later a smooth, pant-clad thigh brushed solidly against Gideon's as she crossed her legs. "Sorry about that," she said casually. "I guess my legs are a little too long for the table."

He had chatted briefly with her during the reception. Cheryl was a nature photographer whose pictures had appeared in *National Geographic*, *Travel and Leisure*, and a few airline magazines. If she hadn't told him, he wouldn't have guessed that she was the wife of the prissy, balding Donald. On looks, she might have been a model. With her jutting cheek bones, long nose, and thin lips, no one would call her beautiful, but striking she was, and she moved with a catlike, self-assured grace that had drawn male eyes to her at the reception like iron filings to a magnet.

As far as Gideon was concerned, however, she could have stood to put on a few pounds. On the living, he preferred his skeletons a little better covered.

"As I was saying, Gideon," Madeleine continued, "I suppose I should have mentioned this earlier—but I'm afraid we won't be able to arrange anything like your normal fees." She gave him a fluttery, winning smile. "If I were to buy you lunch, do you suppose that would do?"

"Madeleine, I'll buy *you* lunch."

When the waitress passed behind him with a tray of wine, Cheryl reached over his shoulder for a glass. As she did, a small, firm breast pressed unmistakably against his upper arm and then stayed there while she spoke to someone at the next table, her arm very nearly around Gideon's shoulder. A few strands of her long, dark hair, held back with a barrette, grazed his neck.

This was something that didn't happen to him very often these days. He had long ago learned that he was attractive to women—six-one, broad-shouldered, with an only slightly middle-aged version of the fighter's body that had seen him through the brief professional boxer's career with which he'd paid his way through graduate school. And the broken nose that had come with it was an intriguing counterpoint to his sometimes pedantic manner, or so he'd been told.

All this he knew. But he also knew that no woman had to check his ring finger to tell whether or not he was married. It was written all over him. He was one of those men who emanated husbandly contentment, and women on the prowl were quick to sense his unavailability. He was taken, happily married, and couldn't have hidden it if he'd wanted to, which he didn't.

Still, his forehead was warm as he tried as nonchalantly as possible to separate himself from the undeniably stimulating pressure of that warm, pokey little mound of flesh. *Now wait a minute*, he lectured himself. *What are you getting embarrassed about? You haven't done anything to feel ashamed of.*

When Cheryl smiled knowingly, and a little patronizingly, at him as he shifted gingerly away, he turned grumpy. Now he felt stodgy, and old-fashioned . . . and just plain *old*.

"Everybody?" Standing in front of the bar, Kozlov was calling for attention. Gideon took advantage of the opportunity to turn his chair still farther around. In doing so, he caught Julie's eye from across the room. She blew him a discreet kiss that instantly whisked away his sulk. He returned it somewhat less discreetly, and Julie gestured something to him. He knit his eyebrows to show he didn't understand.

She repeated the message, emphasizing the movements a little. With a couple of tips of her head she indicated that she was referring to Kozlov and to the welcoming speech that was apparently on the way, then mouthed: "Be . . . good. . . . You . . . promised."

Gideon bowed his head and placed his hand over his heart to show his good intentions.

FOUR

HE had no trouble sticking to them during Kozlov's presentation, a witty, charmingly accented, and unobjectionable condemnation of the existence of close-mindedness in scientific inquiry, followed by an introduction of the five Fellows, who then described the subjects of their papers. The Fellows had known this was coming, so it went smoothly, if dully, each one standing in his or her place and reading a brief, dry abstract in AcademicSpeak.

Julie was first, soberly explaining the importance of "fire management polices that replicate as closely as possible the spatial and temporal heterogeneity of natural fire regimes, taking into account the importance and reality of anthropogenic fires in woodland subsystems and thereby achieving the maintenance of biodiversity in a form adhering as closely as possible to its natural facets and fluxes."

Damn, he thought with pride, *she's almost as good at that stuff as I am.* When she took her seat again and glanced furtively in his direction he gave her a vigorous thumbs-up.

The others followed with equally turgid descriptions of their work, and although he took mental issue with a few things that were said, it wasn't too hard to keep his peace through most of them, including even Victor Waldo's rattling on inscrutably and at length about holistic and naturalistic paradigms that would reconstruct the nature-human dynamic of the postindustrial world.

But Donald Pinckney, speaking last, broke through his self-restraint when he dipped a toe into the treacherous waters of Darwinian theory.

". . . and therefore demonstrate that hunting, properly regulated, positively impacts wildlife populations by preventing game from exceeding the carrying capacity of their habitat areas, thus serving as a valuable adjunct to the mechanisms of natural selection and the survival of the fittest."

"*Nggkk,*" Gideon said.

To his dismay, this strangled, inadvertent squawk, wholly unintentional, dropped smack into a dead spot in the presentation and was heard clear around the room. Donald, with the faintest of frowns, glanced questioningly at him and prepared to continue reading, but Kozlov interceded.

"Mr. Skeleton Detective wants say something?"

No, Gideon didn't want to say anything, but by now his professorly instincts were beyond his control. "Well, it's only that Donald may have made a small . . . a *very* small but nonetheless important, um, misinterpretation of the way that natural selection works."

Donald's pale eyes glittered behind his glasses. "Oh?"

"The thing is," Gideon said, as delicately as he could, "in nature, natural selection works by selectively eliminating the more vulnerable—those animals that are least 'fit' to survive in their current environment. By removing them from the gene pool, the stronger—or I guess I should say the better-adapted—animals are more likely to reproduce, to contribute their genes, and to thus keep the species genetically strong; that is, genetically well-adapted to their environment . . ."

Unnoticed by Gideon, a pursed-mouthed Donald slid silently back into his seat.

"Hunting by natural predators has the same result," Gideon went on, well-launched now. "They're most likely to catch and kill the weak, the old, the slow, the sick, and so on. But modern human hunters, with their intelligence and technology, are a kind of super-predator that's never been seen on earth before. They kill the strongest and ablest animals, which of course means that the less 'fit' animals have a relatively greater opportunity to reproduce and pass on their genes."

"Ha-ha, that's exactly right," a delighted Joey Dillard cried. From the looks of him, he had had more to drink than was good for him. "What it is, is, it's evolution in reverse."

"Well, no, I wouldn't exactly say that. The idea that evolution can reverse itself, while it has a certain poetic appeal . . ."

"I tried, I really did," Gideon told Julie afterward, when they had come back outside to take a few turns around the ramparts, watching dusk turn to night as the sun dropped toward the sea beyond the Western Rocks, a jumble of offshore boulders that had been the end of many a seagoing vessel during winter storms, but in summer served mainly as a picturesque backdrop for the sunset-watchers who picnicked on Garrison Hill as the evening came on. Julie and Gideon could see several groups of them on the bluffs below the castle walls.

"Actually, I thought what you said was quite interesting," Julie told him loyally. "I think everybody did. Honestly."

"Not Pinckney."

"No, not Donald," Julie agreed. "But then he does tend to be a little touchy, a wee bit sensitive."

With a predatory wife like Cheryl, Gideon thought, *who wouldn't be?*

"So, what did you think of his wife?" Julie asked.

"Um . . . his wife?"

"Cheryl? The person sitting next to you? Certain parts of whom were more or less on top of you there for a while?"

"Oh, *that* Cheryl," Gideon said, laughing. "I didn't think you noticed."

"I bet *you* noticed."

"I did, but I hope you also observed that she didn't get to first base with me. Why would she? I can do a whole lot better than Cheryl Pinckney." He swung an arm around her shoulder, pulled her to him, and kissed her warmly. "Have I mentioned to you today that I'm in love with you?"

A gruff "Hey, you two, knock it off there" came from a nearby niche in the walls, where Liz was having a post-prandial cigarette, its end glowing red in the dark. "We're running a G-rated consortium here. This time, anyway."

"Hey, yourself," Gideon growled back, leaving his arms where they were, "go find your own parapet."

But after another lingering moment with their arms wrapped around one another they separated and resumed their slow tour of the ramparts, their fingers entwined.

"*This* time?" Gideon said. "Meaning, 'As opposed to last time'?"

Julie nodded. "It got pretty torrid around here a couple of years ago."

"Rats," Gideon said. "I was hoping it was just something about me that brought out the beast in Cheryl."

"'Fraid not, the beast in Cheryl is pretty easy to bring out. But it wasn't just Cheryl—well, it was, but the hanky-panky was really pretty general. I mean, I know this stuff happens at conferences, but that was the first time I'd ever experienced anything quite like that."

"Not first hand, I hope."

She squeezed his fingers. "Not a chance. Edgar was at the center of it all, and I guess I wasn't his type. He made only one move on me that could be construed as a pass—about as subtle as Cheryl's move on you—and then quit." She smiled. "I suppose I should have been insulted, because I was the only one he didn't keep after. He managed to have affairs—well, to have sex with—all three of the other women. Not that he had to try too hard."

"In *one* week?"

"Well, you know, the man was brilliant, famous, moody, edgy, good-looking in a dangerous sort of way . . . the kind that appeals to a lot of women."

"But not to you, I take it."

"Ugh, no!" He was absurdly pleased by her enthusiastic shudder. "Not that I have any objection to brilliant, famous, and good-looking, but I like my men a lot bigger, and sunnier, and friendlier . . . and I already have me one of those."

You sure do, Gideon thought. *And just you try and get rid of him.* "But I thought Villarreal was supposed to be some kind of loner, a recluse—preferred living with the bears and the wolves to being around people. Was that all hype?"

"No, as far as I know it was true. He spent a lot of the year in the wilds. When he left here he was heading straight out to the Alaskan wilderness to spend the summer all by himself, keeping tabs on a cluster of bear families—you know, tracking their eating, and mating, and migration activities. All alone with the bears, that's what he loved." She shook her head. "But when he was around people—women, anyway—he got very, um, shall we say, social."

"Yeah. Well, who knows, maybe I would too, if I spent my summers all alone, watching bears have sex."

They walked on a few steps, still hand-in-hand. "You said all three of the women," he said. "That means Cheryl, which is not exactly a huge surprise, and Liz—which *is* a surprise, because I wouldn't have pictured her going for a one-night stand—but who else was there?"

"Victor Waldo's wife, Kathie, was here with him too, and she—"

"Ah, that's right. You asked after her when we met him on the boat and he said they were separated, and you and Liz gave each other a couple of 'aha' glances."

"Really? Was it that obvious?"

"Hey, don't forget you're talking to the Skeleton Detective here. Not too much gets by me. So you think they broke up on account of what went on between her and Villarreal?"

"I wouldn't be surprised. She and Victor had a real wingding when it came out. It was pretty bad. I'm surprised you didn't hear them back in Port Angeles."

They had taken four turns around the ramparts now, and had them all to themselves, with Liz having gone back inside, and they stopped to lean their elbows on the parapet, overlooking the lights that were beginning to twinkle on in Hugh Town.

"It started right on the first night," Julie mused, "the night of the opening reception."

You'd have to have been out to lunch, she told him, not to notice that Cheryl and Villarreal had begun circling each other like storks doing a mating dance, about five minutes after they'd set eyes on one another. An hour into the reception, both had disappeared for a while, not even bothering to disguise the fact that they'd left together and returned together. Afterward, their little shared giggles and glances at dinner, and even at breakfast the next day, had left little doubt about what was going on. At first Julie had been embarrassed at their behaving that way in front of Donald, but it was soon obvious that he was used to it, and it wasn't long before Julie was used to it too.

Villarreal's affair with Cheryl lasted all of two days, Sunday and most of Monday, after which it cooled perceptibly. By Monday evening, he and Liz were a pair, a relationship that continued for most of the week, to Liz's transparent delight.

"She really thought he was in love with her," Julie said, shaking her head. "She thought she'd found the man of her dreams. Liz and I were pretty close, and I could see what was going on even if she couldn't . . . anybody could, really . . . and so I tried to calm her down a little, get her to take the long view, but, you know, when somebody is like that . . ." She shrugged. "And anyway, I didn't want to rain on her parade."

"No, of course not. Poor Liz. She's a smart lady, but she's honest herself, and so she can be a little gullible when it comes to other people."

"More than a little, I'm afraid. Edgar was like some kind of predator, as if he thought we were all his private harem. She was the only one who couldn't see it." Another shake of her head. "She couldn't stop talking about him."

Until that Friday, at any rate, when it somehow came out—Julie didn't remember how—that in addition to romancing Liz, he had been grabbing the occasional hour in the sack with Victor's wife Kathie on the side. There had been an extremely uncomfortable scene at dinner that evening, and then later everyone had heard Victor and Kathie screaming at each other in their room. As for Liz, she'd pretty much laughed it off, keeping a stiff upper lip in public, but there had been a couple of long crying sessions with Julie, filled with guilt and self-recrimination.

"Poor kid," Gideon said. "Edgar was really a piece of work, wasn't he? I knew I didn't like him just from looking at him. Now I know why. I also understand why Liz was being so nasty about him on the ship. I wondered at the time. It didn't seem like her."

"Well, now you know. The whole steamy, sordid story. Come on, let's go back to the other side. I want to see the last of the sunset."

They were too late for that. The sun was gone, and the last of the sunset-watchers were plodding home with their blankets and picnic baskets. But the darkening western sky still showed faint layers of orange and rose at the horizon, and the Western Rocks, now jagged, black silhouettes, looked like the menacing maritime-disasters-waiting-to-happen that they were.

"And what did Kozlov think of all the hanky-panky behind the scenes?" Gideon asked. "He couldn't have been too pleased."

"I have no idea. I know he didn't take to Edgar; you could see it on his face. There was always a kind of negative electricity between them, but I think it was what you get when you have a couple of rival superstars. Edgar was a born prima donna, and I'm sure Vasily didn't take kindly to playing second fiddle. I doubt if he was too awfully upset when Edgar decided not to come back."

"So far, I haven't met anybody who was." He turned to look at her. "Julie, how come you never told me about any of this before? The sexcapades stuff?"

"Would you have wanted me to?"

"No!" he said with feeling. "I hate hearing this kind of stuff, you know that."

"Well, that's how come."

"So why tell me now?"

"You asked me a question."

"I did? I don't remember—"

"You said 'This time, as opposed to last time?' That's a question."

"I guess it was. My mistake."

"Anyway, now you know."

"So I do," he sighed, taking her hand again as they turned from the parapet to go back inside. "Now If only I could figure out a way to un-know."

FIVE

VASILY Kozlov had a well-deserved reputation as a glutton for work, and the schedule he had devised for the week confirmed it. The consortium would meet at nine every morning for a working breakfast, take a one-hour lunch break at one, then reconvene until 3:45, when tea would be served on the ramparts, weather permitting, or in the dungeon if not, and conclude with another working session from 4:15 to 6:00. Evening sessions would be held as needed. And Kozlov himself intended to chair every minute of them. The first day, Monday, would consist of a review of current issues and a fine-tuning of the agenda; presentation of participants' papers and discussion of them would follow for the next five days; and there would be a free-wheeling wrap-up on Sunday.

Although Kozlov again charmingly urged Gideon to attend the breakfast session, Gideon had learned his lesson the day before. (He had learned another lesson later on that night, losing twelve and a half pounds at the poker table, mostly to the crafty Kozlov himself.) Thus, as the old clock in the castle's entryway was striking nine, Gideon, having breakfasted on ham-and-egg-and-potato pasties and a double cappuccino at the bright little Kavorna Coffee House in town, was forking over his two pounds to enter the Isles of Scilly Museum on Church Street, the first visitor of the day. Madeleine Goodfellow, he was told by the volunteer behind the counter, would not be in until ten, which gave him a welcome hour to wander the halls.

It was, as Julie had said, his kind of museum. Well-done, but not too big, or ambitious, or flashy. Two floors of local archaeology and natural history, maritime life, shipwrecks, artifacts going back to the sixteenth century, and photographic displays of life on the island a hundred years ago. No high-tech gadgetry, not a single button to push, no 'hands-on interactive learning experiences'; just well-mounted, down-to-earth exhibits with lucid explanatory plates. It even smelled like his kind of museum: floor polish, stone dust, and old things.

Naturally enough, one glass-encased wall exhibit in particular held his interest.

Puritan (Roundhead) uniform, circa 1648. These remarkably well-preserved objects, from the days when St. Mary's was the last redoubt of Cavalier resistance to Parliamentarian forces, were discovered in a dry eighteenth-century well in 1946, clothing the remains of a Cromwellian footsoldier.

"Remarkably well-preserved" was stretching things a bit, but there was enough to give some idea of how the clothed, living man might have appeared: a few faded, darkened shreds of gray-and-white striped trousers, some sad fragments of once-bright-yellow ribbon that had probably been a jaunty waist-sash, and a few leather items—a sword holder and several unidentifiable straps—that were now a tarry black. There was no sign at all of the thigh-high boots he'd probably worn, which suggested that they'd been appropriated when he died. No one had needed his armor, however. There was a near-complete set, lovingly restored and buffed: separate back- and breastplates, a gorget to shield the throat, one of the two tarrets that would have protected the thighs, and a "lobster pot" helmet with a deep, round dent on the left side, a little back from the front. Everything had been tacked to an outline of a man that showed where they would have gone in life.

Gideon stepped back to take it in. Judging from the outline, this soldier of the soon-to-be Lord Protector of England would have been quite short by modern standards, but probably about average for the time. And that deep, round dent in the helmet . . . that was interesting. It looked as if it had been caused by a hammerlike weapon, or perhaps a nearly spent musket ball that hadn't had the oomph left to penetrate the metal. Either way, it would likely have left a sizeable dent in the skull beneath it too, so it might well be that he was looking at evidence of the cause of death. Directly under that dent, beneath the unfashionably short-cropped hair (which was the reason they were called Roundheads), would have been the coronal suture, separating the frontal and left parietal. Too bad the skull didn't survive. It would have been interesting—

"Yes, that's our man," Madeleine's plummy, jolly voice announced, "waiting all these years—all these centuries— for you to come and tell us all about him."

Gideon turned, smiling, to greet her. "Nice exhibit. You've already shown quite a lot about him."

"Why, thank you," she said, beaming. She wore a skirt-suit of violent green that did nothing to minimize her ample proportions. "Ready to go to work? Or would you care to chat for a while?"

"How about work first, chat later?"

"Very good. A true scientist."

She unlocked an unmarked door between wall cases and

they stepped into a typical museum storeroom, with racks of cheap metal shelving, some holding neatly stacked boxes specifically made for museum storage of specimens and artifacts, others holding cartons specifically made for grocery storage of applesauce or tomato paste. There were also objects large and small—Victorian schoolbooks; a well-worn millstone (how had they gotten that in here?); a cannonball; framed, pressed seaweed specimens—stowed willy-nilly in corners, on chairs and tables, and anyplace else they'd go. One of the two library tables in the room had been cleared, except for a serious-looking one-by-three-foot, lidded cardboard carton at one end, and a smaller Prince's fish paste carton at the other. In the center, neatly arranged, were the materials and equipment he'd asked for.

"And here . . ." With a flourish, she removed the lid from the larger carton. ". . . lies our fallen hero."

Inside the heavy cardboard box were some of the long bones lying loose, all of them brown and exfoliating, and only a few of them whole. When he picked up the left humerus, bits of bone flaked off and floated to the bottom of the carton.

"Madeleine, you'll want to stabilize these if you exhibit them. Or even if you don't. Otherwise they'll just continue to degrade. Whoever cleaned them did it without preserving them, which didn't help. Look at all the flakes and crumbs in the bottom."

"It does look pretty bad," she said, concerned. "I should have done something before this. What does one use for human bones? Alvar and acetone?"

"Sure, something like that. Whatever you're used to using on pottery would work." He looked down for a few seconds at the dry, dun-brown remnants that had once given form and strength to arms and legs. "Madeleine, I'm afraid your doctor may pretty much have said it all. He was human and he was male. As for going beyond that, ageing's going to be difficult because the ends of most of the bones have been gnawed off. . . ."

She waited for more, and when he didn't go on, but simply stood gazing at the bones with his hands clasped behind him, she said a bit plaintively: "And that's all you can tell me?"

But he was plunged in thought, looking at each bone, registering details, and oddities and anomalies, and visually moving on to the next, so that it took a few seconds for the question to penetrate.

"Maybe a little more," he said at last. "For instance, I can tell you he wasn't a particularly beefy guy. The bones are relatively slender, with no heavy muscle markings.

"Oh, yes?" she said politely. She'd been hoping for more.

"I can also tell you that he had a rough life." Gideon picked up the partial left femur, the thigh bone, and showed it to her. The upper third was gone, and the lower, or distal, end had been chewed off by rodent scavengers, but the shaft itself was distinguished by an unnatural bend in the middle, with an ugly, uneven excrescence of bone at the site of the bend.

Madeleine looked at it and drew back a little, the corners of her mouth turned down. "It's as if . . . as if it got broken, then somebody stuck it together again—not all that carefully, either—and then stuck all this . . ." She gestured at the roughened area. ". . . all this *gunk* on it to keep it from coming apart again."

Gideon nodded, smiling. "That's a pretty good description of what happened, Madeleine. The femur was broken, all right, and then it healed on its own. This 'gunk' is the protective callus that forms around a break after a couple of months. If the ends of the pieces don't quite match up, as they don't here, it temporarily builds up even more to add strength. This is probably what your doctor thought was a sign of disease."

"What's it made of?"

"Bone. Lamellar bone, stronger than the original." He fingered it. "I don't think it happened too long before he died. The callus is still pretty big. Very little resorption. A year, maybe less."

Tentatively following his example, she touched it too and was surprised. "It's jagged. It's *sharp.* Wouldn't that have been painful?"

"Oh, no doubt about it. The musculature around it would have been inflamed and probably infected. He'd have been in constant pain, and he'd surely have had difficulty walking. This leg would have been a couple of inches shorter than the other. I wouldn't be surprised if he was on crutches."

"And yet here he was off in the Scillies, far from home, wherever home was. A soldier. Marching." She shook her head. "The poor man."

"He had other problems. Look at this." He proffered another bone.

She complied. "How interesting. Er, what exactly am I looking at?"

"This is a right forearm bone, the radius." He laid his finger on a point halfway down the shaft. "Now look at this."

"Oh, I see," she said, peering at the spot near which he'd laid his finger. "That's another callus, isn't it? A smaller one, though. This is a healed fracture too, although it's not as bad as the other."

"The callus isn't as big, no, but the injury is worse. See how the bone below it has this sort of swollen look? That's not normal."

"I'll take your word for it."

"Okay, see this hole?" He inserted the tip of a ballpoint pen into a small, smoothly rounded opening just below the callus.

"Isn't that a natural foramen of some kind? It doesn't look like a puncture."

"No, it's not, but it's not exactly natural, either; that is, he wasn't born with it. It's a reaction to infection, to serious infection; an opening to let the pus drain from inside it. In other words, the fracture healed fine, yes, but the bone got infected—and stayed infected. I imagine this poor old guy was just one mass of infection and pain. That might well be what killed him."

She shivered. "I'm beginning to be sorry I asked you to do this."

"Well, you know, war isn't—" Whatever homily had been on his tongue stopped in mid-sentence. "Oh, Lordy," he said.

Madeleine cringed. "What now, or don't I want to know?"

He had shifted his attention to the proximal end of the bone, the one near the elbow, and now, using the magnifying glass and holding bone and lens close to his face, he slowly rotated it beneath the magnifying glass.

"The end of this one hasn't been completely gnawed off," he told her. "And it's not completely ossified."

Madeleine frowned. "You're talking about the, what is it, the epiphery, the diastysis . . ."

"The epiphysis."

Long bones—arms, legs, ribs, clavicles—grew by depositing material at their ends: the epiphyses. At first this material was cartilaginous, but with time it ossified and fused permanently to the shaft of the bone, which was then done growing. And when the last epiphysis had fused to the last shaft, somewhere in the person's mid-twenties—a bit later for the clavicle—the person was also done growing. The amount of time the process took, researchers had learned long ago, varied from bone to bone, but was highly predictable for each individual bone. So at least for the first quarter-century of life or so, one could fairly reliably estimate age from the skeleton by how much fusion had taken place on the various bones. If they were all completely fused, the person had been, physiologically, at least, an adult; if not, he or she hadn't yet been fully grown.

And this particular epiphysis on this particular person was not. A cleft, thin but plainly visible, still ran halfway around the base of the coinlike disk of bone that formed the top of the ulna; fusion had been incomplete at the time of death.

"So how old was he?" Madeleine asked when he'd pointed this out.

He shrugged. "For white males, it usually closes up anywhere from fourteen to eighteen. There's some variability, of course, but—"

"You mean he's . . . he's not even eighteen years old?"

"Fifteen or sixteen would be my guess."

The grizzled, scarred old veteran that they'd been imagining had suddenly become a teenaged boy, a youth who had hardly lived, who had died wretchedly, in pain and misery, far away from home, probably weeping for his mother or his girl.

He laid the bone back in the box with more tenderness than he'd picked it up. "Just a kid," he said softly.

"Now I'm depressed," Madeleine said. "I could use some coffee. How about you?"

"Same here. Thanks."

"Be back in a minute."

There wasn't much more to be learned from the bones, and there were no pieces to be glued together, not that gluing would have been a good idea anyway until the bones had been stabilized. If he'd had some standardized tables with him, he could have come up with a formal stature estimate from measurements of the long bones, but he didn't. He did, however, have a pretty good feel for such things, and from eyeing and hefting the bones, he was able to arrive at an estimate that he'd hardly stake his reputation on, but in which he had confidence all the same. His estimate was five feet to five-feet-four inches, even shorter than he'd thought from the costume display.

So it was not only a kid, it was a runty, probably ill-fed one at that. Gideon sighed as he fitted the lid back onto the carton.

Now I'm *depressed.*

He pulled up a stool and opened the other carton, the one that had once been home to two dozen jars of Prince's Tuna and Mayo Paste. It now contained five small white paper bags, each crisply folded over precisely three times, and one larger sack from Porthmellon Store (Groceries, Fruit and Vegetables, Beers and Wines). There was place-and-date information printed on each one with a marking pen: *Town Beach, nr Holgate's Grn, 21 May 2002; Rat Island, nr quay, 4 Nov 2003; Woolpack Pt, 15 Jan 2004 . . .*

Each bag contained a single bone or bony fragment, which he laid out on its own bag. He saw at once that his promise to Madeleine—"There's always something to be learned"—was a bit exaggerated. The two smallest weren't human; flattened and streamlined, like miniature paddles, they were probably metapodials, the fingerlike bones from seal flippers. The other four, while human, had little to offer. Two fragments of femur, one near-complete tibia, and half of an ulna. Not even enough to make respectable guesses as to age and sex. The two humeral fragments and the ulna were old, maybe as old as the kid in the other box. And they'd probably been in the sea for a long time, given the nematode encrustations. For them, Madeleine's guess of old shipwreck remains was as good as any.

The tibia—the shin bone—was newer: not brown and fragmenting like the others, but ivory-colored and dense. The proximal epiphysis—the one at the knee—was fused, so he knew at least that it had come from an adult. The distal end of the bone, the one near the ankle, had been snapped cleanly off. He lifted the broken end to his nostrils and sniffed. There was a faint, greasy smell of candle wax; the odor from the fat in the bone, which was always strong at first, then gradually faded with time and eventually disappeared. The fact that it was there at all told him the bone was in all probability no more than ten years old; the facts that it was relatively weak, and that the bone was completely devoid of soft tissue told him it was older than, say, a year, given the relatively warm (and thus decomposition-inducing) climate of the Scillies. Two or three years was his guess.

And now that he'd had it in his hands and felt the roughened muscle insertion points and the general robusticity, he could take a reasonable stab at the sex too: male. His interest increasing as he became more "acquainted" with it, he glanced at the bag that it had come in, in hopes that there might be more data, but there was only the usual cryptic information: *Beach below Halangy Point, just north of the Creeb, 20 January 2005.*

"Coffee," Madeleine announced, placing two lidded sixteen-ounce cardboard containers on the table. "Inasmuch as you're from Seattle, I went to enormous trouble and expense to get you a double-shot latte, so that you feel entirely at home."

"You're wonderful."

"You see, we're reasonably civilized here, at least in some ways." She removed the lids from both cups.

"Clearly, in the ways that count," Gideon said appreciatively, inhaling the opulent aroma. A lot nicer than bone fat, he thought.

"Anything new?" she asked, drawing up a stool of her own and delicately balancing her bulk on it.

It was at the very moment that she asked, while he was

placing the tibia back on the table, that his sensitive fingers "saw" what his eyes should have seen in the first place.

"Damn," he whispered.

"What now?" she whispered, alarmed.

When he peered hard at the bone, it took him only an instant to confirm what his fingers had told him. "Madeleine, this bone didn't break. It was cut—cut, and sawed too."

"Yes? I don't—"

"I think we might be looking at a dismemberment. From not that long ago."

"A dis—" Her lips curled with disgust. She got off her stool and moved a couple of feet away, never taking her eyes off the bone, as if it might come after her. "You're serious, aren't you?"

"Oh, I'm serious, all right. Can you tell me anything about this, other than what it says on the bag?"

Her glasses which hung on their lanyard around her neck, were raised to her eyes—indeed, like a lorgnette—so she could read the lettering. "Oh, yes, I remember. The little beach near Halangy Point. That's at the north end of the island, about two miles from Hugh Town, at the very end of the road. It's an out-of-the-way place; not many visitors find it."

"No, I mean how it happened to be found, who found it, was it buried—"

"Yes, it was buried in the sand. A visitor brought it in when her dog dug it up. We didn't keep her name, we usually don't. If I recall correctly, she said it was about a foot down. That's all I know. I . . . I didn't think there was any reason . . . Gideon, are you *certain*?"

"No, I'm not certain—we only have the one bone—but that's what it looks like to me. You see, when fresh bone is sawed—"

Hurriedly, she raised her hand, palm out, bangles jingling their way down to her elbow. "Stop. Desist. I've had all the forensic anthropology I want for one morning, thank you. I'm afraid it's far too gruesome for me. What are you going to do?"

"Go see the police. What else? Do you mind if I take this with me?"

She turned her head to the side to avoid looking at it, like a baby resisting its mashed carrot. *"Take it. Please."*

As he was putting it back in the sack, she said, "Ask for Sergeant Clapper; he's in charge. The police station is on Upper Garrison Lane, on the way back toward the castle. You can't miss it."

SIX

HE could and did, walking the two-block length of Upper Garrison Lane twice before he realized that the modest two-story house, tucked into the elbow of an uphill curve in the street and half-hidden behind lush shrubbery and a low stone wall, was what he was looking for. No sign out front, no parking area, not a police car in sight. But behind a rolling bank of pink and white narcissus, slightly below the level of the street and overhung by a shabby, glassed-in balcony, he finally spotted a nondescript storefront window that might have been the entrance to a dry cleaner's or a hearing aid center. But a closer look showed POLICE in stick-on letters on the window, and an inconspicuous gray plaque on the stuccoed wall beside it:

Devon and Cornwall Constabulary
Isles of Scilly Police Station
This station is open between 0900 hours
and 1000 hours daily where possible.

He smiled. It must be nice to live someplace where reports of criminality could be dealt with in an hour a day (where possible). Once he opened the door and walked in, however, except for the absence of a reception area, he found himself in a small-town version of any big-city police station he'd ever been in: a short corridor lined with a couple of glassed-in cubicles, mismatched office furniture, too-bright neon ceiling lights, desks cluttered with papers and files, and walls cluttered with plastic-sheeted, grease-pencil calendars and charts, scrawled notes, and public information posters, including an unlikely one advertising "Substantial Rewards for Information Leading to the Prosecution of Terrorists." On a bureau near the door were two old-fashioned bucket helmets and two of the newer checkered police hats that always made Gideon think of taxi drivers.

The cubicle to the left, despite its desk and chair, seemed to be a storage space, copy center, and coffee room. In the one on the right a smiling, clean-cut, red-haired young man in dark blue uniform trousers and a short-sleeved, open-throated white shirt with blue epaulets sat working at a computer, apparently untroubled by an in-basket that was spilling over with forms and memos.

"I'm Police Constable Robb," he said cheerfully, swiveling his chair to face the newcomer. "How may I be of service?"

"My name's Gideon Oliver, Constable. I'm an anthropologist. I was just looking over some bones at the museum, and one of them in particular caught my attention. A tourist brought it into the museum in January. It was buried on the beach near Halangy Point. Her dog dug it up."

"And we're speaking of a human bone here, sir?" Polite attention, but no real interest. As Madeleine had said, the odd human bone turning up now and then wasn't that unusual.

"Definitely, yes, but the main thing is that I think there's a good chance that it came from someone who's been dismembered. My guess is that it's something that happened within the last ten years, probably in the last five, so I thought I'd better bring it in. I'm supposed to ask for Sergeant Clapper."

A stray bone might be nothing to get excited about, but violent crimes, let alone dismemberments, were not common fare on St. Mary's. Robb's mouth hung open for a moment before he replied. "I think Sergeant Clapper is very much the man for that, sir."

He picked up his telephone and explained. "Shall I send him in, sir?"

Gideon heard the rumbled answer come through the door at the end of the corridor, delivered with a won't-they-ever-leave-me-in-peace sigh. "No, I'll come there."

Sergeant Clapper was a broad, heavy man of fifty-five or so in civilian clothes—black corduroy trousers and a white shirt folded back over thick, hairy wrists—with a sad, dull-brown slick of hair pulled across his scalp, a heavy red drinker's face, and tired, seen-everything, don't-even-*think*-of-putting-anything-over-on-me eyes. He stuck out a blunt-fingered, big-knuckled hand that looked as hard as a shovel but turned out to be about as emphatic as something dragged out of a pond in late August.

"I'm Sergeant Clapper."

"Gideon Oliver."

"What's all this about a dismemberment?"

"Well, I have it here." He looked for someplace on Robb's desk on which to put it, and with a sweep of both hands Robb cleared a space. File folders and their contents flopped to the floor.

"Kyle, your desk is a damned disgrace," Clapper muttered.

Robb seemed undisturbed. "Sorry, Sarge."

Gideon opened the bag and put the tibial fragment on the old-fashioned blotter that was now visible on the desktop. When, he wondered, had he last seen a desk blotter, let alone one that was actually stained with ink? The three men stood looking down at the bone. Robb seemed eager to comment but waited for his chief.

"That's it?" Clapper said. "That's your dismemberment?" He made a small dismissive gesture with his hand. Gideon noticed that the fingernails were chewed to scraps and the thick fingers were deeply tobacco-stained, down almost to the first joint.

"Well, it's an indication, a possible indication, of a dismemberment."

"Ah, so it's a *possible* indication, is it?"

Gideon was beginning to get irritated. "Sergeant—"

"American, are you?"

"That's right, I'm here just for the week, for the consortium at Star Castle."

"Oh, yes? One of the participants?"

"Well, no, my wife is a Fellow. I'm just here to . . . I'm just along."

Clapper's lips parted to show a set of big brown teeth. "*Are* you now? Well, well."

Now Gideon *was* irritated. What the hell was that supposed to mean?

"I'm also a professional anthropologist," he said hotly. "I do quite a lot of forensic work. I assure you, I know what I'm talking about."

"No offense, Mr. Oliver."

"*Doctor* Oliver," Gideon said. "Or professor, if you prefer."

Now he was not only annoyed with Clapper, but with himself for letting the guy get under his skin. And ashamed of himself as well for acting like a stuffed shirt. This was not going as planned.

He summoned up what he hoped was convincingly friendly smile. "Well, let me show you what I have," he said mildly, "and you can take it from there."

"Chairs, Kyle," Clapper ordered from the side of his mouth.

Robb was obviously used to being treated like this. Docilely, he cleared off a couple of fabric-seated metal chairs and set them in front of the desk. When the three men sat, Clapper put an ankle-booted foot against the desk front and shoved himself back a few feet. He was putting some space between himself and them to show that he wasn't committing himself to anything yet. This was between his constable and his visitor; he was merely observing.

So be it. Gideon addressed himself directly to Robb while Clapper, looking preoccupied, thumbed open the lid of a red-and-white pack of Gold Bond cigarettes and lit up.

"What this is—" Gideon began.

The telephone on Robb's desk chirped. He picked it up, listened, and covered the mouthpiece. "It's for you, Sarge: Exeter. Policy and Performance Unit, Chief Inspector Cory. What should I tell him?'

"Tell him to sod off, the vile bugger," Clapper growled.

"Sarge, this is the third time in the last two—"

"Tell him to sod off."

Robb removed his hand from the mouthpiece. "Chief Inspector? Sergeant Clapper is in conference with village officials at the moment. May I have him call you back? Yes, I know he did. No, I'll see he does this time. Yes, of course he will. Thank you, Chief Inspector."

"You were saying?" Clapper said to Gideon

"I was saying that what this is, is a left tibia. The tibia is the—"

"Shin bone," Robb said with an eager smile. If he'd been American, Gideon thought, and this had been the 1940s, he might have made a Hollywood living portraying nice, young, small-town soda jerks. He reminded Gideon of all those bright-eyed, painfully alert young students trying to make a good impression on the first day of class. And as he generally liked them, he'd taken liking to the young cop.

"Right. And what we have is the proximal three-quarters or so, that is, the—"

"The end closer to the center of the body. In the case of the tibia, that would be the upper part, near the knee." He pointed. "The patella would be attached right here, then?"

"Kyle." Clapper wearily exhaled a lungful of blue smoke. "We know you're a clever lad who's been to university and you're very intelligent. Now why don't you just let the man tell his story without interrupting after every two words?"

Robb's face stiffened with its first dull show of resentment, quickly snuffed out. "Sorry about that, sir."

"It's not as if I don't know what a shin bone is, now is it?"

"No, sir, I didn't mean to imply—"

Clapper turned away from him toward Gideon. "Do you suppose we can get on with it, *Doctor* Oliver?"

Ah, was that what Clapper's problem was? An ageing, old-guard policeman, ill-educated and burnt out, who'd never risen beyond the rank of constable sergeant, stuck away in a tiny, crimeless village, in the remotest place in all of Merrie Olde England, to run out his time until retirement? And burdened with a young, personable, college-educated youth who was clearly on his way up the ladder on which Clapper had climbed but a couple of dingy rungs at the bottom? Gideon felt his first flicker of sympathy for the older man.

But not as much as he felt for Robb.

"That's right, Constable, the patella would be about there, but it doesn't really attach to the tibia itself, or to any bone. It's embedded in the terminal tendon of the *quadriceps femoris*—the big muscle in the front of the thigh—and actually sits in a little hollow at the distal end of the femur, just above the tibia."

This was said equally to gratify Robb and to irritate Clapper, and judging by their reactions, he'd succeeded. Robb looked at him gratefully, while Clapper heaved a huge sigh and looked at his watch.

Better get on with it, all right, Gideon thought, *before I lose him altogether.*

"This is the right tibia of an adult male who died some-time in the last ten years." He paused, expecting a chal-lenge from Clapper—how do you know it's a male? how do you know he's an adult? how do you know when he died?—but the sergeant merely blew smoke at the ceiling and continued to look fidgety and preoccupied.

"The markings on it indicate a dismemberment, which in turn strongly suggests a homicide, at least to me." He waited again for Clapper to object, and this time he did.

"A homicide, is it now?" the sergeant said with elephan-tine joviality. "Kyle, lad, when was the last homicide we had here in these delightful islands?"

"Don't know, sir. Before my time, that's for sure."

"You see, Professor," Clapper said, "we don't much go in for that sort of thing in this little corner of the world. Our usual run of problems, on those rare occasions when we have them, involves disorderly conduct, antisocial be-havior, noise complaints—alcohol-related things, gener-ally speaking. Although, if I'm going to be honest, I have to admit, there was the case of the purloined piglet from Farmer Follet's van on Market Day last."

"We don't much go in for murder and dismemberment in my little corner of the world either," Gideon said curtly, "but that doesn't mean they don't happen." Without wait-ing for Clapper to reply, he picked up where he'd left off. "The cut that severed the bone was made by a saw. So was this groove right next to the cut—it's a hesitation cut, the kind of thing you get when you're having a little trouble placing the saw at first. But these grooves here"—he pointed to two shallow cut-marks at a slight angle to the hesitation cut—"were made with a knife."

"A knife *and* a saw?" Clapper said with a skeptical lift of his eyebrows.

"Yes, and that's what makes me think this guy was almost certainly dismembered. An old bone with saw marks on it—or some knife scratchings—who knows, that might be nothing more than something that was found and then whittled or sawed for . . . well, for some innocent reason, not that anything comes to mind. But a knife *and* a saw, that's different."

Robb shook his head, puzzled. "But why—"

"You'd want a knife to cut down through the soft tissue, then a saw to get through the bone."

"Ah," an engrossed Robb said, but Clapper looked as restless and dubious as ever.

Gideon plowed ahead anyway. "You can see the difference between the two kinds of cuts by—"

"The knife marks are narrower than the saw marks?" Robb asked with a wary glance at Clapper, who continued to say nothing. "Is that the difference?"

"More or less. The teeth on a saw are 'set'; that is, they're at a slight outward angle to the blade on each side, so the groove that a saw leaves is going to be very slightly wider than the actual blade. On the other hand, a knife has no set, so its groove is going to be a better indication of its actual width. More than that, a knife blade is V-shaped in cross-section, so it leaves a V-shaped groove, whereas a saw—"

"Leaves a square, flat-bottomed one," Robb finished for him, peering at the various notches and nodding vigorously.

"Well, U-shaped would probably be more accurate, if you look closely."

"Yes, I see."

"Besides that, a V-shaped groove in fresh bone is more

likely to close up a little afterward, whereas a wider, U-shaped one won't, which means that not only do saw cuts give an over-impression of blade width, but knife cuts tend to give a slight under-impression."

"What about a serrated knife?" Clapper put in. "That has teeth."

"Not set at an angle to the blade," Gideon said. "It leaves a slightly different mark than a non-serrated one, but it's still V-shaped."

"And why, if you don't mind my asking, are you so sure the big cut, the one that cut it in two, is from a saw?" Clapper asked in the spirit of a defense attorney who found himself short of serious ammunition but had every intention of obstructing anyway. "Why not an ax? That'd be my choice. Speed things up a bit, wouldn't it?"

"No, this is a clean cut. There would have been some crushing, some splintering, with an ax, and probably more than one blow to get through the bone. And only a saw would have left these parallel striations in the cut end. They show the direction of the saw cut, by the way, which was from back to front. And—"

Clapper's sigh was monumental. He got up to grind out his cigarette in the metal ashtray on Robb's desk, then went to the window behind the desk and looked out at the garage of the house next door, a bored and restless man.

"And there's another way you can tell too," Gideon went on, partly for Robb's continuing edification, but mostly for the hell of it. He took the bone back from the young constable, who had been holding it while he followed Gideon's remarks, and touched his finger to a thin, quarter-inch spike extending from the cut end. "This is the breakaway spur that you get with saw cuts. The bone snaps off from its own weight just before the saw blade gets all the way through."

"Yes, the same thing happens when one saws a piece of wood, doesn't it?" Robb said. "Unless, of course, one turns it over and finishes sawing through from the other side."

"Right, but when you're dismembering a corpse, as the sergeant correctly suggested, you're probably going to be a lot more interested in speed than in neatness."

Clapper turned from the window and perched his bulk somewhat precariously on the sill. "Where did you say this was found? On the beach? Up near Halangy Point?"

"Yes, a little north of the creeb," Gideon said, to show him he was dealing with someone who knew the lay of the land, not merely some know-nothing outlander. *What the hell is a creeb?* he wondered.

"Buried," Clapper said. A statement, not a question.

"Yes."

Clapper lit up another Gold Bond. " 'Buried' as in the active voice or in the passive?"

"Pardon me?"

"Are you saying 'Someone buried the bone in the sand'? Or simply 'The bone was buried in the sand,' as, for example, if it had washed ashore from who knows what distant land, and then been covered over during a storm?"

Gideon revised his estimate of Clapper's educational level. "I don't have any way of knowing."

"Ah."

When the telephone trilled again, Robb listened a moment and reported. "It's for you again, Sarge." He made a sympathetic face. "Exeter again." His voice went to a respectful whisper. "It's Chief Superintendent Dibbs himself this time."

Clapper rolled his eyes. "And does Chief Superintendent Dibbs himself strike you as being in a fun-loving frame of mind?"

"Not really, sir."

The sergeant rose heavily from the window sill and clumped back toward his office, muttering. He was a slow-moving man with a stately, surging stride, like an astronaut moving through a zero-gravity environment. "Exeter is where headquarters is, Dr. Oliver; the Devon and Cornwall

Constabulary main office," Robb explained when the door had closed behind the sergeant. "They've been giving Sergeant Clapper a bit of a difficult time."

"I'm sorry to hear that."

"I suspect he'll be in there a while."

"Shall I leave the bone with you, then?"

"I think that would be best. Can we reach you at the castle if need be?"

"Any time. I'll be here till the end of the week."

The two men stood and shook hands. "Thank you very much for taking the time and trouble to come in, sir, we appreciate it." He grinned. "And thanks for the osteology lesson. We'll be in touch now, sir."

Heading back down Upper Garrison, a grumpy Gideon doubted it. He knew Clapper's type all too well. A cynical, disillusioned cop nearing sixty, who disguised his cynicism with a leaden-footed jocularity, who was more interested in keeping a low profile and not making any waves than he was in solving old, anonymous murders. He wasn't going to take the chance of stepping into anything that might seriously complicate his life. The easiest, least risky path for him at this point would be to simply let the matter slide, to not even open a case file—it was only a single bone, after all—and that was the path he was going to take.

SEVEN

BUT Gideon was dead wrong. He'd never run into a cop like Mike Clapper before, a fact that was made clear to him the following day.

With Julie, he was having lunch at Tregarthen's Hotel, another establishment, like Star Castle, with proud historical associations, but of a literary sort: plaques on the walls proclaimed that both George Eliot and Alfred, Lord Tennyson, had spent time there.

They ate in the airy, Danish Modern bar, its cool blues and golds a nice contrast to the brooding, dark-wood ambience of Star Castle. After a light meal of steamed clams and a couple of glasses of Skinner's Cornish Blonde beer—citrusy and wheaty, and the waiter's excellent suggestion to accompany the clams—they took their coffee outside to the one of the umbrellaed tables on the terrace overlooking the Old Quay and the outer islands. Julie had considerately failed to mention his promise of the day before to pay for lunch out of his poker winnings, for which he was grateful. They watched the Scillonian ferry disembark its first passenger-load of the day and were on their second cups, silently enjoying the wisps of cloud, the sun-dappled water, and the faint tinge of white mist on the horizon, when Gideon spotted Police Constable Robb going in the hotel's front door, quite handsome in full uniform; blue tunic, bucket helmet, dark tie and all. Robb saw him at the same time and came over for a friendly hello.

"I'm glad to see you, Dr. Oliver," he said after he'd been introduced to Julie. "I was hoping to have a chance to speak with you. I'm in for a quick sandwich. All right if I join you?"

"Sure, pull up a chair."

"I'll just order inside. Faster that way. Back in a tick."

"He seems as nice as you said," Julie remarked as he disappeared inside.

"Oh, a good kid, very nice. It's Clapper that's the hard case. I'm telling you, I'd have slugged the guy if he'd treated me the way he treated Robb."

"Yeah, right," Julie said, and they both laughed.

When Robb returned with a ham sandwich and a can of English lemonade, the first thing he did was strip off his coat and helmet and lay them neatly on an unused chair.

"Ah, that's better." Glaring at the helmet, he massaged his temples. "That thing is like wearing a pail on your head."

"You can't wear the soft cap?" Gideon asked. "I saw a couple in your office."

"Oh, generally, we do, when we wear a cap at all. But I've only just come up from quay duty—seeing in the ferry—and the tourists, you know, they like to see them. Well—" He smiled and shrugged. "'A policeman's lot is not a happy one.'"

"'Taking one consideration with another,'" Julie recited, which pleased him, and together they sang a few more lines of patter from *Pirates of Penzance*.

While he ate they engaged in small talk. What did Julie

do? (She was a park ranger. "How interesting!") Where was Robb from? (Bournemouth, on his last three months of a two-year assignment to St. Mary's.) What was life like in the Scillies? (Quiet.) But Gideon could feel him edging closer to whatever it was he was anxious to talk about, and finally he got there.

"I hope you'll come by and see the sergeant about that bone again," he said as he finished the first half of the sandwich and used a napkin to pluck a crumb from the corner of his mouth. "I'm sure you could be a great deal of help on the case."

"What case?" Gideon asked. "He didn't seem very interested in opening one yesterday."

"I grant you, his manner can be a bit, er, unfortunate at times. Sometimes I have to step in and smooth the waters a bit."

"As you're doing now?" Julie asked.

"As I'm doing now. But underneath his rough exterior, you see—"

"There lies a heart of gold," Gideon said.

Robb laughed with patently real amusement. "Well, no, I wouldn't go so far as to say that, but four out of five days he's quite approachable, quite genial, even."

"Obviously, then, I hit him on day five."

"In a way, yes. Exeter had been nagging him all morning. That always puts him in a foul mood."

"I see. It wasn't my personality that set him off, it was just my rotten timing."

"Very much so," Robb said, nodding eagerly. "His attitude is entirely different today, entirely. You'd hardly know he was the same man. He's had me open a case log on the matter, and he's been hard at the computer, searching for possible leads on that bone ever since."

Gideon was astonished. "He has? What brought about this change?"

"Well, you see, he telephoned headquarters about it, as required in possible homicide cases. The usual procedure would be for them to send a detective constable from St. Ives to determine if foul play is really a possibility. If so, a detective inspector or perhaps a chief inspector, from Truro or possibly from Plymouth, would be assigned as SIO—that is, as senior investigative officer—"

Gideon hadn't remembered that Robb was so talky. "I'm afraid I don't see—"

"Well, the thing is, I gather they pretty much laughed at him—'*One* piece of bone from who knows where, with a few marks on it?' and so on—and implied that the detective force had better things to do, and he was entirely free to pursue it on his own. So that put a different light on it, do you see? It's his case now, not theirs."

Gideon pondered. "Look, Constable, did he tell you to ask me to come in again?"

"No, I can't say that he did, but—"

"Then I don't see the point. I'm not going to go barging in where I'm not wanted." He realized as he said it how pompous it sounded and tacked on a gentler addendum. "Of course, if he does ask me, I'd be happy to."

"I'm sure he *will* ask you, but, knowing him, it'll take a few days for him to get around to it. And inasmuch as you said you'd only *be* here a few days, I was afraid it might be too late by then. Thought I should strike while the iron's hot."

Their waiter came by with Robb's check and more coffee for Julie and Gideon. Gideon sipped and considered. "I don't think so," he said. "I just don't feel comfortable—"

"Oh, go ahead," Julie said. "You know you want to. If someone's really been murdered, you're not going to be happy walking away from it when you probably *could* be of some help."

Gideon shook his head. "Nope, I don't think so." Being

pressed from both sides was making him more stubborn than he might have been otherwise.

"Dr. Oliver," Robb said.

"Gideon."

"And I'm Kyle," Robb said with his sweet smile. "Look, may I tell you a little about the sergeant? Do you have a few minutes?"

"Sure," Gideon said, curious in spite of himself. Julie, always interested in what promised to be a human interest story, nodded as well, although it was likely to make her late for the consortium's afternoon session.

Robb pushed aside the last quarter of his sandwich, drained his lemonade, and collected his thoughts.

"Well, you have to understand . . ." But he decided he needed another beginning and started again. "This is hardly the sort of thing I'd ordinarily tell anyone, you see, let alone a relative stranger, but . . ." Another false start. He thought for a moment more before hitting on the opening he wanted.

"Sergeant Clapper," he said, "is not what he seems."

THAT was putting it mildly.

Harry Michael Clapper had had quite a life before becoming a policeman. The son of a London liquor wholesaler, he had joined the army at an underage seventeen, spending over twenty years in the service. He had been wounded and twice decorated for bravery during the Falklands War and had retired in 1988 as regimental sergeant-major, about as high as a non-commissioned officer could go. He had knocked around for a while after that, and then, in 1990, at the advanced age of 40, he had submitted an application to the Devon and Cornwall Constabulary to become a police officer. To his own surprise he was accepted. He breezed through the local training program in Exeter, came in first in his class at the fifteen-week residential course at the National Police Training Centre in Bramshill, and was assigned to Torquay as a traffic constable.

While still in his two-year probationary period, he had gotten a rare chief constable commendation—the first one that had ever been given to a probationer—for actions over and above the requirements of the service. Off-duty, out of uniform, alone, and weaponless, he had broken up an armed robbery, subduing the two perpetrators and sitting on them (literally) until a couple of police cars, summoned by the Australian victim, could arrive.

On completion of his probation he was transferred to the Criminal Investigation Department and posted to Plymouth as a detective constable. There, he not only completed university but compiled an extraordinary record of cases successfully closed that made him the only person in the department's long history to earn Officer of the Year honors three times. He was the subject of several Sunday magazine articles and was part of a BBC television special ("The New Sherlock Holmeses: England's Greatest Detectives"). By 2000, he had advanced to detective chief inspector—

"Wait a minute," Gideon said. He was shaking his head incredulously. "Hold on, Kyle. Are we really talking about the same Mike Clapper? He was a famous detective? He was a chief inspector? What's he doing as a constable sergeant out in the Scillies? What happened to him? Was he demoted?"

"Not exactly," Robb said. "But just when he was at the top of the heap, a lot of things began going wrong for him. His life pretty much came apart."

First, and probably most important, his wife of nearly thirty years died after a long, exhausting battle with cancer. Then, only a few weeks after her funeral, he received word that the position of detective superintendent, for which he'd applied months earlier, had gone to a much younger man with little more than half his experience and nowhere near his record of medals, commendations, and successes. What he did have was training in community relations and three years' experience as departmental ombudsman—two areas that, as far as Clapper was concerned, had nothing to do with real police work, the meat of which was persistence, legwork, and the dogged, life-encompassing determination to put the bad guys away.

After that it was all downhill. Clapper turned bitter and became increasingly solitary. Once the pride of the department, he became perceived by his higher-ups as an anachronism: a stubbornly old-fashioned copper who had stayed beyond his time and whose hard-nosed approach to the job was outmoded and discredited. His positions on what policing was all about—and especially what it wasn't about—had brought a string of in-house complaints from the chief of Community Relations, the representative of the Gay Police Association, and the head of the Diversity Enhancement Task Force. More than that, his increasingly negative attitude was becoming a bad influence on the younger members of the force. And on top of that—

Robb hesitated. "Well, he began . . . he had . . . other problems too."

"Alcohol?" said Gideon.

"Exactly. He was drinking too much."

It was time for him to go, and various efforts, some subtle, some not, were made to retire him, either voluntarily or otherwise. But with two years left to qualify for a full pension, he wasn't about to be "made redundant," and there was no way to force him. After considerable dickering, an unusual compromise was reached. Clapper would be transferred from the large port city of Plymouth to the obscure, virtually crime-free outpost of St. Mary's, where he could harmlessly serve out his time without getting into trouble or offending anyone. But for him to assume the position of the Scillies' "neighborhood beat manager" required that he be downgraded from detective inspector to constable sergeant. This he reluctantly accepted, with the proviso that his grade for pension purposes remain that of chief inspector. To this the department agreed, and to the Scillies he came, and here he had been for the last six months, out of the mainstream and pretty much going through the motions.

"Not that much beyond going through the motions is generally required here," Robb said with a smile. "We're not what you might call a hotbed of crime. But you can imagine how tough it must be on the old man to be reporting to people in Exeter who don't know the half of what he does."

"Well, I admit," Gideon said as their waiter came to pick up their payments, "I'm impressed. About the only thing I had right about him was that he was counting the days to retirement."

"Which isn't hard to understand," Robb said. "Things haven't been easy for him."

"They can't have been too easy for you either," said Gideon. "I didn't get the impression he was the easiest boss in the world to work for."

"Oh, not so bad. One has to make allowances. One has to consider who he *is*. It's been a privilege to work with him, really. I've learned a lot."

"I admire your staying power," Gideon said.

"Well, yes, it was a little hard at first," Robb admitted, "but after a couple of months on the island he mellowed. He likes the idea of living at the police station, for one thing."

"He *lives* at the police station?" Julie said, surprised.

"Well, above it. Above the store, as we say," Robb said with a smile. "Upstairs, on the first floor. My wife and I do, too. There are several flats up there. It used to be a common arrangement years ago, but you don't see it much anymore, except in out-of-the-way places like this. And then . . ." He hesitated. "The fact is, he's gotten himself a lady-friend who more or less lives there too. That's *really* mellowed him. For one thing, she's gotten him off the sauce. He's a teetotaler now, which has made all the difference in the world. He's put his life together again. But any time he has to deal with Exeter"—he shook his head— "he's an unhappy man."

They got up from the table and walked to the terrace's metal railing to look out over the water at the outer islands for a few moments. The sun was warm on their faces, the breeze cool. "That's Samson on the left," Robb said, slipping on his tunic, "and Tresco over there, and Bryher lies between them. Beautiful, aren't they?"

"Lovely," Julie agreed.

"Enjoy the view while you can. This is what we call fog season, you know, and it looks like it may be a bad one. It's already starting to build out there. I suspect we'll be socked in pretty soon now." He sighed, put on his helmet, adjusted the chin strap, and tapped it into place with his palm. "Ouch."

"But it's so becoming on you," Julie said.

Robb smiled his thanks. "So what do you say, sir? Will you come by the station? Anytime now would be fine. He'll have come back from lunch."

"Okay, I'll be there in half an hour or so. And Kyle—I want you to know I appreciate this. I hated to just let it drop."

"You're welcome. Mostly, I'm doing this for the sergeant. I know that working on a real murder case again would do him a world of good. Otherwise, you know, I'd never have said . . . I wouldn't have told you . . ."

"I understand. But listen, you're sure he hasn't gotten any calls from Exeter today?"

"None," Robb said laughing. "He's as gentle as—"

"A lamb," Gideon finished for him.

"An old lion with most of his teeth pulled would be closer to it," Robb said, and then, in friendly warning: "But not all of them."

EIGHT

SERGEANT Clapper was awaiting him at the entry to Robb's cubicle, leaning casually against the frame of the glass partition, sipping from a chipped mug of coffee and chatting with Robb, who was seated at his desk, sorting desultorily through the mess of files on it.

"Here's the very man," was his indisputably genial greeting. "PC Robb was telling me you might be coming in again about that bone of yours." He was in uniform today: open-throated, short-sleeved white shirt with blue-and-gold epaulets decorated with chevrons; dark blue trousers; and heavy, polished black shoes.

"Well, yes, I thought that maybe there was a little more to talk about," Gideon said.

"Indeed, yes. I was thinking the same thing. I was extremely interested in what you were saying yesterday, you know, but then we were interrupted by that . . ." He made a growling noise deep in his throat. ". . . that sodding telephone call, and when I came back you'd up and left, hadn't you?"

That's not quite the way I remember it, Gideon thought, but it didn't seem meanly intended, so he let it pass with no more than a murmur. If that was the way Clapper wanted to recall it, that was fine with him.

"I've been thinking about it," Clapper went on, motioning Gideon to follow him to his own office, "and I've done a bit of checking in the—oh, coffee?" he said, pointing to the coffeemaker in the unoccupied cubicle.

"I'm about coffeed out, thanks," Gideon said.

"A wise decision," Clapper said, grimacing and placing a hand on his belly. "Kyle, you can come along too, lad," he called over his shoulder. "I know you're interested."

Walking behind him, keeping pace with his slow, billowing stride, Gideon saw that Clapper was an even bigger man than he'd realized, matching Gideon's six-one, but probably pushing 250 pounds. Not that much overweight, really. Brawny was more like it. Basically, he was a constitutionally thickset man to begin with, with an unusually broad thorax and a wide pelvis. He'd make an interesting skeleton, Gideon couldn't help thinking.

His office was at the end of the little hallway, just past a door that said "Interview Room." It was no larger than Robb's cubicle but with real walls instead of glass partitions, and a door that opened and closed. There was the usual clutter here: charts and maps on the walls, and files scattered across the desk—but not a single one of the many plaques and commendations he had received, according to Robb, no framed copies of the magazine articles that had been written about him, nothing that would indicate he had ever been anything more than the constable sergeant in St. Mary's.

There were a few old, framed photographs on the walls—groups of smiling constables with their arms linked, but apparently they'd been left there by his predecessor, inasmuch as none of them included Clapper. Or Robb, for that matter. On his standard-issue desk, in addition to the paperwork and a pair of reading glasses, were a logoed mug (Chirgwin's Gift Shop) holding pens and markers, and a filigree-framed photograph (his new "girl-friend"?) facing away from Gideon. Two metal visitor chairs that matched one another but not the desk were wedged into the narrow space between desk and wall. There was a single waist-high metal bookcase with a few thick manuals in it, and on the top shelf the bag in which Gideon had brought the tibial fragment, apparently still containing the bone.

"Now, then," Clapper said when they'd sat down—Gideon and Robb having had to angle their chairs to make room for their legs—"how long did you say the bone had been there?"

"Probably under five years."

"Because, you see, I've been searching back through our local records for any outstanding mispers, and while—"

"Excuse me? Whispers?"

"Mispers, missing persons," Robb explained.

"Yes," Clapper said, "and while we have none on file here, the national misper register at the Yard turned up two possibilities—people that might, or might not, have disappeared during visits to the Scillies."

"You've been doing your homework," Gideon said. He knew that information of that sort—"might or might not, have disappeared during visits to the Scillies"—didn't jump out of the computer at you. You had to dig.

"Not too hard when you know the ropes. But, you see, one is from eight years ago and one goes back twelve. You're certain it couldn't be either one?"

He saw that Clapper really was in a better mood today. Yesterday's questions had been challenges, confrontations. These were genuine requests for Gideon's opinion.

"No, I'm not certain at all," Gideon said. "Consider it an educated guess, no more. There are a whole lot of variables that make it hard to pinpoint the time. For one thing, I'm not that familiar with climatic conditions here— moisture, temperature variation—"

"So it *could* be as much as twelve years old?"

"Yes, it could." He'd certainly been wrong by that much and more before. "What do you have?"

"The eight-year-old one is . . . let's see . . ." He shuffled a file into view on his desk. ". . . an eighty-eight-year-old woman from London with senile dementia who wandered away from her tour group somewhere between St. Ives and . . . what?"

Gideon had been shaking his head. "Not her," he said. "First, I'm pretty sure it came from a man. Second, it's not from an eighty-eight-year-old. The texture of bone changes with age—it gets all rough and pitted as you get older."

"Really?" an entranced Robb said. "Is that so?"

"Oh, yes, and that tibia's too smooth. It's a younger person's bone—"

"A young man's bone, is it? Well, then, what would you say to a eleven-year-old lad who disappeared from his uncle's . . ." Clapper's face fell. "No, again?"

"No, again. Not that young. Sorry." Gideon got up, brought the tibia back to the desk, and explained about epiphyseal union while a disappointed but moderately interested Clapper lit up a Gold Bond and Robb listened as if his life depended on it. "As you can see, the proximal epiphysis is completely fused to the shaft—not a trace of a line separating them. The age range for that to happen is sixteen—fifteen at the very earliest—to twenty-two or so. This absolutely can't be an eleven-year-old's bone. He's in his mid-twenties at the earliest, and probably older than that."

"Sixteen to twenty-two," Clapper mused, "for that particular bone. You knew that off the top of your head, so to speak?"

"Sure."

"You know the age ranges of all these different epiphyses?"

"Well . . . yes, I guess I do. All the ones used in ageing, anyway."

"And they're all different? Even the ones on opposite ends of the same bone?"

"Pretty much."

Clapper, studied him, nodding, his head wreathed in smoke. "Fancy," he said.

Gideon, not knowing what to reply, replaced the bone in the bag. "So where would you say we go from here, Sergeant?"

Clapper leaned back in his chair. "Well, now, that's the question, all right, innit?" he said slowly. "We have here a fragmentary bone, the condition of which implies dismemberment, which in turn implies homicide—"

Gideon noted that this was accepted as a given; another difference from yesterday.

"—but we know of no one it could possibly belong to."

"That seems to be about it."

"Yes. So what I ask myself is, I ask myself, why couldn't it have come off a passing ship, as so many other bones found on the beach have done?"

"Maybe it did. Personally, I'd have my doubts. No marine life encrustation on it. And from what I understand it was buried a couple of feet down. Pretty unlikely for that to have happened naturally, from shifts in the sand. So I'd have to guess he was murdered, cut up, and buried right here on the island."

"But—" Robb hesitated until Clapper nodded his permission to continue, and then barreled ahead, the words pouring out. "But isn't that a premature conclusion? The lack of encrustation would merely mean that the bone hadn't lain in the ocean for a considerable period of time, isn't that right?"

"Right," Gideon agreed.

"Well, that wouldn't necessarily mean it hadn't come

from offshore, would it? How do we know that it's not from a passing yacht of which we have no knowledge? That someone wasn't murdered and dismembered on a boat, then brought ashore onto the beach and buried—at night, I should think—after which the murderer simply went back to his boat and sailed away, with no one the wiser?"

Clapper began to answer, but changed his mind and let Gideon do it.

"I kind of doubt that, Kyle," Gideon said gently. "If you've already killed someone at sea, and even dismembered him, why risk coming ashore with the body to bury it? Wouldn't the safest, easiest thing be to simply dump the remains into the ocean? If they were already dismembered, they could be dumped separately, miles apart. The probability of any of them ever being found would be infinitesimal, much, much smaller than the chances of finding remains buried on a beach."

"Oh, yes, of course," Robb mumbled, embarrassed. "Yes, you're quite right. The murder would have occurred here, yes."

Gideon expected Clapper to make one of his cutting remarks about the value of university education and modern police training, but he demonstrated once again that he wasn't the Mike Clapper of yesterday by letting the chance pass. Instead, he thought it all over. He nodded slowly to himself. He pondered. He drummed his fingers on the desk. He was without a doubt one of the most deliberate people Gideon had ever come across. "I'll be honest with you, Professor. Dismemberments are new to me. Never worked on one. So where would *you* say we go from here?"

It was the question he'd been waiting for, and he'd carefully considered his answer. "Look, I know this doesn't look like much of a case—a single bone, and not even a whole one at that—but if you have one piece of dismembered body, the rest is very likely to be nearby."

Clapper nodded, puffing away. "That's probably so."

"Right. The pieces were probably put in plastic garbage bags or something similar and stuffed into a car, then driven to the beach, almost certainly at night, dumped out of the bags, and buried."

"Why take them out of the bags? To make things harder for the police in the event they were ever to be discovered?"

"Yes. The smarter ones do that. For one thing, if they're left sealed in garbage bags, it takes much longer for them to skeletonize. Clues remain. For another, finding human body parts in a plastic bag—even skeletonized ones—is a pretty good giveaway that dirty deeds have been done. Whereas the occasional bone fragment or two can be overlooked."

"As this one was," Clapper said. He pondered some more. "So there our man was, with a boot full of human remains, in a great hurry to be rid of them, and he takes the time to remove them from their bags—and wouldn't that be a filthy, miserable job?—before burying them. Even in the middle of the night, on a quiet beach, I'd say that takes a cool customer. The road runs quite near the beach up there, don't you see."

"I'd say so too. But cool or not, he *would* be in a hurry, and he wouldn't want to risk driving around with what he had in his trunk any more than he had to. So the chances are good that the rest of the body is buried nearby. Would you consider doing some exploratory digging at Halangy Beach?"

Clapper laughed. "If I had a staff, I would. But there's only young Robb and myself—which in effect means only young Robb, because I wouldn't be much of a hand with a shovel anymore."

"I'd be glad to pitch in too. There are signs to look for when you're hunting for—"

Clapper held up his hand. "I have a better idea, Professor. If you're free for the next hour or two, there's someone I'd like you to meet. I think he might be just the chap to help us."

"I'm free, all right." Whatever this was about, Clapper

was taking it seriously, and Gideon was pleased. And Robb had certainly been right: the big, jovial, animated man he was looking at was barely recognizable as the sarcastic, burnt-out cop of yesterday.

Clapper stubbed out his cigarette and stood up, looking as near to positively enthusiastic as Gideon had seen him. "That's fine. Fancy a short, bracing walk to the harbor, followed by a jaunt over the bounding main in a luxury yacht?"

"Nothing I'd like better," Gideon said.

"Excellent." He was already shrugging into the tunic that he'd taken from a hanger behind the door. "Kyle," he said pleasantly on the way out, "get hold of Trus Hicks on the blower and tell him we'll be on his doorstep in half an hour, will you? Tell him what it's about." He picked up one of the hats—the soft, military kind, not a helmet. "And ring up the cox to let him know we're on our way to the boat, there's a good lad. Going to St. Agnes, ain't we?"

CLAPPER'S "luxury yacht" turned out to be a garish yellow-and-green, twin-hulled metal boat that served both as police launch and water ambulance for the islands. The cox—the pilot—was waiting for them, and as soon as they were aboard he started it up. Gideon was surprised at the 747–like roar and power of the twin jet-thrust engines. Within seconds they were out of Hugh Town Harbor and scudding south across the famously wicked currents of St. Mary's Sound, heading for the island of St. Agnes with the boat's prow a foot in the air.

"Wow," he exclaimed, hanging on to the railing for dear life.

"We'll have you there in three and a half minutes," the pilot shouted with pride, leaning forward as if to coax yet a little more speed from it. "At full-tilt, we can get to just about any of the off-islands in under nine minutes."

The launch had a small enclosed cabin for patients

needing treatment or prisoners needing restraining, to which Clapper and Gideon retreated, partly because it was quieter than the deck, and partly because the wind had a bite to it from the thready mist that was beginning to form low over the water, in line with Robb's earlier prediction of fog. Once seated on the wooden benches that ran around its perimeter, Clapper asked: "Ever heard of Truscott Hicks?"

"I don't think so."

Clapper seemed moderately surprised. "Know anything about cadaver dogs?"

"Dogs that locate bodies? Not much. I've been on cases where they've been used, but they've already done their work by the time I get involved."

"Well," Clapper said comfortably, popping the lid of his cigarette box and dragging one out with his lips, "you're about to learn everything you ever wanted to know about them." He lit up and took a drag. "And then some."

The pilot's estimate of three and a half minutes was on the money, but there was a twenty-minute holdup during which the launch was forced to putt back and forth offshore while the short, narrow stone quay was occupied by two farm tractors with flatbeds unloading the day's deliveries—everything from milk and bread to a sofa (not new) and a television set (likewise)—from the daily supply ferry. When the unloading was finished, the tractors had chugged off in a dusty haze, and the ferry had backed out and departed, they pulled up alongside the quay and the pilot threw a rope over a nearby stanchion.

"We won't be long, Ron," Clapper said, climbing out onto stone steps worn concave by four hundred years of friendly visitors and unfriendly invaders. "Time enough for a pint at the Turk's Head, if you don't dawdle."

The pilot nodded soberly. "I shall take your sage advice, Sergeant."

The tide was at its highest, with a thin sheet of water sloshing over the uneven old stonework, so they had to watch their step. Gideon was again struck with Clapper's stately man-on-the-moon walk. In an odd, elephantine way, he was extremely graceful, totally in balance. Maybe it was the low center of gravity that hippy, pear-shaped form gave him. At the foot of the quay, where they stepped onto the land of the one-square-mile island itself, there were a few metal signs tacked onto an unpainted shed. All except one were for family-run guest houses and bed-and-breakfast places (there were no hotels on St. Agnes, Clapper said); the other was an advertisement for where they were going:

Bed-and-Biscuit Canine Boarding Establishment
Lowertown Farm Road
Tel 422380
Minimum Stay One Week
Proprietor Mr. Truscott Hicks

"Truscott Hicks," Clapper explained as they began walking up the path from the quay, "knows more about dogs than any man I've ever met. He was a famous dog trainer in the seventies. Wrote a few books, had his own show on the telly, gave courses all over the world, and so on. Well, about the time he got tired of that, his son—a copper up in Barnstaple at the time—told him about how they were starting to use dogs to detect firearms, explosives, drugs, and so on. Trus took an interest, took some courses on the Continent and on your side of the Pond, and made himself into a first-rate expert. First paid canine consultant of the Devon and Cornwall Constabulary, founding member of the Canine Forensics Association, and so forth and so on."

They were passing the Turk's Head Pub that he'd mentioned to their pilot (Turk's Head being a common name for pubs, deriving either from a type of seafarer's knot or, with more grim connotations, from the Crusades, depending on whom you asked) and a couple of men, sitting at an outdoor table over their pints, waved.

"See who's here, Alf. What brings you to our fair part of the world, Constable Sergeant? A bank robbery? A triple murder? An anarchist plot to blow up the parsonage?"

"Just out and about enjoying the fresh air, lads," Clapper said pleasantly. "Lovely day, innit?"

At the Turk's Head they turned left off the road onto a footpath that skirted the low bluffs above the beach. "Shorter this way," the sergeant said. "Now where was I? Well, I myself first met Trus, oh, about five years ago. I called him in on a case when I was . . ." He faltered. "Well, you see, this was—"

"When you were a detective chief inspector in Plymouth?" He was getting along well with Clapper, and he thought this might clear the air even more.

Clapper tucked in his chin but didn't break stride. "Someone's been talking out of school," he muttered. "PC Robb, would that be?"

"He's proud of you, and proud to be working with you, Sergeant. And I understand why. You've had a hell of a career."

"And did he tell you why I'm spending the remainder of this illustrious career as a sergeant in the most remote outpost of England?"

"He implied there'd been, uh, differences with administration."

Clapper laughed, not disagreeably. "I'd say that describes it."

Gideon responded in kind with one or two humorous accounts of his own struggles with administration in the groves of academe, and by the time they arrived at another modest "Bed-and-Biscuit Canine Boarding Establishment" sign at the head of a curving lane, they had slipped without noticing into first names.

The lane curved down toward the water and ended at the front steps of a green-roofed, white farmhouse on a gorse- and heather-covered bluff, below which was a small, white beach strewn with driftwood and edged by grassy dunes. The small sign on the front door said, "Please ring and enter. Be sure to close door behind you."

They did as instructed, finding themselves in a small foyer at the foot of a half-flight of stairs, and bringing instantly down on themselves a pandemonium of frenzied barking, yapping, and yipping—moderated by a single wise, resonant *whooof*—that seemed to come from every corner of the house. There followed the patter of many feet on wood flooring, and a pack of eight or ten small dogs— terriers, pugs, toy spaniels—threw themselves in what seemed like pure, noisy, gleeful ecstasy against the baby gate at the top of the stairs, barking away. A second later a huge Great Dane padded up behind them—the whoofer— and towered over them, adding his own deep voice to the chorus.

From down the hall came a soft, neutral voice: "Quiet." Nothing authoritative or threatening, not really a command at all, just a courteous request, but the barking stopped the way a switched-off radio stops. "Sit." And with an audible thump, as abruptly as if their back legs had been swept out from under them, every one of them went down on its haunches (the Dane accidentally sat on a Yorkie, which caused a brief commotion) and stayed there, heads smartly turned to the left, from whence the voice had come, as if posed for a cute doggie calendar photo.

A moment later, a mild-looking man of seventy appeared behind the dogs, preceded by the sweet, cloying odor of pipe tobacco from the ancient briar that was held loosely between his teeth. Gideon's immediate impression was that he was looking at someone who was about as contented as a human being could get. With his gray, thinning hair, his polished-apple cheeks, his schoolish spectacles, and his not-so-expertly hand-knitted vest, in the neck of which the knot of a plain blue tie was visible, he might have been a retired Oxford don. From the way he smiled down at his charges, it couldn't have been more clear that he was living his sunset years exactly as he wished to, surrounded by the companions of his choice.

He plucked the pipe from his mouth and smiled kindly down at them. "Mike Clapper! Sergeant Mike, the very man, as I live and sneeze. Come all this way just to cheer up his poor old mate, struck down by the cruel and remorseless hand of age."

"Come on business, Trus," Clapper said briskly.

Hicks rubbed his hands together. "Well, then!"

"Not that there's any money in it for you, you understand."

"The story of my life," Hicks said with a sigh. "And this young fellow must be the renowned Professor Oliver, whose monograph on exhuming skeletal remains has been my bible on the subject for many years."

"Thank you," said a flattered Gideon. "Actually, it was more Walter Birkby's monograph than mine. I was the junior author on that one."

"Modest too. Very becoming. Come in, gentlemen."

He unclicked the baby gate—the dogs stirred, but didn't dash for the opening—and let the two of them in, and men and dogs followed him in a line down a hallway to a comfortable but undistinguished linoleum-floored living room with a matched set of 1960's–style department store furniture. Hicks sat Gideon and Clapper on the sofa and, without asking, went to get them tea, while the dogs, each apparently with its preferred place, clambered into the seats or onto the arms of the chairs. Some curled themselves like cats over the chair backs. The Great Dane laid himself down, Sphinxlike, in front of the fireplace.

When Hicks had returned with the tea things on a tray and had squeezed himself into an armchair between three look-alike black spaniels, two of which clambered into his lap, Clapper briefly laid out the facts.

"One of those little cove beaches up north, eh?" Hicks said. "Those would be, what, a hundred, a hundred-and-fifty yards wide?"

"Something like that," Clapper said. "No wider, anyway. Want to have a go?"

Hicks dug the bit of his pipe against his cheek. "Well, sand isn't the easiest medium in the world, you know. It's too porous, you see, too many ways for the scent to escape. You get a huge scent pool, and the dog has to work extremely hard to pinpoint. And then, of course, sand is notorious for shifting, so there's the added problem of . . . mm . . ." The pipe bit went back in his mouth. Absently, he stroked the ears of one of the spaniels on his lap.

"You don't think it can be done?" Clapper asked, his disappointment showing. Gideon imagined his own was showing too.

Out came the pipe. "Body's been there a good five years, you say?"

"Probably less," Gideon said. "More than one, though."

Hicks pondered. "Well, that might be stretching things a bit, but yes, why not? We can certainly have a look-see. The dog will enjoy a run on the beach, in any case. What say we do it tomorrow morning?"

Gideon and Clapper readily agreed.

"Good-o." Hicks thrust the pipe back into his mouth and got to his feet, spilling dogs onto the floor. "These you see are all guests and house pets. My old working dogs prefer living outside. Come and meet them."

"Do you still have Heidi the Wonder Dog?" Clapper asked, getting out of his chair.

"Why, Mike, what a thing to say. Of course I still have her. I'd never give up Heidi. I'd never give up any of them."

"Well, yes, I only wondered if—that is, I thought perhaps—"

"She's alive and well," Hicks said, "and no doubt eager to see you."

When they left the room, the dogs started to scramble after them, but Hicks murmured, "Down. Stay," over his shoulder, and down they went and down they stayed, after practically screeching to a halt.

"I just thought of something, Trus," Clapper said. "The fog's supposed to be worse tomorrow. Fog season, you know. Is that going to be a problem?"

"Dear me, no. For you and me, perhaps, but not for a dog. It's smell they depend on, not sight. It might even make it easier, because moist conditions enhance scent. And then the dogs are happier when it's cool."

The three men walked through the kitchen and out the back door of the house, into an acre of grassy moorland that included an inviting pond and a couple of shady clumps of small elm and sycamore trees, all safely enclosed by a wire fence. Valhalla for dog heroes, Gideon thought.

There were four of them: a Doberman pinscher, two German shepherds, and a Border collie, and all of them came bounding over gracefully when Hicks made a clucking sound with his tongue. These were not like the yappers and yippers indoors, who had clamored for the attention of strangers. Three of the four had eyes only for Hicks. With their shapely heads turned adoringly up to him, they weren't begging for food or even pleading for attention. All they wanted was the joy of his presence. The fourth, the Border collie, pranced around them, snapping gently at their feet to herd them together, as its genes demanded.

"This one's Heidi, am I right?" Clapper said, bending to rub the ears of one of the German shepherds, which permitted the attention with the abstracted air of a pasha tolerating the devotion of a supplicant. "Hello, there, love,"

Clapper said affectionately, and to Gideon: "It's Heidi here that put an end to the biggest arson racket that Plymouth ever saw. What a nose on this old girl."

"She did that, all right," Hicks agreed. "It was Heidi that put us onto the lean-to where they'd stored their petrol—for setting their fires, you see, even though there'd been no petrol there for more than five months and it was completely open to the elements. Did it entirely on what vestiges of scent remained."

"Amazing," Gideon said. "Will we be using her tomorrow?"

Hicks stared at him. "What an idea. No, Heidi is an accelerant-detecting canine. No, no, we need a cadaver dog, or as we prefer to call it in these politically correct times, a human remains detection dog."

"I didn't realize they specialized to that extent."

"Well, of course they specialize. How could a—" He was obviously shocked at Gideon's ignorance, but politeness stopped him from expressing it. "For example, Kaiser here"—he kneaded the scruff of the other shepherd's neck—"is strictly a water search dog. Keenest nose in existence for locating a body at the bottom of a pond, but wouldn't know a cadaver in the open if he stumbled over it. And Trixie there—" At the mention of her name the Doberman shivered with pleasure and pushed her sleek muzzle into Hicks's hand. "—well, this beauty has been known to hunt down an automobile with explosives in its boot after it had driven two miles through dense Torquay traffic."

"Amazing," Gideon murmured again.

"No, our expert tomorrow will be Tess." He pointed at the midsized brown-and-white Border collie, which continued politely mock-nipping at their heels, presumably to keep them from wandering off and getting lost and thereby getting her in trouble. "Tess is a tried-and-true cadaver dog—pardon me, a human remains detection dog—inasmuch as she's trained to find skeletons, and even single bones, as well as decomposing corpses. But she couldn't track a lost hiker—a lost *live* hiker—to save her soul. Not her fault, of course; it's the way she's been schooled. She's been taught to alert to nothing *but* human remains. She'll even ignore animal remains."

Gideon only barely caught himself before saying "Amazing" again. "Huh," he said, "and I thought they were all just general-purpose tracking dogs, search-and-rescue dogs, with some specific training tacked on."

"Good heavens, no," Hicks exclaimed. "They're not tracking dogs at all, never were. Tracking dogs require *tracks*, don't you see. Either literal tracks or some specific scent article belonging to the person. And they generally require some specific starting point. But *these*"—he used the stem of his pipe to jab at the animals—"are air-scent canines. They don't look for an individual person or object but for a specific type of smell. They can start from anywhere, they don't need scent articles, they—" His rosy cheeks turned a little redder. "Gentlemen, I beg your pardon. I'm boring you, I'm sure. It's only that I don't get a chance to talk about it very much anymore."

"Ah, well, we're bearing up," Clapper said stoically.

"It's extremely interesting," Gideon said. "There's a lot more to it than I thought."

"Oh, that's only the start," Hicks said, recognizing Gideon as the curious scientist he was. "There's a remarkable field of knowledge here. Come into the house for another cup of tea, or something stronger, if you like, and I will astound and edify you."

"We're for it now," Clapper muttered crossly on the way back in.

NINE

HICKS began simply enough. What a dog had that a person didn't was not only the ability to discriminate between extremely similar scents, but to locate the source of smells much more precisely than any human being could possibly hope to. It came naturally. What the dog was doing when he located a buried human bone was no different than what he did when he dug up a beef bone that he'd buried in the backyard months before. He doesn't "know" where he buried it, he simply picks up the scent of a decaying bone on the air. Other animals, such as cats, actually have more scent receptors than dogs—was Gideon aware of that?— but of course the dog's emotional and behavioral characteristics made it infinitely more amenable to training and working in the field.

Interesting enough, and so far so good, but when Hicks got into the chemistry of putrefactive olfaction (chemistry had never been Gideon's strong suit) he rapidly left Gideon behind. ("Some say that the dog responds to the outgassing of volatile fatty acids and ionic compounds, but I maintain—

have always maintained—that it is at the level of the major histocompatability complex, where unique protein markers form, that differentiation between these markers results in recognition.")

"Ah," said Gideon dully, while Clapper dozed peacefully, "amazing."

ONCE Hicks had a full head of steam going, he was unstoppable, so it wasn't until five-fifteen that Clapper and Gideon, dazed with canine lore, were let loose, and five forty-five by the time Gideon climbed Garrison Hill in the gathering mist and got back to Star Castle. In his room, on the table by the casement window, was a note from Julie:

> *Hi, Prof,*
>   *Hope your session with the sergeant-major went better than yesterday's. Having put in a hard day's work furthering human knowledge, a few of us have headed for the Bishop and Wolf for a relaxing pre-dinner pint or two.*
>   *Dinner's not till seven, so come join us!*
>
>   *XXX, J*

The Bishop and Wolf had been the consortium's pub of choice during its first convening two years earlier, and Julie had pointed it out on their walk through Hugh Town when they'd arrived. The oldest building in the village, an attractive, mid-seventeenth-century stone inn with pansy-filled window boxes that added a whimsical and unlikely Bavarian air to the façade, and a hanging sign that showed a gigantic, slavering wolf crouching over a bishop's mitre–topped lighthouse (the pub had been named for the Bishop and the Wolf, two of St. Mary's earliest lighthouses). Situated in the center of the village, on the little square where the Strand and the Parade angled together, it was only a five-minute walk from

Garrison Hill, so that it was a few minutes before six when Gideon pulled open the door and entered an old English pub, traditional in the extreme: cozy and plain, with nets, glass globes, and odds and ends on the walls; dark, old wooden tables; and a fitting, not-really-unpleasant fug of beer, wine, and cigarette smoke in the air.

They were at two pulled-together square tables near the back wall: Julie, Liz Petra, Rudy Walker, Victor Waldo, Donald Pinckney, and Donald's man-eating wife, Cheryl, who looked bored, bony, and exotic in a flared white pantsuit that appeared to have come from the cleaners' five minutes before. The barmaid was in the act of taking orders, probably for their second round. Only Joey and Kozlov weren't there.

"Hi, all." Gideon asked the barmaid for a pint of best bitter and pulled up a chair between Julie and Victor, well out of Cheryl's range.

"Oh, Gideon, hi, sweetheart," Julie said. "How did it go today? I was just telling everybody about the bone."

"A human bone, I understand?" Donald said. "A tibia?" He was wearing another button on his shirt: *I didn't claw my way to the top of the food chain to eat vegetables.*

"Partial tibia of an adult male," Gideon said, "with signs of dismembering at the distal end."

"Signs of dismembering?" Victor echoed. "What would be the 'signs' of dismembering?"

And so he had to go through it again. His explanation was met with more interest than he might have expected, except from Cheryl, who, still nursing her earlier drink—a straight-up martini—was exchanging lingering, supposedly covert glances with a husky bodybuilder-type in a muscle shirt a couple of tables away. An olive on a toothpick slipped suggestively between her lips and out again.

"And do they have any idea to whom it might belong?" asked Donald, resolutely avoiding taking notice of his wife's goings-on.

"As of now, no. No unsolved murders, no records of any

missing people it could belong to. No theories as to whose it is. Still, it's somebody's. Mike introduced me to a dog-handler on St. Agnes, and tomorrow we'll go up to Halangy Point and see if we can find any more pieces. If we do, Mike said he'd find me a place at the police station where I can go over them."

" 'Mike'?" said Julie, her eyebrows going up. "My goodness, you *did* get along better with him today, didn't you?"

"Robb was right," Gideon said. "He's actually a pretty decent guy."

The barmaid came with their drinks: ginger beer for Victor; white wine for Julie, Liz, Rudy, and Donald; another martini (with three olives on the toothpick) for Cheryl; and Gideon's ale in the time-honored dimpled glass tankard.

"Murdered and dismembered," Liz said thoughtfully after taking her first sip. "You don't suppose . . . I wonder . . . Well, no, never mind. It's a silly idea."

This naturally prompted interest all around, and she was prevailed upon—it didn't take much prevailing—to continue. "Do you remember the last time we were all in this pub?" she asked. "Well, everybody but you and Gideon, Julie." She waited, slowly rotating her wineglass on the scarred table, but no one came up with an answer.

"It was the final night, after Edgar gave that talk at Methodist Hall, remember? The one where he got into it with that Pete Williams guy, that writer who hung around all week."

"Yes, that's right," Cheryl said, her first contribution. "Edgar was livid. Deservedly so, if you ask me. That reporter was vicious."

Her attention seemed to have returned to the conversation, but she was paying no attention whatsoever to Gideon. She wasn't even working at *not* paying him attention. It was simply as if he weren't there. *She's written me off as a dud*, he thought, not certain whether he ought to be relieved or offended. A moment's consideration told him he was relieved. *I* am *getting old*, he thought.

"That reporter treated him in exactly the way he deserved," Rudy said to Cheryl. "Edgar had it all coming to him, and then some." He muttered on a little more, but all Gideon was able to hear was ". . . arrogant, condescending . . ."

Rudy and Villarreal had not gotten along, Gideon remembered Julie telling him. "If you think Donald and Joey get under each others' skin, you should have seen Edgar and Rudy," she'd said. Apparently their views on the American wilderness—"open it up to everyone and everything," according to Rudy, and "shut it down to everyone and everything," according to Villarreal—were too much at odds for them to stomach one another, and potshots and barbs had flown between them all week long, with Rudy doing most of the needling. But Villarreal had been possessed of a ready, caustic wit, Julie had said, and, generally speaking, Rudy had gotten the worst of it.

There had been a time, Gideon thought sadly, when Rudy had had a sharp and ready wit, too.

"Whether he had it coming to him or not is not the point," Liz said now, gathering steam. "The point is that he said he wanted to kill him, do you remember? He said it right in front of us. Twice, if I remember right. Well, who's to say . . ."

"Liz!" Julie exclaimed. "You're not serious. You're suggesting Edgar actually *did* kill him? I mean . . . *murder*?"

"That's just what I'm suggesting."

"It wouldn't surprise me," Rudy said, but it was hard to tell if he was serious.

There followed a general chorus of doubt and incredulity. Gideon, silent, reflected that, as cheerful and kindly as Liz was, getting her back up was obviously not a good idea, even if you went out and got eaten by a bear afterward.

And she stuck to her guns. "I *am* serious. Hear me out now. Has anybody heard anything about Williams since that night?" She stared challengingly at each of them in turn, and everyone admitted that they hadn't.

"Don't look at me," Gideon said. "I never heard of him at all until the day before yesterday."

"All right," Liz said. "Nobody's heard of him since then. Has anyone heard anything about the book he was working on? Has it come out? We all keep up with the environmental literature, we'd certainly have read about it. A book like that, it would have made a splash."

No, they allowed, they hadn't heard news of the book. Still . . .

"Cheryl, let me have your BlackBerry," Donald said to his wife.

"What for?"

"Just let me have it."

"Jesus," she sighed, digging it out of her purse. *This was definitely not a marriage made in heaven*, Gideon thought.

Donald took the device. "It should be easy enough to settle. We'll Google him and see if he turns up."

"Google a name like 'Pete Williams'?" Rudy said. "You'll get a million hits."

Donald frowned. "That's a point. Does anybody know where he's from?"

"London," said Liz. "But that's not much help either. Does anybody remember the name of the book? No? Well, does anybody know the names of any of his other books?"

"There weren't any other books. This was his first one," Victor said.

"You mean he wasn't a professional writer?" Donald asked. "I assumed—"

"He published a few magazine articles," Victor said, putting down his ginger beer, "but he was . . . What was he? . . . An auto mechanic."

"An *auto mechanic*?" Donald said, deeply aggrieved. "I gave him hours of my time!"

"Yes, he worked in a garage," said Victor, "but he was a student at one of the colleges. He'd been working on that book of his in his spare time for years. We got to talking about it when he interviewed me. He asked me for advice on publishing, and I gave him some suggestions for—"

"*Movers and Shakers of the Earth*," Cheryl said. "That was the name of it."

"That's it," Donald agreed. Using his pinky he punched it in on the tiny keyboard and waited. "Yes, it's—no, it's nothing. It was a chapter in a book by Alistair Cooke, that's all. But it's not a book title on its own." His serious expression as he looked up at the others suggested he'd discovered something of significance. "It never came out, and it's not scheduled to come out in the foreseeable future."

"Is that *right*?" Victor said, eyes wide, head swiveling from person to person.

"Now, wait a minute," Julie said. "A lot of books never come out. That doesn't mean the author's dead. And a lot of books take more than two years to write."

"I can vouch for that," Gideon muttered.

Liz turned to him. "Look, you said the bone was from an adult male. Why *couldn't* it be him?"

"I didn't say it couldn't be. I don't have any real reason to think it isn't. But I also don't have any real reason to think it is. You have to admit it's an awfully long shot, based on pretty flimsy evidence—or rather nonevidence."

"You don't have any other hypotheses to go on," Liz said.

"That's true enough."

"You could always mention it to Sergeant Mike tomorrow," Julie suggested. "He'll certainly know how to look into it if he wants to."

"Very good, I'll do that," Gideon said, searching for another subject to move on to. "So how'd the poker game go after I left last night?"

"Sounds like a Hoover, doesn't she?" Robb said admiringly.

"Certainly does," Clapper said, and then for Gideon's benefit: "A vacuum cleaner."

Hicks stood there, chewing on his pipe, keenly watching her. "All right, then," he said, "seems to me she's defined the limits of the pool. Appears to run from this rock over here, halfway down to the water, and then over to those low dunes over there." With the stem of the pipe he had outlined an area of about twenty by thirty yards. "Time now to get specific."

The pipe was jammed back in his mouth. "Tess!" he said, more sharply than he'd spoken to her before. Reluctantly, she surfaced, coming to a stop and raising her head a little from a clump of dune grass. "Slow down, girl, calm down." He tapped his thigh. "Come."

She lifted her head a little more and looked doubtfully at him, obviously beset by warring instincts, and for a second it looked as if she might disobey, but with a soft whimper she came to his side, nuzzling his hand with her sandy nose to make amends.

"Now we'll get a bit more businesslike," he said to the others. "We'll search the area in a grid pattern to make sure we cover every inch, instead of this frantic to-ing and fro-ing. If there's something here, she should be able to pinpoint it."

"*Should* be able to," Clapper muttered.

"They're not infallible, Mike, you know that. No more than you or I. Well, you, anyway."

Without benefit of a leash to connect them, dog and handler began to move slowly and systematically over the defined area. When it was time to shift directions, Hicks would murmur "Turn" or "This way" and the dog would turn with him, while Clapper, Robb, and Gideon watched from the perimeter.

"Like a dance, innit?" Clapper said, getting a cigarette going.

"It's beautiful, really," said Robb. "The way she follows."

After about five minutes, the dog suddenly sat down and softly whined.

"She's located something," Clapper told them. "That's the alert he trains them to give. Now he'll ask her to show the exact spot."

"She won't actually dig it up, will she?" an anxious Gideon asked.

"No, no, she knows better than that."

"Good girl," Hicks said to the dog. "Now then. Touch."

Tess immediately jumped up, placed a graceful forefoot on the sand, and pawed gently and elegantly away, like a high-strung horse.

Hicks knelt to plant a thin metal rod with an orange flag on it. "X marks the spot," he said, pleased and smiling. "Who wants to do the honors?"

Robb and Clapper deferred to Gideon, who knelt and began clearing sand with his hands, spreading rather than digging. It was as soft as he'd hoped, if a bit colder, and it took less than a minute to uncover a smooth, spiraling, sea snail–shaped knob of bone, as clean of flesh and ligament as a specimen from a biological supply house. "That," he said, sitting back on his haunches, "is the distal end of a human right humerus—the elbow. Thank you, Tess, well-done."

The dog, her face on a level with his own, grinned at him and yawned prodigiously, her bright pink tongue curling back on itself into an almost-complete circle.

Robb immediately got out his pad, his camera, and a metal tape measure, and set about industriously drawing, photographing, and writing down the circumstances of the find.

With his fingers and the paintbrush Gideon began clearing sand from the rest of the bone. "If we're right about it being a dismemberment—"

"So now we're back to *if* we're right?" Clapper growled

predictably; not with any conviction, but from mere force of habit.

"—the chances are we'll only find three-quarters of it or so. The top few inches will probably be missing, the same way . . . Ah, there we are, see?"

He ran his fingers down it. "Male," he announced. "And adult, of course. As expected."

"How did you know that?" Clapper asked, looking down from what seemed a great height. He was wearing a voluminous, calf-length topcoat, which gave him even more of a looming quality than usual.

"Male because of the robusticity," Gideon began, "and as for age, as you can see, the distal symphysis is—"

"No, how did you know the top part would be missing?"

"Oh, I didn't know, I was just going with the averages. Dismemberments have a pretty typical pattern: upper arms cut from the torso just about where this one was, hands cut off above the wrist, legs severed a few inches down from the hips, head chopped off at about here—" He tapped his own neck. "Feet separated—"

It was all a little too graphic for the imaginative Robb. "A bone like this, it doesn't look so bad, but when you think about someone actually doing it . . . what a horror it must be . . . a nightmare." A shudder ran visibly down his back.

"It is. They do it in a bathtub when they can, to contain the gore," Gideon said, continuing to brush sand. *How did a peaceable, laughably squeamish guy like me, whose primary academic interest was early Pleistocene hominid locomotion, get to the point where I could so easily and knowledgeably discuss the methods of choice of homicidal monsters whose terrible minds and motives I couldn't begin to comprehend?* It was far from the first time he'd had such a thought, and no doubt far from the last.

"Actually, I've never dealt with a freshly dismembered body"—*and let's hope I never do*—"but I've gone back to the scene of the crime a few days later—the bathroom where it was done, I mean. And gory is hardly the word for it. Blood everywhere—the walls, the ceiling . . ." At the memory, he couldn't quite repress a shudder of his own.

Clapper noticed. "Grisly work," he said sympathetically.

"Messy in the extreme. The bathtub makes it easier to clean up, but of course blood traces are almost impossible to get rid of. If we knew where this guy was sliced up into sections, there'd probably still be traces, even after all this time."

"At Bramshill," Robb said with a frown, "they told us dead bodies don't bleed."

"That's not always the case, lad," Clapper said.

"That's right," Gideon agreed. "Oh, there aren't any great gouts of blood if you cut or stab them, because the heart's not pumping anymore, so there's no pressure, but they certainly can bleed if the blood's still in them and it's still liquid. The way a garden hose would continue to leak if you cut into it, after you turn it off."

"Like a fresh piece of meat, you might say," said Clapper helpfully. "Oozes, like, don't it?"

"And when you're cutting up a corpse, and hefting the segments, and trying to get them into sacks," Gideon added, "you're juggling some pretty heavy, awkward pieces of meat—a male torso weighs eighty or a hundred pounds, a single leg weighs about thirty—so you're bound to get quite a lot of blood all over everything."

"I see," whispered a pallid Robb, and then, barely audibly, "thank you."

Gideon had had enough too. "Look, why don't we just concentrate on what we have here in front of us?" he muttered roughly, his head down, continuing to scrabble in the sand with his fingers. *Nice, clean, dry bones, not a sign of gore.*

"You're expecting to find the forearm bones here with

it, then?" Clapper asked. "If the body was cut up the way you said?"

"I was hoping so, assuming he deposited the entire fleshed arm here, but anything could have happened to them by now, and it's starting to look as if—no, no, here we go." His fingers had found something, and with a few strokes of the brush he uncovered two smaller, thinner bones. "They've just shifted in the sand a bit, but here they are: radius and ulna."

"Cut off through the wrist," said Robb, impressed, "exactly as you predicted."

"Seen one, seen them all, I suppose," Clapper said. "You'd think the blighters would cut through the joints, wouldn't you? Disjoint, as you might say."

"Disjoint!" said Hicks with a grimace. "Sounds like something you'd do to a chicken."

Gideon laughed. " 'Disarticulate,' we like to say."

"Well, whatever you call it," said Clapper, "it would be a lot easier than all this hacking and chopping and sawing of bones, and a good bit neater, too."

"But not a lot faster," Gideon said. "This is the quickest way. Getting through the articulations is a slow, tricky process, and, anyway, you couldn't do it without a pretty thorough knowledge of anatomy."

He placed the three bones in a sack that Robb provided and got to his feet, brushing off his knees. "That's it for this cache, I think. The hands are probably elsewhere, possibly with the feet. They seem to do it that way a lot."

"Shall we have the old girl carry on, then?" asked Hicks. "See what else she might turn up?"

"Lead away," Clapper said. "Kyle, we'll leave you to do the sifting here."

"I'll get started right away, Sarge," Robb said, setting down the bucket, unrolling the length of screening, and producing a trowel.

"Search," Hicks said to Tess.

Any expectation that she would repeat the lightning-quick results of her first effort was soon dashed. A cursory exploration of the beach at her own rapid pace produced no pool of scent. Nor did the first hour and a half of a slower, more methodical search with her master doing the guiding, after which Hicks, citing "olfactory fatigue," declared she needed food, water, a play break, and a rest. By that time Robb had rejoined them: his sifting had produced nothing.

Looking at his watch—it was a well after 1:00 P.M.—Clapper suggested they could use a food and watering break themselves, but Hicks said it would be better if Tess wasn't away from the scene for too long, and Robb said he wasn't hungry, and if it was all right, he'd like to stay on and assist Hicks.

"That's fine with me," Gideon said. He was hungry, but he was more eager to get someplace where he could properly examine the bones; preferably somewhere indoors and out of the increasingly dank fog. "If anything else does turn up, I think you get the idea of how to unearth it, Kyle, so why don't you go ahead and take care of it yourself?"

His graduate students would have been justifiably outraged to hear him say this, considering how often he reminded them of the importance of being in on the exhumation whenever possible. But in this case, with the bones dismembered and scattered, there was little to be learned from their precise placement. Besides, the natural shifting of beach sands made it even less likely that their positional relationships would have any similarity to the way they were originally buried. Besides that, in order to maintain even their present positions in the unstable sand and keep them from getting covered over again by dislodged fill, he would have had to erect a set of retaining walls, which, in the present circumstances, wasn't worth the doing.

And besides, he was freezing.

"Really, would that be all right?" Robb was thrilled.

"Doesn't seem as if there's all that much to it," Clapper rumbled. "Brush 'em off, pick 'em up, and put 'em in a bag. It's the dog that does the work, innit?"

"If the hand or foot bones turn up, make sure you do a thorough search for the small ones," Gideon said. "Some of the carpals and tarsals are pretty funny-looking, like irregular little stones, so pick up anything along those lines. Oh, and be sure and sift really thoroughly around any hand bones, Kyle; he might have neglected to pry off a ring, or even a watch, and it might still be around."

"Can you handle that all right, lad?" Clapper asked.

"Oh, I think I can just about cope," said Robb, but with so sunny a smile that Clapper couldn't have taken offense if he'd wanted to.

"And if you have a problem," Clapper said, "you know how to reach me."

"I'll do that, sir. And have no fear, Professor, I'll document and photograph everything exactly as it lies in situ."

"In situ," Clapper repeated, shaking his head. "My, my." And then with a sigh, "I'm sure you will, lad, I'm sure you will."

E L E V · E N

"PETE Williams?" Clapper echoed distantly, chewing determinedly away at his double-portion haddock-and-chips lunch, periodically washing it down with a swallow of non-alcoholic ginger beer.

"He's a writer who got into a hassle with Edgar Villarreal the last time the consortium met, two years ago."

"And who's Edgar Villarreal?" Clapper asked without much interest, using his knife to plaster the last of the "mushy peas" onto his fork.

Sergeant Clapper ate in what Gideon thought of as the classic English manner, holding his knife like a scalpel to cut things (so elegant), and then employing it to lather stuff on the back of his fork, which was then stuck in his mouth upside down (so inelegant). And since the English rarely put down either implement during a meal, when they chewed it was impossible not to think of Oliver Twist sitting over his paltry meal in the workhouse, holding knife and fork upright on the table. On the other hand, Gideon was ready to admit, Americans wasted a lot of motion changing hands twice every time they had to cut a piece of meat.

Gideon explained about Villarreal as he continued to work on his ploughman's lunch of Cheddar cheese, half a baguette, relish—"pickle," as they called it—pickled onion, and a bit of lettuce-and-tomato salad. He was a relatively fast eater, always finishing before Julie, but Clapper put him to shame.

"And he actually threatened to kill him?" Clapper asked as Gideon finished the story. "With witnesses?"

"No, I wouldn't call it a threat, and he didn't say it to the guy's face. He was with some of the other members right here at the Bishop and Wolf and muttering in his beer—" Gideon lifted his own half-pint of bitter and sipped. "—and he said he'd like to kill him, which, I agree, wouldn't ordinarily mean much of anything, but Williams seems to have disappeared off the face of the earth since then, so I thought it was worth mentioning to you. You might want to see what you can find out about him."

Clapper laughed. "Oh, right, give me fifteen minutes and I'll have it done."

"I gather there's a problem? I mean, I know it must be a fairly common name—"

"Fairly common? Gideon, 'Williams' is the third most common name in Great Britain, following closely on the heels of 'Smith' and 'Jones.' And if I'm not mistaken, 'Peter' comes right after 'William' and 'John' as a Christian name."

"Still, I thought you'd want—"

"I do, of course I do. But I'd have appreciated it if you could have come up with a more unusual name." He hauled out a notepad. "Where is he supposed to live?"

"I think somebody said London."

"Naturally," Clapper said wryly. "And he's a writer, you say?"

"Well, not really. I gather this was his first book." He

snapped his fingers as the previous night's conversation at the Bishop and Wolf came back to him. "He was an auto mechanic, he worked in a garage. That should make it easier, shouldn't it?"

"Yes, that's excellent," Clapper said, yawning. He entered a final scribble in his notepad, reached for a menu, and pulled it to him. "Now then. Fancy a spot of pudding? Let me recommend—bloody hell, that's mine."

His cell phone had signaled. It was stowed in the pocket of his topcoat, which hung from a coatrack, its hem trailing on the floor, so he had to unwedge himself from behind the table and get up to answer it. "Is that so? Well, I'll let you tell him yourself." He handed the phone to Gideon. "Kyle."

"Dr. Oliver?" Robb piped happily. "I don't like to interrupt your lunch, but we've found some more. Only about a foot down. Appear to be hand or foot bones, I'm not sure which. Maybe both. Those little finger bones—"

"Phalanges."

"And then some of the funny-shaped little ones you mentioned. And also the bottoms—I mean the distal ends—of the tibias, or maybe it's the, er, ulnas, depending—"

"That's great, Kyle. Okay, we'll be right there."

Clapper took back his phone, clicked it shut, and cast a last wistful look at the menu. "So much for pudding," he said.

THE new hoard that Tess had uncovered, now resting on the length of screening, did indeed consist of a mix of left and right hand and foot bones, plus the distal ends of both tibias, one fibula, and one ulna.

"I count thirty-five hand and foot bones altogether," Gideon said, kneeling over them. Are you pretty sure you got them all? Could any of them have migrated a few feet one way or the other, beyond where you looked?"

"Not according to Tess," said Hicks. He was sitting on the sand, elbows around drawn-up knees, smoking his pipe. Tess sat beside him, watching with polite interest.

"I dug up a pretty big area," Robb said uncertainly. "How many should there be?"

"Twenty-seven in the hand, twenty-six in the foot. And parts of both hands and feet are here, so that would be a total of, ah—"

"One hundred six," Clapper promptly supplied.

"The rest have probably been washed away," Hicks offered, "or possibly the shrews got them, or the crabs."

"Or the seals," said Gideon, "or the crows, or the gulls. Or other people's pet dogs. Well, it's not a bad haul, considering." He got to his feet and brushed off the knees of his trousers. "If Tess is finished, then, I'd like to have a chance to look it all over in detail. Mike, you said you had someplace for me to work?"

"Actually, the final quadrant hasn't been searched," Hicks said, unwrapping one arm from his knees to point to the rock-littered upslope at the far end of the beach.

Gideon followed his gesture. "That's pretty unlikely to turn up anything, Mr. Hicks. Too many rocks, too much brush. People digging holes for dead bodies prefer easier terrain."

"Yes, that was my thinking. That's why I left if for last, in case we couldn't get to it. Poor Tess is thoroughly knackered at the moment, I'm afraid." He massaged the ruff of her neck. "And I'm feeling my age as well. I think we'll pack it in. Maybe we'll try again tomorrow."

Clapper shook his head. "That's doubtful, Trus. If the fog gets much worse, which I don't doubt it will, even Ron won't be able to get you here tomorrow."

Hicks got creakily to his feet. "Well, we'll see, shall we?" He paused. "I don't suppose the Devon and Cornwall Constabulary would have it in them to buy a hungry old man his pottage, now would they?"

"Absolutely," Clapper said. "I apologize, Trus, I wasn't thinking. You must be starving. You too, Kyle. Kyle, I want you to take Mr. Hicks to any dining establishment of his choice, courtesy of the department, and give him a truly memorable lunch. Anything he wants. And remember: expense is not a consideration."

"Why, thank you, Michael," Hicks said. "I'm quite touched."

"Anything up to and including a pound," Clapper said grandly.

"WILL this give you enough room, then?" Clapper asked. They had just finished arranging the unoccupied cubicle opposite Robb's office, clearing the desk of storage files and assorted debris and shoving the stacks that were on the floor up against the walls to provide more room around the desk.

"It'll do fine," Gideon said, placing the sacks of bones on the desk.

"We can put the coffeemaker elsewhere, if you want."

"No, leave it on the desk, it won't bother me."

"I wouldn't recommend drinking any, however, at least not in the afternoon after it's been out a while. Takes a bit of getting used to."

"Mike," Gideon said, laughing, "stale coffee and bone dust go together like bees and honey. Don't worry about me."

"Very well, then. Anything you need to get you started?"

"Yes, a magnifying glass. And I need something to measure with—a ruler; a tape measure too, if you have one. Calipers would be too much to hope for, I assume."

"They would, indeed."

Gideon blinked up at the fluorescent tubes overhead. "And an adjustable desk lamp, if there is one—something to counter the flat lighting."

Clapper nodded, moving toward the doorless entry of the tiny cubicle.

"Oh, and where's the tibial fragment I brought over on Monday? Is it in here someplace?"

"No, it's still in my office. I'll bring it."

While he was gone, Gideon sat down, opened the bags, and began arranging the bones, sorting left from right, and placing them roughly in their anatomical relationships. When Clapper returned, Gideon took the partial left tibia—the upper four-fifths of the bone—from him, and set it against the partial left tibia—the lower portion—that they'd found today. Carefully, he set cut end to cut end. As he then demonstrated, they fit together so perfectly that, kept upright, they didn't have to be held in place.

"There you go," he said with satisfaction. "Couldn't be a neater fit, could it? You can even see how the breakaway spur from the one from the museum fits right into that little cleft in the new one. These are from the same person, absolutely no question about it."

"Well, that's a relief, innit?" Clapper lazily poured a splash of coffee into a mug that he took from a pegboard on the wall and sat down across the desk from Gideon. "I'd hate to think there was a whole series of dismembered corpses littering our pristine beaches."

"Are you saying you definitely agree that that's what we're dealing with? A dismembered corpse? You're convinced?"

Clapper stared at him. "Well, of course I am. What else would I think?"

"I just wanted to be sure. You never said so in so many words, and you sure weren't that convinced a couple of days ago."

"A couple of days ago, there was one measly piece of bone, species and context unverified, brought in unannounced by a man who claimed to be some sort of anthropologist. But now . . ." He gestured at the array on the table.

"Does this mean you'll be turning the case over to headquarters?"

"Not bloody likely!" Clapper burst out, then collected himself. "That is to say," he said serenely, "not at the present time. Let us first see what results ensue from the pursuit of our inquiries."

That suited Gideon, who was getting to enjoy working with Clapper. "Fine. Let us begin pursuing them." He glanced over the thirty-odd hand and foot bones. "No obvious age or sex differences—and no duplication," he said. "And everything matches the original tibia in condition and general appearance. No reason to think there's more than one person here."

"I thought we'd just established that."

"Yes, but it's the kind of thing you like to establish more than once."

With the goosenecked lamp that Clapper had brought now on the desk casting its light sidewise to accentuate textures, he turned the birdlike bones, one at a time, this way and that, for their first examination. "No obvious trauma or pathologies . . . well, except for a little osteoarthritis in some of the joints. That probably puts the age, oh, up in the thirties or forties, at any rate."

Clapper, in the act of lighting a cigarette, looked up from under his eyebrows. "Thirty or forty years old, and the poor bugger already has arthritis?"

"Sure. So do I. So do you."

"Get away! My joints are perfectly fine." He waved his arms in circles to prove it. "I'm in my prime, couldn't be primer."

"Mike, I hate to tell you this, but you're not in your prime. You never were. Your bones get stronger and healthier as they grow—say to twenty-five or so; thirty at the outside—and then, wham, it's downhill from there right up to the end. The minute they reach maturity they turn around and start deteriorating. Osteoarthritis, atrophy, osteoporosis . . . there is no prime, as far as your skeleton goes, or if there is, it lasts about five minutes, and the chances are you were doing something else at the time and you missed it."

Clapper blew out his first lungful of smoke. "Now there's a charming thought."

"And as for the rest of you, it doesn't last all that much longer. You know those free radicals and antioxidants that start building up as you get older? Those are just your body's way of trying to get rid of you. Nature doesn't want you hanging around using up resources any longer than necessary—which means just long enough to get your DNA into the gene pool so the human race keeps going. So it does what it can to keep you healthy till then. After that, you're on your own. If you're not contributing any more DNA to the species, the hell with you. The sooner you're out of the picture the better." He laughed. "Hey, have another puff. Mother Nature will appreciate it."

Clapper scowled at him, but he was amused. "Oh, I can see I'm going to enjoy hanging about with you." He looked for an ashtray but didn't find one. "Try and carry on without me for a minute, will you?" He went to his office in search of an ashtray and came back with a metal one logoed *The Goat and Compass, Norwich.*

"Well, now here's something," Gideon said as Clapper sat down, the ashtray in his lap. With his thumb, Gideon was stroking a smooth, dime-sized area on the lower margin of the right tibia, the part that connects to the ankle. "You don't see these very often in modern skeletons, other than Asians."

Clapper peered at the spot but obviously saw nothing. Still, he was interested. "You're saying this bloke is from Asia? You can tell from that little spot?"

"No, I'm not saying that at all. Well, not necessarily. You see, I'm fairly sure it's a squatting facet, though admittedly not a very distinct one. Asians have them more frequently than other people because—"

"Because squatting is more common in the East," Clapper supplied.

"Right." Gideon checked the other tibia. "Yes, this one

has it, too. I'd feel more confident about their definitely being squatting facets if we had a talus—the ankle bone just below this one—because then we'd look for a matching facet on the medial portion of the trochlear surface, where the two bones abut. But as you see, we don't have a talus."

"Pity, that," said Clapper. "But assuming that you're correct, and that these are indeed squatting facets, what is there to be made of them?"

Gideon put the tibias down. "Well, that, at some point in his life, this guy did a lot of squatting. Squatting requires dorsiflexion of the foot—" He demonstrated with his hand, laying it flat on the table, palm-down, then raising it with a sharp bend of the wrist. "—and habitual dorsiflexion results in bone remodeling that produces squatting facets . . . like these."

"I see," Clapper said dryly, emitting twin plumes of smoke from his nostrils. "You're telling me that we're dealing with a habitual squatter here. A serial squatter, as it were."

It was the kind of labored drollery that would have annoyed Gideon two days ago, coming from the newly met Sergeant Clapper, but now he knew Clapper better and he laughed. "All I can tell you is what I find. This guy had some kind of occupation, or hobby, or maybe a cultural upbringing, that involved a whole lot of squatting. If it helps identify him, great. If not, I can't help that."

"Couldn't just be someone who spent a lot of time in the loo, could it?"

"Mm," Gideon said abstractedly. He had gotten out of his chair and picked up the ulna now—the larger of the two forearm bones—and was slowly running his fingertips down it with his eyes closed. Like most anthropologists, he relied on his fingers almost as much as his eyes. It was touch, along with sight, that revealed the unobtrusive little ridges and facets and depressions that could tell the story of a lifetime—as well as the nicks and notches and cracks that might well throw light on the last few seconds of it.

In this case, it was a ridge that had captured his interest, a small, sharp ridge near the top of the ulna—the larger of the two forearm bones—that ran diagonally, front to back, for not much more than an inch, a little below the elbow joint. First his middle finger and then his thumb slid lightly over it.

"This is the supinator crest," he said after a very long silence during which Clapper had sighed, and yawned, and finally gathered himself up in preparation to leave.

"Oh, yes?" Clapper replied politely, partway out of his chair.

"Yes," murmured Gideon, who at this point wasn't paying any more attention to Clapper than Clapper was paying to him. "Everyone has it. But this particular one is extremely well developed." He was, in effect, talking to himself, something he was prone to doing when looking at bones. Julie accused him of talking to *them*, but it was himself he was addressing; he was firm about that.

"Now, the supinator crest," he continued, "naturally, is the origin of the supinator muscle, or at least of the deep layer of it . . ."

"Naturally."

". . . which is the primary muscle involved in supination . . ."

"Well, I could have told you that."

". . . of the hand, especially when the arm is in an extended position. Now that *is* interesting."

Clapper, who'd remained half-in, half-out of his chair, dropped down again. "Maybe you'd better run through that again. *What's* interesting?"

"Well, supination—" Aware that Clapper, like most people, might be a little hazy about the term, again used his own hand to illustrate, once more placing it palm down on the table, but this time flipping it over sideways with a twist of his forearm so it rested on its back. "That's supination of the hand." *Like turning a doorknob*, he almost said, before remembering that doorknobs were few and far between in` Europe, where handles were preferred. And turning a door handle—pressing it down, really—mostly involved the muscles of the upper arm and shoulder.

Clapper shook his head, puzzled. "So?"

"So whoever owned this bone did a great deal of just that movement, only with some stress associated with it. And it occurs to me—now this is just a shot in the dark, with nothing solid to go on, you understand. I'm not asserting anything, I'm not even hypothesizing, really . . ."

"I imagine," Clapper mused to the walls, "that if I sit here long enough, eventually he'll come round to telling me what it is that's occurred to him."

"Well, only that supination"—he turned his hand over again—"is the motion that's involved in using a screwdriver, or to some extent in screwing on a radiator cap, or battery cap, or in—"

"Or in," Clapper said, catching on, "all manner of tasks having to do with maintaining motor cars." Thoughtfully, he picked a shred of tobacco from his tongue. "You really believe, then, that this might be our automobile mechanic, Pete Williams? That Villarreal actually murdered him over some silly academic dispute?"

"Well, I'm not about to go that far," Gideon said. "For all we know he's still happily walking around London and working on his book at night, so let's find that out first, but right now"—he repeated what Liz had said to him at the Bishop and Wolf the previous night—"we sure don't have any other hypotheses to go on."

Clapper pondered this, taking a last drag on his cigarette, grinding it out, and then nodding while smoke poured from mouth and nostrils. "But where would the squatting facets come in?"

Gideon shrugged. "Auto mechanics spend a lot of time

hunkering down to look at the undersides of cars, and at the wheels and things, don't they?"

"I really wouldn't know."

"I wouldn't either. Either way, though, they could come from something completely unrelated to what he did for a living."

"Mm," said Clapper. "Well, it's something to look into. I'll see what can be found out about Mr. Williams's current existence or lack thereof. And what about this Edgar Villarreal? Where would we be likely to find him?"

"Not in this world, it seems," Gideon said, and explained.

"Eaten by a bear!" Clapper said with a grimace, but at that point they were interrupted by the laughing entrance of Kyle Robb, who burst in triumphantly cradling two large paper sacks in the crooks of his arms. "Mr. Hicks was much revived by lunch, as was Tess, and they decided to finish up that last quadrant today after all, and look what the good little doggie has turned up!"

"*Two* more caches?" Gideon asked. "I wasn't really expecting any—not from there."

"Only one," Robb said, placing the bags on the desk, "but it's a big one, couldn't fit in one sack." He stepped back. "Have a look, why don't you?"

Gideon tore the sacks down their sides and gently spread out their contents. "These are the bones of the thorax, the upper body. And a lot of it is here, Kyle. Scapulas, clavicles, vertebrae, ribs . . . the top parts of the humeri, too. There's plenty to work with. This ought to tell us a lot."

"I thought you'd be pleased," Robb said, as proud of himself as if he'd personally nosed them out. "I've cleaned them up a bit for you."

"Thank you."

"I'll pick up, lad," Clapper said when the telephone rang, and went into Robb's cubicle to do it.

Presented with all these unexpected bones, Gideon felt like Silas Marner viewing his hoard; he practically wanted to rub his hands together. "First," he told an observant Robb, "we'll want to—"

"It's for you," Clapper called, holding out the receiver.

Mumbling something, Gideon wandered abstractedly into the other cubicle and took the phone.

Julie was on the other end. "Hi, it's me."

"Umm . . . hi, sweetheart."

She laughed. "I see the expedition was successful. You found some bones, didn't you?"

"What? Yes, how did you know?"

"Well, partly because you're there in the police station, and you said that's where you'd be if you found something to work on, but mostly because you sound like your mind's about a million miles away, and that's the way you sound when you're deep in bones."

"Yes, well, as a matter of fact—"

"Gideon, you didn't forget about the picnic, did you?"

"Uh . . . picnic?"

He heard a small sigh. "Madeleine Goodfellow invited us all to a picnic-reception and dinner on Holgate's Green. You do remember that, don't you?"

"Of course I do," said Gideon affrontedly. "Jeez, Julie, I'm not *that* absentminded." Indeed, he did seem to have a vague memory to that effect.

"Yes," she said dryly, and he knew that she was smiling, "of course you do. Only it's not on the green; it's too foggy. It's indoors, at the museum. That's where I'm calling from. It started half an hour ago. You *are* coming, aren't you?"

"Well, sure, I am. The time just got a little away from me, that's all." He cast a last, long, lingering look at the bones in the cubicle opposite. "See you in fifteen minutes."

AS Clapper had predicted, the fog had continued to thicken, swirling in tendrils of graveyard gray, like mist on a stage set. Walking from the police station to the museum, he could actually see it part in front of him, like water before the prow of a ship, and then close again behind him. "Haven't seen muck like this in donkey's years," he heard one dimly seen passerby complain to another. It was only a little after six, three hours until dark, but the store windows were already lit and the street lights were on, although they did little but contribute an occasional sickly, sulfurous, yellow nimbus to the all-enveloping gray goop. Even the footsteps of others and the occasional whispered snatches of conversation he heard were dulled and muffled by the atmosphere. "This is cool! It really creeps you out," the distorted voice of an invisible child exulted.

With only six feet or so of visibility, it was easy to imagine oneself back a hundred years, on some gloomy, fog-swirling London street, with cutpurses and body snatchers lurking in the alleys and street girls and fishmongers hawking their goods on the sidewalks. At the thought, he laughed aloud, no doubt startling anyone within range. The thing was, there was surely only one person you could reasonably call a body snatcher in Hugh Town at this moment, and his name was Gideon Oliver. As for fishmongers, there actually was one, or rather a fish-and-chips van, customerless and forlorn, parked near the town hall, barely visible in the blurry glow of its single lightbulb.

As he left the town center, the lights grew fewer and the illusion of Victorian times more pervasive, so much so that when the van, now a block behind him, gave up for the day and banged its shutters closed, he took the noise at first for the clop of horses' hooves. He pulled his jacket closer around him. Although his collar was turned up, his neck was wet with moisture that ran down from his hair. Absently, he touched the façade of one of the seventeenth-century buildings—he had the unconscious habit of grazing his fingers along ancient buildings as he went by them on old streets; for the anthropologist in him, it was a small, nurturing point of contact with the past—but this time he jerked his hand back. The rough-cut stone blocks were as slimy as eels. He shivered.

I'm getting a little creeped out myself, he thought, looking forward to the dinner now. It was going to be good to talk about something other than homicide and body parts. He would listen without a peep of dissent even to Victor's twaddle about Western thought–dominated non-relational ways of being.

Alas, it was not to be.

TWELVE

HE was only halfway down the stairs to the museum's lower floor, where the buffet was set up, when he was spotted by the invitees, who were standing around the appetizer table, sipping their drinks, crunching potato chips—crisps, as the English called them—and raw veggies, and engaging in what appeared to be animated conversation. Madeleine, in particular, was nattering cheerfully about something; almost singing, her fluty voice jumped an octave at a time, her bracelets jangling in accompaniment.

Liz was the first to see him. "Speak of the devil, there's the man now!" she exclaimed, to be followed by an eager swiveling of heads in his direction and a blizzard of questions and comments, all flung at him at more or less the same time.

"Hey Skeleton Detective, how the hell did you figure out it *was* Williams?" a more than usually outgoing Rudy Walker asked.

"So did Edgar really murder him, then?" Joey Dillard

wanted to know. No button tonight, but he was wearing a sweatshirt with *PETA: People for the Ethical Treatment of Animals* in big blue letters across the front. There was an easy slur to his speech that made Gideon think he'd been getting steadily into the liquid refreshment for the last half hour or so. By now he'd heard that Joey had a tendency to get a bit pickled when the opportunity arose.

"And cut him up in little pieces?" Victor Waldo added with a happy little shudder.

"How exactly did he do it?" Cheryl Pinckney asked with equal avidity. "Kill him, I mean? Could you tell? With a knife, with a gun, did he poison him, did he cut his throat—"

"What are the police going to do about it?" her husband interrupted, his brow wrinkled. He was wearing a button in apparent reply to Joey's sweatshirt: *Support PETA: People for the Eating of Tasty Animals.* "Don't tell me they're going to want to come and . . . and *grill* us?"

"Of course they are," Victor contributed. "They'll have to investigate. They can't just assume *Edgar* did it. I assume we'll all be suspects." He appeared to be thrilled with the idea. "Am I not right, Gideon?"

In the expectant moment of silence that followed this barrage, Gideon wondered briefly if it was too late to get away with pretending not to have heard any of it, or better yet with snapping his fingers as if he'd forgotten something (like the absentminded professor he was, after all), muttering something to himself, and turning around and heading abstractedly back up the stairs . . . never to return.

No, he thought, looking at the group of eight avid, upturned faces, and one sympathetic, mildly amused one (Julie's), there was no way to get out of it now. They certainly had a legitimate interest, and he might as well face them now as later. He just wished they weren't going at it with such morbid relish.

Still on the stairs, he paused, one hand on the railing, took a breath, and began. "Well, first, the idea that those bones are Pete Williams's is strictly a guess at this point. I mean, there are thousands of visitors a year here, and no one really knows how many—"

"But it's your best guess, right?" Liz cut in. Tonight she was decked out in a fringed, open-weave purple afghan over stonewashed bib overalls and a tie-dyed T-shirt. More than one person had suggested that Liz's wardrobe came largely from the landfills she worked in, and Gideon had to admit that they had a point.

"Well, yes, it's our best guess because it's our only one, but—"

"Oh, please, get real. Vistors, schmisitors, who else could it be? I mean, I know Edgar's innocent until proven guilty and all, but the guy came right out in front of everybody and *told* us he was going to kill him, we just didn't believe him." She gave an incredulous little snort of laughter that had just a touch of nasty satisfaction in it. "God, is this bizarre, or what?"

"Liz—"

Kozlov gave him a little breathing room. "Come, come," he proclaimed with hearty Russian authority, "man is hungry. Give him chance, let him eat. Plenty time for talk. First, eat."

"That's an excellent idea, Vasily," Madeleine trilled. "Why don't we all get our dinners and sit down?" She clapped her hands. "Come, everybody, enjoy. Our museum ladies have done a splendid job, as you can see. I particularly want to thank Louise Boger and Myrna Vandermeer for assisting with bringing the food inside, and for their artful arrangement of it under trying conditions." She led the group in applause, at which the two white-haired ladies who had been hovering behind the buffet table responded with flustered little gestures of diffidence and gratification.

In truth, the buffet looked a bit out of place, as if it didn't know what it was doing in the slightly fusty, exhibit-crowded museum basement, squeezed in between the main floor display, a thirty-foot, crimson-sailed nineteenth-century gig called the *Klondike*, and a display of nineteenth-century sail-making tools. Prepared by the museum's Ladies' Auxiliary with outdoor eating in mind, it was very much a typical English picnic of the potluck variety. There were bowls of varying sizes and colors heaped with couscous salad, rice salad with diced peppers, and tricolor pasta salad; finger sandwiches filled with cheese and tomato, ham salad, ham and cheese, cucumber and butter, and tuna; carrot and celery sticks; individual bags of potato chips with sour cream and salsa dip; sliced, cold pizza; loads of French bread; soft drinks, beer, and hot tea in an urn (no coffee); and two bottles of Pimm's No. 1, along with the lemonade with which to turn it into a reasonable facsimile of Pimm's Cup, a concoction no proper English picnic would be without.

Gideon got himself a bottle of Old Speckled Hen pale ale, which had been sitting in a bed of ice—in sensitivity to the peculiar drinking tastes of Americans (not his)—and stood to one side with it while the others got in line at the buffet. Julie, as he expected, waited with him.

She brushed the back of her hand against his wrist. "So how's it going, big guy?" she asked, smiling. "You look a little stunned. They kind of blindsided you there, didn't they?"

"Kind of. I guess I didn't expect you to tell them about Williams."

"I didn't. How could I tell them? I didn't know myself."

"You didn't? I didn't tell you on the phone?"

"Only that the dog had turned up some more bones. Not that you thought they were Pete's."

"Well, who told everybody, then?"

"Madeleine." She picked up a couple of cardboard

plates and handed one to Gideon, along with a plastic knife and fork wrapped in a paper napkin.

"Madeleine? How the heck did Madeleine know?"

Julie shrugged. "It's a small town. News gets around." She began working her way down the table, putting a little of almost everything on her plate, in line with her current philosophy of healthy eating: lots of variety, but all in tiny portions. This "French" approach, lately recommended by their nutritionist friend Marti Lau, had recently replaced Julie's devotion to an Atkins-style low-carb diet. Gideon gave it about a year, which would be about standard.

"I guess so," Gideon said, shaking his head. "It made it from the police station to here before I did." He helped himself to two cheese-and-tomato finger sandwiches, two of cucumber, a heaping scoop of couscous salad, and a bag of Brannigans Roast Beef and Mustard Flavor Thick Cut Potato Crisps. He was still able to eat just about whatever he wanted without putting on weight, knock on wood. So was Julie for that matter, but keeping up with the latest diets seemed to entertain her, and that was fine with him, as long as he wasn't required to join in, which he wasn't. The way they handled it was that whoever took on the cooking that night called the shots. As to dining out, they were on their own. A reasonable and satisfactory arrangement.

The dining table, made up of two folding tables pushed together end to end, was squeezed into the narrow space on the other side of the *Klondike*. To reach the remaining two chairs they pretty much had to climb up and over some of the others, but everyone was in good humor, and eventually they got there, Gideon at the "foot" (assuming Madeleine, at the far end, was at the head), with Julie around the corner from him on one side, and Kozlov on the other.

The group, seemingly realizing that they had more or less ambushed him on the way down, gave him ten or fifteen minutes of respite for eating and chitchat, which he appreciated. But then, one by one, the individual conversations died away and heads began turning politely in his direction, smiling and anticipatory. Time for the gruesome details, please.

Gideon smiled back. The food and drink had done him good, and simply seeing Julie had revived his spirits, as it always did, and he was ready to talk about the day's developments. He finished the last of the Old Speckled Hen, drinking from the bottle, and began.

"Let me start at the beginning. Working with the dog on the beach where the first bone was found, we turned up three more caches of human skeletal remains, all almost certainly from the same individual: one of bones from the right arm and forearm; one of hand and foot bones from both sides; and finally, one with most of the bones from the torso—ribs, shoulder girdle, and so on."

"No skull?" Rudy asked. "No teeth?"

They were an anthropologist's questions. Of all the bones in the body, the skull—which was actually twenty-one bones soldered more or less solidly together, plus one (the mandible) connected by a hinge—offered the greatest likelihood of a positive identification. And excluding DNA, the teeth, with all their irregularities, patterns, and dental work, were the feature that most often led to a definitive identification.

"Unfortunately, no," said Gideon. "No pelvis either. Altogether, I'd say we recovered, oh, a third of the skeleton."

"So where's the rest?" Donald asked.

Gideon shrugged. "Washed away, taken by carnivores, who knows?"

"Couldn't they be buried on one of the other beaches?"

"Sure, but which one?"

"Almost the whole of St. Mary's is rimmed with beaches," Madeleine said. "It would take months to search them all. Besides, for all we know, the rest might be buried inland. Or just taken out in a boat and dropped in the sea."

"That's right," Gideon agreed. "I think we just go with what we have. We're lucky to have that much.

"But how you know is Pete Williams?" Kozlov asked.

"We don't know it—"

"But you *think,* yes?"

"We don't even think it, Vasily. As Liz said, it's our best guess, but it's no more than that. A guess, and only a working guess at that."

He told them about the supinator crest and the squatting facets. He could see that it was something of a letdown.

"That's nothing," Donald said accusingly. "That's no kind of proof."

"Which is what I've been trying to tell you."

"Maybe he had some other kind of job turning knobs or something," Cheryl said. "Wouldn't that give you a supinator thingie too?"

"Yes, probably."

"So it doesn't mean anything," Cheryl said, the first time Gideon had heard her agree with something her husband had said. "It could be anybody."

"No, that's not the way you look at it," Liz said. "You have to consider the probabilities. Pete Williams has disappeared—that is, none of us have heard of him since the last conference," she added to cut off Gideon's protest. "The last any of us saw of him was right here on this island, two years ago. Most of us here now were there when Edgar threatened to kill him—"

"Oh, come on, Liz, not again," Joey said, stumbling over his consonants a little. He was soused, all right. "He didn't threaten him, it was just, you know—"

"It was just Edgar saying, and I quote: 'I keel 'eem, dat leedle peepsqueak,'" Liz persisted, unwilling to let go of an appealing hypothesis.

"Yeah, he *said* it, but he wasn't really—"

"No, now that I think about it, she's right," Victor said. "He *was* steaming. We had our poker game afterward, and he was so mad he could hardly sit still; punching himself on the knee, talking to himself. Remember? He spoiled it for everybody—our last night together."

"That's so," Rudy agreed.

"Aw, now, look," Joey said, "he had a short fuse, sure, but that doesn't—"

"Now then," Liz cut in. "Think about it. Pete Williams was an auto mechanic. Auto mechanics have well-developed supinator crests. Most other people don't, even allowing for the occasional knob-twister. So when you put all that together—the death threat, the missing man, the skeleton on the beach, the supinator crests—it's pretty hard not to come up with Pete Williams as the first person on your list."

"Is making sense," said Kozlov.

"As far as that goes, I'd have to agree," Gideon said. "It's a long way from proof positive, but it does make sense. Mike thinks so, too. So tomorrow he'll start tracing Williams, seeing if he's still alive. If he is, that's the end of it. If no one's seen him for two years, then maybe we have something. In the meantime, I'll get back to the skeleton and start doing some serious analysis. I already have the sex, but I'm hoping to pin down race and age, and to come up with estimates of height, build, old injuries, and so on. If they do match what we find out about Williams's description—"

"Well, we can help you with that right now," Joey said with the elaborate precision of a drunk trying to prove he wasn't drunk. He pushed his glasses, which had slipped down his nose, back up. "We all know what he looked like. Thirty or so, kind of average build, maybe five-ten—"

"Stop, stop!" Gideon yelled, so suddenly that the museum ladies, now in the process of going around pouring tea, froze trembling in their tracks.

"What did I . . . what did I do?" a startled Joey asked. The tic below his eye was going full blast.

"I don't want to know what he looked like."

Donald frowned at him. "You don't want to know? But how . . . but how can you—?"

"He means he doesn't want to know until *after* he's examined the bones," Rudy interjected smoothly. "If you know beforehand, it's likely to affect your perception. You find what you're looking for; the infamous principle of expectancy."

He smiled fleetingly at Gideon. They had both had the principle of expectancy drilled into them at the same time and place, at the feet of their major professor, back at the University of Wisconsin. Gideon smiled back. He was glad to see Rudy looking a little less miserable than he had the other day; not so different, in fact, from the old Rudy, if you ignored the smudged eyes, the gaunt frame, and that gold chain.

Donald nodded, and the others seemed to get the point as well.

Accepting a cup of tea from one of the ladies, who were now in motion again, Gideon continued: "If the rest of my findings do match Williams's description, and if he really has been missing for the last two years, then the next step would probably be to get some DNA samples from his family, assuming he has a family, and compare them to DNA from the bones. If they match, that settles it. If they don't, we need some more guesses."

"From bones in ground for two years, you get DNA?" a surprised Kozlov asked.

"Oh, yes, even from bones much older than that. They've retrieved DNA from 350,000-year-old fossils. You see—"

"Of course!" Kozlov smacked himself in the forehead. "Stupid. DNA is chemically inert molecule. Nonreactive. Big, long half-life, not going break down any time soon."

"That's right," Gideon said, chiding himself for the childish explanation he'd been about to give. Kozlov's music-hall accent made it easy to forget that he was a brilliant man with deep and wide-ranging interests—self-educated or not.

"The business with the supinator crest and the squatting facets is interesting, Gideon," Rudy said. "Any other occupational indicators?"

Another anthropologist's question. It was good to see Rudy's old interests reawakening. Occupational indicators, or behavioral indicators, or skeletal markers of occupational stress were what anthropologists called the features in bones that provided clues to the person's activities in life: squatting facets, for example.

"That's all I've seen so far. I haven't had a real chance to look at the shoulder girdle and ribs yet, though. That'll be tomorrow. Want to help out?" he asked with sudden inspiration.

For a moment Rudy looked pleased, but then he shook his head—a little sadly, it seemed to Gideon. "Nah, I'd only get in the way; I've been out of things too long. Besides, I've got the consortium."

"Of course. I wasn't thinking."

"But thanks for asking. I appreciate it."

"What I want to know," Victor said, "is why we keep saying this skeleton, this person, was *murdered*. We don't know that, do we, or am I missing something?"

"We haven't found any direct proof, no," Gideon said. "Not yet, anyway, but—"

"But if you can think of another reason for cutting somebody up into little pieces and then burying them in a bunch of different places on a deserted beach, I'd love to hear it," Liz said.

Victor thought for a moment. "I have to admit, nothing jumps to mind," he said, straight-faced.

THIRTEEN

WHEN it came to work, Maude Bewley was not the sort to procrastinate. The more of tomorrow's work you did today, the less work you'd have to do tomorrow; that was her motto. This was the reason she was still puttering around in the Star Castle kitchen at ten o'clock at night. By doing some of the breakfast preparation now, she'd have that much less to do in the morning. She wouldn't have to come in until it was time to put on the bacon, which meant she could stay in her warm bed an extra half hour, a welcome treat that her joints would appreciate. Having seen to the juices and milk in the refrigerator, she set out the warming pans in the dining room, making sure there was fuel in the burners; laid out the silverware, dishes, and cups; filled the urn with water and its basket with pre-ground coffee (not a one of these Americans wanted tea, even in the morning!); and stepped back to survey her handiwork. Very nice. Everything looked clean and appetizing.

She went back into the kitchen to put up her feet and

have a nice, steaming cuppa and a snack at the corner table. She'd gotten chilled right through to the bone walking up to the castle from her flat in town this morning—this bloody fog!—and never had totally warmed up. She got a fairy cake from the refrigerator, poured the milk and tea into her cup, plunked in two teaspoons of sugar, and sat down with a sigh, pulling up another kitchen chair for her poor feet. As Kozlov's cook and housekeeper, the work itself wasn't too hard on her feet, and the additional guests weren't really a problem because the girl from Bryher was coming in every afternoon for three hours to tidy up their rooms and help with the kitchen work.

But the walking up and down Garrison Hill Road all the way from Buzza Street every day, usually twice—that was killing her. Mr. Kozlov knew it, too, which was why, nice man that he was, he'd been pestering her about moving into one of the rooms in the castle. She'd thought about it. Imagine living in a castle! There would be real advantages, too; not only the ease, but think of the money saved. Only what was she supposed to do about her sister Grace, who lived with her in the flat in town? Grace was getting old now, and she'd never been very independent, even when she was a girl. Timid, easy to intimidate, that was Grace. What would she do on her own, after they'd roomed together for the last twenty years? Oh, she had her job at the bank, so money wasn't the problem, but she needed someone to look out for her, Grace did. Someone to sort of intercede with the world on her behalf.

Besides, being in this dreary, chilly old place day and night with nobody for company but that bossy, creepy Mr. Moreton and Mr. Kozlov himself? Brr. You could barely get a civil word out of Mr. Moreton, and as for Mr. Kozlov—nice as he was, she was lucky if she understood two words out of every ten.

She wafted the cup gratefully under her nose, sipped, and swallowed. She could have been drinking tea all along, of course, but Maude Bewley preferred to put off pleasure until the labor was out of the way. So it was a reward, as you might say. And so much more enjoyable this way, with the work over and done with. She peeled the paper from the cake, bit through the soft raspberry icing, and washed the mouthful down with tea. She could feel the hot, sweet liquid flow all the way to her stomach, radiating outward, soaking into her body and easing her bones. With the second sip, her head began to nod. With the third, she was asleep.

The dream, like all dreams, began in the middle. She was lying under an enormously high waterfall. Not in the stream of water itself, but behind it, protected by a shelf of rock far above her. She herself was on another rocky shelf, midway down the face of the cliff. The shelf was small, just big enough to hold her, and it was high above the bottom, hundreds of feet, but she wasn't frightened. It was quite pleasant there, and she dreamed she went to sleep and dreamed again. In her dream's dream the pleasant waterfall, without changing, somehow became sinister and heart-stoppingly threatening. She fought to wake up and dreamed she did. Looking up, she saw a huge, amorphous, blobby thing poised at the top of the fall, a gigantic, formless presence that filled her with dread. To her dismay it tipped over the edge and came plummeting down on her. Unable to move, she squeezed her eyes shut and stopped breathing. She heard the thing whoosh by her, and she knew she had to wake up—really wake up this time—before it hit the bottom, or she would die when it struck.

She heard it hit, however—a slushy, thunky sound, not the ear-splitting crash she'd expected—and she didn't die. She did wake up, however.

She found herself on her feet, disoriented, the fragments of the shattered teacup still skittering on the slate floor. No longer cold, she was sweating now. She had the terrible feeling that it had been more than a dream, that, just outside, some *thing* had plunged by the kitchen's high casement windows to smash itself on the paving stones of the narrow, moatlike passageway that ran around the castle just inside the inner retaining wall of the ramparts. A few years ago, in fog much like this, a gull, unable to see, had flown smack into the upper part of the castle and done just that. She had been in the kitchen finishing up the lunch dishes at the time, and she had heard it plunge by the window, or perhaps seen it out of the corner of her eye. She had gone out to investigate, almost stumbling over the bloodied, broken, still-living creature lying on its back, and the experience haunted her still.

Could it have happened again? Only whatever it was, if there really was anything, had sounded bigger than any seagull. Well, she wasn't going out into that passageway this time, not in this nasty murk. She'd once seen a big rat running around out there, or rather heard a rat, or something that sounded like a rat. The whole thing was probably just her dream anyway—this awful fog had upset her mental balance—and if it wasn't, let somebody else find it this time.

She gathered up the pieces of the broken teacup with a wet cloth, shrugged into her still-damp coat, and went home.

FOURTEEN

A cheerful, softly whistling Gideon Oliver arranged the bones into as near a proper anatomical relationship as the remains would allow. What with Robb's delivery of the final two sacks yesterday, there was quite a lot of material now, more than he'd realized. The skull and pelvis were lacking, yes, but he guessed he had something close to forty percent of the skeleton laid out on the table in front of him. Plenty to work with.

Because it was nine o'clock and the police department was open to the public for its daily hour, Robb and Clapper were busy with island police matters (a report of a lost cat, a complaint about a neighbor's wind chimes), and he was on his own, which suited him. Not that he really minded their being around, but this way he could mumble, exclaim, and go "Hm" to his heart's content without having to explain what he was doing. Things would go faster. He could get right down to business.

And he did. As a serious scientist, a well-regarded expert, a board-certified diplomate in forensic anthropology, the last thing he wanted to do was to examine these remains with the express purpose of determining whether or not they matched the fragmentary description of Pete Williams that he'd heard from Joey last night: age, about thirty; height, about five-ten; build, average.

But of course he was also very much a human being, so naturally it was the first thing he addressed. He started with build, the least specific, least useful, and most unmeasurable of the three characteristics, but also the easiest one on which to reach some conclusion. Inasmuch as bones, especially at muscle-insertion points, reflected muscular development—the bigger and stronger the muscles, the more robust and rugged the bones they attached to—their general ruggedness was an indicator of the muscularity of the living person. And it took but a few moments' study for him to conclude that this once-living person had been neither especially powerfully built nor particularly puny. In other words: average. Like Williams. Also like almost everybody else. Conclusion: It might indeed be Williams. Or it might not.

Of course "build" comprised more than muscularity. There was also weight. Had the owner of these bones been obese? Skinny? Medium ("average")? Unfortunately, there was no way to tell. Fat people's bones looked like thin people's bones. So no useful decision on that score either.

That left age and height. Stature, as finicky anthropologists (including Gideon) insisted on calling it, was most certainly something you could determine from skeletal remains. You could make an astonishingly good estimate of stature from any of the long bones, including partial ones, or, with a bit less certainty, even from the metacarpals, the finger bones, or the vertebrae. The more of these bones you had, the more accurate the estimate, and Gideon had a lot of them sitting right in front of him. That was the good news. The bad news was that he didn't carry around in his head or on his person the tables, formulas, and regression equations required to make the calculations. He did carry around—one never knew what one might run into—a copy of ForDisc, a CD containing a sophisticated forensic anthropology computer program from the University of Tennessee that took all the grunt work out of it. You just measured the bones, clicked in the results, grabbed a quick sip of coffee while the computer plugged them into the proper regression formulas, and up popped your stature-range estimates, down to the millimeter. The only problem was, ForDisc was useful only on complete long bones, of which he had nary a one.

There were, however, published formulas for estimating stature from partial long bones; less reliable, naturally enough, but better than pure guesswork. Last night, realizing that he would need them, he had called the departmental secretary and asked her to overnight-mail a couple of textbooks that contained the necessary Steele and McKern formulas. He now also made a mental note to call the museum and ask Madeleine for the sliding and spreading calipers she'd mentioned. An osteometric measuring board was probably out of the question, but it wouldn't hurt to ask. In any case the formulas wouldn't arrive until tomorrow, or possibly even the next day, so for the moment there was nothing he could do other than eyeball the bones, which didn't tell him much. The guy had not been a giant, and he hadn't been a dwarf—that was about it. Five-ten was very much in the ballpark, but it was a big ballpark. More than that he couldn't say at this point.

Ageing an adult (and Gideon had already determined these were mature bones, reflecting an age at least in the mid-thirties) was a different matter. No calipers, no formulas, no regression equations, no discriminant function analyses; you just looked carefully at certain skeletal structures, and if you were familiar enough with the changes they typically underwent in adult life, as Gideon was, you could make a respectable guess as to how old the person was when death struck. Not all bones showed these changes with equal clarity. The pubic symphysis—that is, the area where the two halves of the pelvis came together—exhibited them most clearly and predictably (why, exactly, nobody knew), and was therefore the most useful of the skeletal age-indicators, but Gideon didn't have a pelvis to work with. He did, however, have quite a few ribs—eight, to be exact—and ribs, although not quite as trustworthy as the pelvis, could give you a pretty fair idea of age.

It worked like this: The upper seven ribs did not directly join the sternum—the breastbone—but were connected by struts of cartilage. Without these flexible struts, inflating and deflating the lungs (otherwise known as breathing) would be a far more painful and difficult job than it was. (The next three lower ribs were each connected to the one above, and the lowest two to nothing at all in front.) As one got older, however, this "sternocostal cartilage" began to build up calcium salts and to very slowly ossify, particularly at the end that attached to the rib. As this lifelong process continued, the rib-ends reflected the new stresses placed on them with certain predictable changes. Generally speaking, in going from young to old, they went from billowy-smooth to granular and jagged, from round-rimmed to painfully sharp-rimmed, from flat and wavy to deeply concave. As one of Gideon's students had put it, "Anybody can tell. They just plain get older- and uglier-looking. Like people."

So they did, but with some understanding of these characteristics one could do better; one could arrange them into stages and use them for a reasonably reliable estimate of age, within a ten-year range at any rate.

And the estimate that Gideon came up with was fifty,

give or take five years; certainly not the thirty he'd been anticipating. He went to pour himself a first cup of coffee from the pot that Robb had made a few minutes earlier (fresh, it wasn't exactly Starbucks, but it wasn't sludge either), spooned in some powdered creamer, and talked this over with himself. Could Joey's guess at Pete Williams's age have been fifteen or twenty years off? Possible, but very, very unlikely. Or were the rib-ends he'd just looked at atypical and therefore misleading? The standard ranges were, after all, merely averages, not hard-and-fast parameters, and human beings, as everyone who studied them knew, loved to violate averages. Neither Gideon nor any other anthropologist would stake his reputation on an age determination based strictly on his reading of rib-ends or, for that matter, any other single criterion.

But there were other criteria as well, and another ten minutes' perusal of the bones convinced him that his age estimate had been on target. Aside from the generally "older and uglier" look of the long bones, there were signs of compression and lipping of the lower thoracic vertebrae. (He didn't have the lumbar vertebrae, in which he'd expect these signs to be even more advanced.) Equally telling, there was some lipping of the glenoid fossa of the scapula—the ovoid depression in which the ball of the humerus nestled, forming the shoulder joint. That was part of the general, unavoidable wear and tear that went along with getting older. And on the body of the scapula—he held it up to the light—yes, there were translucent patches developing; almost like looking through eggshell in places. That went along with getting older, too. Bone demineralized with age, and the scapula, one of the thinnest, flattest bones in the body to begin with, showed it especially clearly.

So everything supported the mid-forties to mid-fifties age range. In any case, the guy was no thirty-year-old, of that he was now certain. The possibility that this was Pete

Williams, perhaps a bit strained to begin with, grew even dimmer, despite those oh-so-clever conclusions he'd come up with about supinator crests and squatting facets. A pity, too; it had all fit together so neatly. One more theory that had bitten the dust when faced with the ugly facts. So he was back to square one on identifying the guy.

Ah, well, coming up with a definitive identification was Clapper's job, not his. All Gideon could do was to provide clues. He topped off his coffee, and went back to take a closer look at something on one of the ribs that had caught his interest.

"THAT little nick, that insignificant little scratch?" Clapper demanded, staring skeptically at the rib Gideon was holding out to them. "That's what you brought us in to see, interrupting our vital police work?"

"It sure is, Mike," said Gideon. "I thought you might have some interest in the cause of death. We're not simply assuming homicide any more. We have the direct evidence. That's a knife wound you're looking at. He was stabbed."

"It isn't much to look at," Robb offered. "You can hardly see it. Just a little ding, really, no more than half an inch long."

"Not even that," Gideon said. "Two millimeters in length, and just barely penetrating the cortical bone, the outer layer. But that's what stab wounds in bone look like. Flesh and organs are easy to penetrate; living bone isn't. Knife points don't typically get in very far."

Robb had taken the magnifying glass that Gideon had offered but Clapper had declined, and was studying the tiny incision. "I see. It isn't really what you'd call a ding, is it? The edges are very sharp, very straight. And the shape is . . . well, it's sort of triangular, isn't it?"

Gideon nodded. "And judging from that, and from the breadth of it—at the top it's almost as wide as it is long—

I'd say it was probably a fairly big knife with a heavy spine, not some little pocket knife. From the kitchen, possibly something along the lines of an eight- or ten-inch utility knife, although I'm way out on a limb there, so don't quote me on that."

Clapper folded his arms. "If you say it's a stab wound, I'll accept it, but how can it be the cause of death? Obviously, the rib blocked the knife from entering the body cavity, and you don't die from a nicked rib, or are you going to tell me that you do?"

"No, of course you don't, but there's more. Look."

He had cleared a space on the table, in which three other ribs lay, and on two of them he pointed out similar nicks. "He didn't die from these either. But this one . . ." He slid over the longest of the ribs and held it up for their inspection. "This is the fourth rib on the left side, and here about midway back, you see not a little puncture like the others, but—"

"A spur!" Robb exclaimed. "Like the one on the tibia."

"Well, not quite. That spur, if you remember, was a stubby little spike on the sawed edge of the bone. This one extends from about the middle of the rib's bottom, and it's longer. It's more like a thin, curved sliver, a—"

"It looks as if it's been peeled away from the rest of the bone," Robb said, "bent back but not enough to break it off."

"Yes, that's a good description, that's what happened." Gently, Gideon fingered the inch-long sliver. "This cut wasn't made by the point—well, it may have been started by the point—but, basically, it was made by the blade, which sliced through the thin lower edge of the rib on its way by. Try that on a piece of dry bone, and it would just break off, but when bone is green—that is, living—it's flexible; it gives, it doesn't break, and you get a shaving, like this."

Robb frowned. "But he wouldn't have died from that either. Or would he?"

"Not from that itself, no. You don't die from broken bones, let alone nicked bones, no matter how severe. It's the soft tissue damage associated with it that does you in. And this had plenty of soft tissue damage associated with it. See, to create a slice this wide, the knife would have had to be shoved in pretty far—six or seven inches anyway, assuming it's shaped anything like a typical kitchen knife—which means that it would have slipped right on through the fourth intercostal space, kept on going through the left superior lobe of lungs, and wound up deep in the left ventricle of the heart." He put the bone down. "And when that happened, he would most assuredly have lain down and died."

Clapper nodded. "So we have our cause of death."

"Well, not for sure. For all we know, he was already dead from some other wound or blow that doesn't show up on the bones. But there's not that much difference. If I wanted to use our usual weasel-words, I'd say that trauma of this nature is not compatible with continued life. That would cover it."

Robb was fascinated with the bone sliver. "Such a little thing," he murmured. "It's hardly noticeable."

"You'd notice it if it was you," Clapper said, and to Gideon: "Four stab wounds. That's a lot."

"Yes, it is," Gideon said, "especially considering that we have only eight ribs here. There are stab wounds on half of them."

"Out of how many ribs altogether?"

"Tw—"

But Robb was quicker on the draw. "Twenty-four," he announced promptly. "Twelve on a side. And men and women do have the same number."

Clapper rolled his eyes. "What a joy it is to work with such a fount of knowledge." He groped for the box of cigarettes in his shirt pocket, flipped open the lid with his thumb, and lit up. "Truly, I am blessed."

"Sorry, Sarge," Robb said, laughing, "It just popped out. I can't help myself sometimes."

"You should try harder," Clapper said. "Twenty-four altogether," he mused, letting out a lungful of smoke. "So if the ratio holds, we probably have something on the order of a dozen stab wounds, would that be a reasonable guess?"

"No, I wouldn't want to guess at the number," Gideon said, "but I think it's pretty safe to assume, given what we have, that he was stabbed a whole lot of times. A very violent death."

Clapper nodded soberly. "A crime of passion. Someone was very upset with our Mr. Williams. Assuming that this turns out to be Pete Williams."

"Oh, as to that, I don't think it will. Williams was supposed to be around thirty—although that may turn out not to be correct. But in any case, this guy was a good twenty years older than that."

Predictably, Robb's interest quickened. "Can you tell us how . . . ?"

"Sure, some bones age predictably enough to give you a pretty reliable range." He was going to demonstrate with the sternal rib ends, but that got a little abstruse, so he picked up the scapulas instead and held them up to the ceiling lights. "See, bone demineralizes and thins out as you get older, and whereas in a twenty- or thirty-year-old, you wouldn't see any light through . . . any light through . . ."

His voice faded out. This was the first time he'd held the two scapulas up side by side, and as he did his mind shot off on a tangent of its own. There were some significant differences between the two shoulder blades. "Looks like he was left-handed . . ." he murmured, and then, after a few moments: "No, it's almost as if these are from two different people. No, it isn't that. It's more like . . ."

Again, continuing to peer at the scapulas, he fell silent. Thirty seconds passed.

"Hello?" Clapper said. "Is anybody home?"

"Mm," said Gideon. Another thirty seconds went by.

Clapper sighed and ground out his cigarette. "Shall we go?" he said to Robb. "It appears that Elvis has left the building."

FIFTEEN

THE only room in Star Castle that was large enough to comfortably hold seven people, other than the dining room and the dungeon bar, was the cozy second-floor lounge, and it was there that the consortium held its meetings, seated not at a conference table but informally, in a rough circle, on what were probably the very same overstuffed Victorian armchairs on which Queen Victoria and her retinue had taken tea there that hallowed afternoon in 1847.

It was 9:45 A.M. The second urn of post-breakfast coffee, prepared by Mrs. Bewley, was on the seventeenth-century sideboard, and the light had gone on indicating that it was ready. Various items of administrivia had been disposed of, and it was time to get down to the serious business of the day: the reading and discussion of Donald's paper on the many social and ecological benefits of properly regulated sport-hunting. But one member had yet to arrive.

"So where's Joey?" Liz asked.

"Well, you know, big night last night," Kozlov said, tipping an imaginary glass to his lips with an amiable wink. "Maybe not so good feeling. We start anyway, okay?"

"If you like," said Donald, who was just as happy not to have Joey there to carp at his presentation anyway. "Julie," he said coyly, "may I have your promise not to report on my paper to your famous husband? I wouldn't want to upset him again."

"My lips are sealed," said Julie, amid general laughter. *I wouldn't want to upset him, either,* she thought.

From his attaché case Donald removed a sheaf of papers of alarming thickness, placed them on the butler's table in front of him, lovingly patted them into a neat stack, cleared his throat, cleared his throat again, and began.

"Man's hunting heritage predates the agricultural revolution of the Neolithic era by millions of years. Without the prehistoric hunter's contribution to early hominoid society, human social mores and family structure could hardly have developed . . ."

The room was filled with a faint, sad, sighing sound, partly from human lungs, and partly from slowly compressing seat cushions, as his colleagues resignedly settled themselves in for what looked like a very long haul.

ALONE again, Gideon sank into a chair beside the table, angling the scapulas in front of his face to look diagonally down their dorsal surfaces.

"Now what do we have here?" he said, happily and aloud, almost as if he expected them to answer him.

Which, in a way, they would.

MRS. Bewley rinsed the last of the breakfast things that were too big for the dishwasher, put them on the drying rack, and dried her hands with a dish towel. She was troubled. Generally, she couldn't remember her dreams five minutes after she woke up, but the one last night, if it was a dream, was still with her. She hadn't been able to get the idea that something had happened out there, just beyond the kitchen window, out of her mind, although she hadn't worked up the nerve to mention it to Mr. Kozlov or Mr. Moreton.

"This is silly," she told herself firmly, stroking dry-skin lotion into her reddened hands. "You're a capable, grown woman. If there's something out there, which there probably isn't, you can go and see for yourself. Besides"—and this was a thought she'd successfully fought to keep from the surface of her mind, although she now recognized it as the source of the nagging guilt that had been with her since she'd awakened—"someone might be hurt."

She took a final drag from the cigarette she had burning in an ashtray on the windowsill, got her sweater on, squared her shoulders, and went out to look.

GIDEON was sitting at the table, hunched over the two scapulas, when Clapper appeared at the opening to the glassed-in cubicle.

"Well, Gideon, you were right. Whoever it is that you're communing with, it's not Pete Williams. I just got word. The gentleman is alive and well in London."

"Mm," said Gideon, not looking up. His elbows were on the table, his chin supported in his hands, his eyes on the scapulas.

"Amusingly enough, by the by, he does work for a garage, or rather a franchise of them, but your informant got it slightly wrong. He's an accountant, not a mechanic." A rumble of laughter came from his chest.

"Yes, I know."

The laugh was cut short. "You know? How do you know?"

"How do I know what?"

"How do you know he's an accountant?"

Gideon finally looked up. "How do I know *who's* an accountant?"

Clapper stared silently down at him, his big hands on his hips. "I think I'll go out and come in again," he said mildly. "We can start all over."

Gideon leaned back in the chair. "I'm sorry, Mike. I wasn't paying a lot of attention."

"You weren't paying *any* attention," Clapper grumbled. "Pete Williams," he said, enunciating with great clarity, "still walks among us. And he is not an automobile mechanic, he's an accountant. Accountants, to my knowledge, do not spend a great deal of time twisting screwdrivers or anything else. *Ergo*, no supinator crest. *Ergo*, the chap we have before us on the table is not Pete Williams."

"Yes, I know it's not Williams. That's what I meant before. When I said I knew."

Clapper sighed. "I'm not getting any less confused. You know it's not Williams? *How* do you know it's not Williams?"

Gideon was as subject as any other forensic anthropologist to engaging in the secret vice and great pleasure of the field; namely, boggling the minds of policemen large and small. He let a deeply satisfying beat go by before replying.

"I know," he said with a sweet and childlike smile, "because I know who this is."

SIXTEEN

CLAPPER'S reaction was all that he'd hoped for. "Get out!" he shouted so violently that Robb, who was hanging up the telephone in the office across the corridor, nearly toppled his chair. "You're out of your bloomin' mind!"

"I don't think so, Mike," Gideon told him. "I think we're looking at what's left of Edgar Villarreal."

"Edgar . . . Edgar . . ." Clapper turned around and stomped back to his office.

"Did I offend the man in some way?" Gideon called pleasantly across to Robb.

"No, no, he's just gone back to get his cigarettes. Is it really that Villarreal chap?"

"I think so. Come on over, if you want. I'll tell you about it."

But the telephone rang again, and Robb dropped back into his seat just as Clapper, true to Robb's word, came back out of his office shaking out a match, and talking around the freshly lit cigarette in his mouth. "Now, did I misunderstand, poor, dumb copper that I am, or did you not tell me, in this very room, only yesterday, that Edgar Villarreal was et up by a grizzly bear in the wilds of Canada some two years ago? Consumed, digested, and excreted in minute pieces?"

"Alaska," Gideon said. "Yes, I did. I'm pretty certain now I was wrong. He's in fairly minute pieces, all right, but it was a saw that did it, not a bear. The people in Alaska were wrong."

"How could they be wrong about a thing like that?"

"I'm not sure," Gideon said. "But if I'm right, they were wrong about more than that. After he left here, Villarreal was supposed to have faxed Kozlov a letter from the States, resigning from the consortium. That's why—that was ostensibly why—he wasn't here this year. And as soon as he got back to the States, he was supposed have gone right off to his summer base camp to study bears. Which is where one of them supposedly got him."

"And you don't think it happened that way?"

Gideon gently touched a scapula. "I don't think he ever went home," he said soberly. "I think he's been right here at Halangy Point Beach all along."

"But how do you explain the fax?" Robb called.

"What does it prove?" asked Gideon. "Anybody could have sent it. And what else is there to show that he was really alive after he left here?"

Clapper sucked furiously on his Gold Bond and expelled a haze of smoke from his mouth and nostrils. He was thinking hard, Gideon could see. "If you're right . . . *if* you're right, then someone went to some pretty elaborate lengths to mislead everyone."

"It looks that way, yes."

Clapper thought some more. "All right, then, go ahead. What makes you so sure about this?"

"All right. First of all, you have to know that Edgar Villarreal had once been an agricultural worker, a fruit picker."

Clapper began to say something, but then clamped his mouth shut.

"His parents were Cuban immigrants who worked in the citrus groves in Florida, and Edgar worked right with them for a long time—from the time he was five until he was seventeen, if I remember right."

Clapper nodded. "Continue."

Gideon cleared a small area around the scapulas. "If you look here, on both these bones, immediately medial to the supraglenoid tubercles, which are these—"

"Let's keep it simple," Clapper muttered.

"Okay, right. This general area"—using the right scapula, he fingered the ovoid, concave surface of the glenoid fossa—"is the place where the head—the ball—of the humerus fits."

"The shoulder socket, you might say."

"Exactly, and this small, flattened area at the top of it—"

"That? You'd better not tell me that's another squatting facet."

Gideon laughed. "Well, but that's what it is, in a way. It's been worn, or polished, into the bone as a result of another bone moving against it during a certain kind of activity. Only in this case it's not squatting, of course. This is what you'd get in a person who spent a whole lot of time with his arms raised and moving above shoulder-level, okay? And look, here on the head of the humerus, exactly where it would come into contact with that facet, you can see a slight flattening. You can feel it better than you can see it."

"I'll take your word for it."

"Fine. Well, that goes along with the arms-above-the-shoulder idea. With me so far?"

"Yes, of course I see what you're getting at. But Gideon, agricultural workers are hardly the only people who hold their arms up. So do barbers, or orchestra conductors, or, or—"

"Sure, but I'm only getting started. Give me a chance. Now, these are a couple of the cervical vertebrae—C6 and C7. They'd be right at the base of the neck. The lipping on the bodies of these vertebrae strongly suggest that this person regularly extended his neck and head dorsally—" He tipped his own head sharply back to demonstrate. "And I don't think a barber or an orchestra conductor would be doing that too much. But a fruit picker on a ladder would, when he leaned his head back to see the fruit."

Clapper smoked silently and frowned. He was coming around.

"Now here's the clincher," Gideon said. "Most right and left scapulas look pretty much alike, but these are really different. The right one is pretty standard; your basic, everyday shoulder blade. But the left one is anything but. Look at how much bigger the acromial end of the scapular spine is, and—"

A hollow, rumbling growl from Clapper made him change course. "Let's just say there are several indications of a lot more stress being placed on the left shoulder girdle than the right. Well, migrant citrus workers typically carry those long heavy ladders they work with over their left shoulders. Not only that, but that's where they hang the bag of fruit as they pick, and a full bag of oranges weighs ninety pounds. That's a lot of stress, Mike." He waited for Clapper's reaction.

Clapper had finished his cigarette. He stubbed it out in the Goat and Compass ashtray. "Can I ask a question?"

"Of course."

"A full bag of oranges weighs ninety pounds."

"Yes."

"And is that also something you just happen to know? I mean I'm just curious, but doesn't seem the sort of fact a person would just happen to—"

"I don't just happen to know it," Gideon said, laughing. "Back in the eighties, an anthropologist named Curtis

Wienker did a paper on the skeletal anomalies that go along with this kind of agricultural work. My prof in graduate school made it the core of his seminar on applied anthropology, so I remembered it, and Kyle let me use his laptop to look it up again on PubMed, and that's where I saw the ninety pounds. That's where I got most of the rest of what I'm telling you, too."

"I'm relieved to hear it," Clapper said.

"There's one more thing," Gideon said. "This rough, bulgy area on the left scapula is an old enthesopathy, an inflammation, at the point where the tendon of the trapezius inserts. That too is usually a result of stress, heavy stress, and when you consider the function of the trapezius and the—"

"Tut-tut-tut-tut-tut, you're losing me."

"In a nutshell, Mike, if you went around reaching up with your left arm to pick fruit—thereby rotating your scapula—while your left shoulder was already bearing the weight of that heavy bag, this is exactly what you'd expect that shoulder to look like."

Gideon put the bone down and leaned both hands on the table. "I rest my case."

Clapper nodded slowly and sat down in the other chair, thinking it over, patting his breast pocket in search of the cigarette pack that he'd left in his office, but not bothering to get up to get it. "But what of the squatting facets? Where do they come in?"

"Well, I was wrong there too—"

"They're not squatting facets?"

"No, they are squatting facets, but they probably didn't come from squatting. Remember, what causes them isn't necessarily squatting as we generally picture it. Specifically, you get them from repeated dorsiflexion of the foot." Again, he illustrated as he had the day before, placing his hand palm-down on the table, then bending it sharply upward. "And—think about it for a moment—climbing up and down a ladder, especially with a heavy bag on your back, would involve a whole lot of highly stressful dorsiflexion."

He, too, sat down. "It all fits, Mike."

"Yes, it does. It's also all circumstantial."

"Well, naturally. I can't positively ID this guy—not so far, anyway—but what would you say the odds are of finding a dismembered fruit picker buried on a beach on St. Mary's?"

"Well, now, maybe not so poor as you think. There's a lot of agriculture here. A lot of farms."

"Yes, but what are the crops?"

"The crops? Ah, well, mm . . ."

"Flowers, bulbs, and potatoes," Robb called as he hung up the phone. "And then they harvest kelp, too."

"There you are," Gideon said. "Unless they grow their potatoes on trees here, he's not a local."

"I take your point," Clapper said with a smile as the phone rang again and Robb picked it up. "All right, this deserves some looking into. I believe I'll start by seeing what there is to be learned about Mr. Villarreal's supposed demise in the wilds of Montana."

"Alaska," Gideon said.

Robb held out the telephone. "Sarge, it's for you."

"Take it for me, lad."

"No, he wants you. Sounds serious. Something's up."

"All right, all right, I'll take it at my desk." Clapper slapped his thick, corduroyed thighs and thoughtfully stood up. "Very interesting, Gideon. Back in a tick."

A minute later—Gideon hadn't gotten around to getting out of the chair yet—Clapper came barging out of his office and into the corridor, but it was a different Clapper, far more akin to the coarse, rough character Gideon had met the other day. "I'll need you, Kyle! Let's get going!"

Robb was on the telephone with another caller. He put his hand over the mouthpiece. "It's not quite ten, Sarge. The office is still open."

"You've done enough bloody nursemaiding for one

day," Clapper shot back. "The office is closed. Switch the telephones to the service, let Anna do something useful. Pack it in. Now!"

"Straightaway, sir," Robb said, practically jumping out of his chair. He uncovered the mouthpiece. "I'm sorry, miss, we'll have to ring you back on that."

"What's up, Mike?" Gideon asked.

"Not your concern," Clapper snapped without turning around to look at him.

Robb paused at the table that held the two different kinds of headgear. "Which hat, sir?"

"Screw the effing hats," Clapper snarled, striding toward the front and roughly motioning for Robb to follow. At the door he turned back to Gideon with a parting growl. "If you go out, make sure you pull the effing door good and shut after you."

Gideon, deciding that further conversation with Clapper at this point was not in his best interest, silently watched them go.

On a guess, he thought, *I'd say that call was from Exeter.*

BUT in fact the call had come from Star Castle, and the man who had made it stood waiting for them in the fog, at the base of the age-worn stone staircase, hands delicately folded in front of his discreet little paunch, as Robb pulled the van up in the grassy parking area at the entrance to the castle.

"I am Mr. Kozlov's majordomo," the pasty, dark-suited man with the pencil mustache said. "My name is Mr. Moreton. You've come about the unfortunate deceased gentleman. You'll want to see Mr. Kozlov. I'll take you to him." He turned to precede them up the stone steps. "If you'll be so good as to follow me."

"No, we don't want to see Mr. Kozlov, we want to see the unfortunate deceased gentleman," Clapper said.

A very slight lift of his eyebrows showed that Mr. Moreton considered this a contravention of etiquette, but he acceded without dissent. "Certainly." He continued majestically up the steps before them.

They followed him across a short stone bridge that crossed a dry moat, then under the "ER 1593" carved into the great lintel, and through the castle wall onto the grounds. Robb, if Clapper remembered correctly, had toured the place not long before, when it was open to the public as part of some anniversary having to do with the accession of Charles II—or was it the execution of Charles I?—but it was the first time Clapper had been inside. Yet it was Robb who looked with curiosity at the historic walls around them. Clapper didn't go in much for history.

Once through the massive entryway they continued single file on a narrow pathway, perhaps five feet wide and paved with granite blocks, that ran between the fifteen-foot-high stone retaining wall—the inner wall of the ramparts—and the castle building itself, forming a deep, claustrophobia-inducing passageway around the building and apparently serving as a storage area for dustbins, gardening equipment, piles of stone for repairing the retaining wall and the paving, pottery shards, and similar odds and ends. A few heavy outpipes, waste pipes of one kind or another, ran from the building into the rampart's wall, about ten feet above the passageway. Higher up, the top of the castle disappeared into the fog, making the well of the passageway seem even deeper and more tunnellike.

"You wouldn't know the name of the unfortunate gentleman, would you?" Clapper, a step behind Moreton, asked.

"Mr. Joel Dillard, a member of the consortium. The doctor arrived about twenty minutes ago. He's in the kitchen now, if you wish to—"

"Twenty minutes? You took your time calling the police, didn't you?"

"Mr. Kozlov didn't think it was a police matter. A simple fall. But Dr. Gillie said, in a case like this, where there's been a violent death, the police must be notified. We certainly didn't intend to violate the law. If we have, please accept—"

"All right, all right," Clapper said gruffly. There were only three doctors on the island and all of them served both as deputy coroners and as police surgeons. Davey Gillie was one of the better ones, probably the very one Clapper himself would have called to the scene to make out the death certificate, as procedure required for any sudden death, suspicious or otherwise.

"Next time something like this happens—" Robb began, as they turned the first corner of the building. They were still in the well of the passageway.

"Next time!" Mr. Moreton cried with feeling. "Let's hope there's no next time!"

"Next time, call 999," Robb went on gently. "That's the best thing to do."

Not necessarily, Clapper thought. In this case it was probably better that he hadn't. Once he called this in to headquarters, there would be a crime-scene team, and very probably a couple of detectives, out from Truro within the hour to look things over, and the fewer paramedics and technicians and such that had been mucking around, stepping in the blood and all, the better.

"You found the body?" Clapper asked Mr. Moreton as they turned the second corner.

"No, our housekeeper, Mrs. Bewley."

"Don't let her leave. We'll want to talk with her."

"Yes, of course." He slowed and stopped at the next corner. "The gentleman . . . the remains . . . are just beyond. Is it all right if I don't—"

Clapper pointed to a nearby door. "Go in there and wait. That's the kitchen, is it?" He'd seen Davey Gillie at a table, writing.

"Yes, sir, the kitchen," Moreton said gratefully, scurrying for the door. "Shall I get Mr. Kozlov?"

"Get Mrs. Bewley. No, wait, get them all. Everyone in the house. Ask them to wait in the kitchen as well."

Mr. Moreton nodded and opened the door.

"Thank you, Mr. Moreton," Robb called, earning a sullen glare from Clapper.

The two policemen turned the corner together, but Clapper then stopped at once, putting out his arm to stop Robb as well. "Now that's what I call a bloody mess," Clapper said disgustedly.

"Good God," a shaken Robb whispered.

Joey Dillard's body lay sprawled, partly on its back, partly on its side, on the stone paving, one blackened, dulled eye open, the other one half-lidded. One foot, shoeless, was propped awkwardly against the retaining wall, the leg that went with it twisted unnaturally under him. A bent, broken pair of glasses hung pathetically from one ear. There was a great deal of blood, matted in his hair and soaked so heavily into his sweatshirt that most of the logo on it, something about Ethical Treatment, couldn't be read. More blood coated the paving, tarry and congealed.

"He's been here a while, I'd say, sir," Robb said as professionally as he could manage, despite the quaver he could hear in his own voice. "You can see one of his eyes, and the cornea's just about opaque, so that's two to three hours at a minimum, and the blood is well on the way to drying. I'd say eight to twelve hours."

"My goodness," Clapper responded meanly, "did they teach you all that hard stuff at Bramshill?" He raised his eyes toward the still invisible roof of the castle. Robb thought he was merely rolling his eyes, but no; Clapper was looking for something. "You've been here before. What's up there?"

"Up there?"

"No, down here," Clapper snapped. "If I say 'up there,' what else can it mean but 'down here'?"

Robb gulped. This was as vinegary and dyspeptic as he'd ever seen Clapper, and his resentment and anger were starting to get the better of the awe in which he generally held the Great Man. Well, almost. But what the hell was the ferocious old bugger's problem this time?

"Well, there's not really anything up there, Sarge," he said neutrally. "See about twenty-five, thirty feet up, where the stone facing ends, and then there's another floor, set back a little, with shingles on the outside? That's the third floor—where all the guest rooms are, I think."

This time Clapper really did roll his eyes, making it clear that the information he was hearing wasn't what he wanted to know, and Robb hurried nervously on. "Well, at the top of the stone facing up there, just above the level of the windows, there's a sort of walkway all around the outside, under the eaves. You get out onto it from the third floor by walking up five or six steps and going out this little door—"

"Aah!" Clapper said, and Robb relaxed a little. "Yes, I can see there's a little railing there. That's where he fell from, Kyle."

"Certainly possible, sir."

"No, it's definite. Come a little closer—that's enough, no nearer to the body than that. See that outpipe above us? If you had your wits about you, you'd have observed by now that it's been broken. One end emerges from the building, quite awry, and the other end, also awry, drains into the retaining wall. Between them is a space of approximately eighteen inches, from which, by power of intellect, we may take for granted the existence of a missing eighteen-inch section of pipe. Now where do you suppose that missing section might be? Where would a smart, privileged, university-educated youth like yourself look?"

"I don't know, sir," Robb said, his face stiffening.

"I don't know, sir," Clapper mimicked. "Well, have you thought of looking at the body? You don't suppose that the aforementioned missing section of pipe and the length of wonderfully similar-looking pipe that peeps ever so subtly out from under his hip could be one and the same?"

"Oh," Robb said. "I . . . I didn't see it before. He must have struck it on the way down and carried it with him."

"From which you conclude . . . ?"

"That he . . ." Robb glanced up at the wall of the building before continuing. "That since there are no windows directly in line with the body, it follows that he fell from that little walkway."

"As the night the day," said Clapper. "Or, more likely," he added, "that he was pushed."

"You're saying that you think we have a suspicious death here, Sarge?"

"Well, think about it for a moment. Yesterday we dug up a beachful of bones belonging to a murdered man who, if we are inclined to believe Gideon—which I am—was a member of this consortium of Kozlov's. And today—no, last night, from the looks of him—*another* member of said consortium suffers a violent and mysterious death. Considering the normally peaceable nature of our little part of this green and pleasant land, what would be your conclusion?"

"That there's a relationship between the two events."

"Exactly, Kyle," said Clapper, who was showing signs that perhaps he'd considered that he'd harassed Robb more than he should have. "A connection. Possibly he was murdered. Possibly it was a random accident—a slip, a fall. Or possibly . . ."

Why are we just standing here? Robb wondered. One of the things they *had* taught him at Bramshill was that speed was of the essence, that sus-death clues grew cold, and often useless or irretrievable, very quickly. And yet here was Clapper, lost in his musings, letting the minutes go by.

"Sir, I left the CSI gear in the van. Shall I—"

Clapper snorted. "What, and when the 'real' detectives get here, have them complain that we've cocked the whole thing up, stomping around with our hobnailed boots? No, no, no, we'll call this in to headquarters as ordained, and they'll have Detective Superintendent Vossey and his supersleuth minions out from Truro inside of half an hour. We'll leave it to them, Kyle. We don't go a step closer."

Robb's spirits plummeted. His first chance at a significant crime-scene investigation, he thought bitterly, with the bloody corpse lying right there in front of them, untouched except by the doctor, and . . . He clamped his lips together. "Shall I at least execute the duties entailed in first-officer-on-the-scene uniform standards, sir?"

Clapper sighed. "Kyle, I don't even know what that means. But no. All I want you to do is execute a telephone call to headquarters and tell them what's happened. Then come find me in the kitchen."

Robb turned and left without a word.

Now what does he *have to be so mopey about?* Clapper wondered, watching the younger man trudge angrily off. He took one last, long look at the body, turned, and went into the kitchen that was a mixture of sooty, sixteenth-century stone walls and twenty-first-century stainless steel kitchen equipment, where Mr. Moreton had dutifully gathered the denizens of the house, all of whom were seated around an old table, drinking coffee and looking suspicious and untrustworthy.

"Where is Dr. Gillie?" he asked. "I want to speak with him first."

"I put him in my office," Mr. Moreton said. "It's more private."

Kozlov, whom Clapper knew by sight, clarified. "By stairs. Through dining room. There." He pointed toward the kitchen's door to the interior.

Once in the dining room, the smell of pipe tobacco

reached Clapper's nostrils. He stopped and automatically reached for his cigarettes, lit up a Gold Bond, and continued into a cramped foyer, off of which was a tiny, cluttered alcove that looked as if it might once have been a coatroom. The doctor sat behind the desk, screwing the cap onto an old-fashioned tortoiseshell fountain pen. He looked up, smiling, a long-nosed, horse-faced man in an old tweed jacket, with a pipe in the corner of his mouth.

"All right, what have we got?" Clapper said.

"Why, hello there, Davey-lad," Gillie said, addressing himself, "so nice to see you again. I hope you're well."

"Sorry, Davey, I'm not in much of a mood today." He stood, waiting.

"No, really? All right then, I'd better mind my manners. Well, you've looked at the body?"

Clapper nodded.

"Then you already know what we have." He straightened the form on which he'd been writing and read aloud: "'Cause of death, crushing head injuries; manner of death, undetermined; contributing causes of death, none indicated.'" He looked up with a shrug. "Been dead twelve to twenty-four hours, from the looks of him; rigor is quite pronounced and hasn't begun to break up yet. So if what Kozlov told me is so—that he was alive and well as late as eleven o'clock last night—why then, we'd have to put the time at right around then, say somewhere between eleven and one. Body temperature, assuming that it was normal to begin with, is down fourteen degrees Celsius, so that fits nicely enough as well."

"Other injuries?"

"Contusions and lacerations here and there, quite consistent with a fall. I would expect some internal trauma as well, when he's undressed and examined. Oh, and he died right where he lies. No one's moved him. The livor pattern makes that clear. I'd assume he fell from the catwalk up above."

"And hit the pipe on the way down?"

"*Grabbed* the pipe on the way down, I should say. There are rust stains and abrasions on his right palm. It would seem to have broken his fall and taken some of the force out of it. Otherwise—falling twenty-five feet directly onto stone like that—his head wouldn't merely have cracked, it would have exploded like a watermelon."

"Yes. 'Falling,' you said? What about 'jumping' or 'being pushed'?"

Gillie took the pipe from his mouth and pressed the bit into his cheek. "It's always possible, I suppose, but the man had been drinking heavily last night—you can still smell it on him—and that's a pretty narrow catwalk up there, and the railing's not even waist-high. I see nothing that suggests anything beyond an accidental fall."

"Oh? And what would he have been doing wandering out there on that narrow catwalk in the middle of the night?"

"Smoking a cigar."

Clapper's cigarette stopped halfway to his mouth. "Smoking a cigar? How do you know?"

"Because I asked Mrs. Bewley. 'Mrs. Bewley,' says I, 'what would he have been doing wandering out there on that narrow catwalk in the middle of the night?' She told me that he smoked these nasty black cigars that everyone hated—when he had one, even in his room, you could smell it all through the place—so that he often stepped out there to have one in peace without bothering anybody or being bothered by anybody."

"Including at night?"

"Especially at night. After dinner. Look, Mike, I've been here twenty-two years now, and we've never yet had a homicide, let alone a murder, but you obviously think this needs looking into, so if you want me to do a postmortem—assuming the budget can stand it and I still remember how to perform an autopsy—I could do one for you tomorrow, much as I hate the bloody job. Not that I expect anything to come of it, you understand."

"There are a few background elements you're not aware of, Davey."

"How mysterious," Gillie said. "And am I permitted to know?"

"Not at this point," Clapper said curtly.

Gillie smiled. "What a charmer you can be, Mike." He folded the report, slipped it into a jacket pocket, and stood up. "I'm done with the body. Would you like me to call Algy and have him get it to the chapel?"

Algy Rennet was the coroner's undertaker for the Isles of Scilly, and "the chapel" was the Chapel of Rest, a small room at St. Mary's Hospital that served the community as a mortuary.

"No, as a matter of fact. I want it left here."

"*Here?* Out in the open? But—"

"I don't want him moved. Kyle is speaking with Exeter right now. They'll have the Truro people here by helicopter in no time, and the deceased gentleman will soon be on his way to Treliske, where the Force pathologist is probably sharpening his gruesome instruments even as we speak. He'll do the postmortem."

"I see," said Gillie, showing his first sign of irritation. "Local talent not up to the job, eh? Well, I suppose they have a point. I haven't done an autopsy in two and a half years. My bad luck to live someplace where nobody kills anybody else."

"It's nothing to do with you, Davey. It's the way it works in a sus-death. Standard procedure, it's in the book."

Robb came into the room, with a quizzical expression on his face, as if he didn't know how Clapper was going to take what he had to say.

"Spit it out, Kyle. What'd they say? Who'd you talk to?"

"I talked to Detective Chief Superintendent LeVine himself, who referred me to Detective Superintendent

Vossey in Truro, who said—none too kindly—'Have you looked out the window?' "

"Have you . . . what the bloody hell is that supposed to mean?"

"The fog, Sarge. They can't land any helicopters here from Truro or anywhere else. No planes, no boats, nothing."

"Well, what do they expect me—"

"They expect you to handle the case yourself. You'll have to keep them up to date with a running case log, of course, but it's your baby, Sarge. You're the chief investigating officer." He chanced a smile. "And I'm your team."

This information produced a change in Clapper that was straight out of old horror movies, where the full moon finally goes down and the misty dawn breaks at last. The hunched, misshapen figure straightened. The glowing red eyes became cool blue again, the drooling fangs sank back into their gums, the fur on the backs of his hands vanished. A normal, smiling, reasonably amicable human being reemerged.

"I see," he said, letting it sink in for a few moments and relishing every second of it. "Well, well. Davey, go ahead and make that call to Algy. It looks as if you get to do your autopsy after all."

"Calloo, callay," said Gillie around his pipe.

"And you, Kyle, lad—"

I'm "lad" again, thought Robb. *That's better.*

"—don't just stand around, there's a lot to be done. Go and get the kit—no, first get on the blower to our summer help, all three of them. Tell them to climb into uniform and get over here—Gordon will go along with the body and remain with it, and you, Martin, and Sean will assist me in a proper investigation of the scene. Never mind what they taught you at Bramshill, I'll show you how the real coppers do it. . . . Kyle, I may have been a bit short with you before—"

"Not that I noticed, Sarge," Robb said, smiling. "About as mean as usual."

"Good, I suppose I'm imagining it. Now, before any-thing else, get the camera and get some pictures—no, first better run up to the catwalk and do a preliminary; see if there's anything like a cigar stub, or ash therefrom, before the wind blows it away. Wait, don't run off yet. I'll want everybody in the house kept available for interviews, start-ing with the housekeeper. Oh, but first seal the door to the catwalk and the passageway and have one of the boys make sure no one violates it. Oh, wait, before you do anything else . . ."

SEVENTEEN

LEFT alone with the bones, Gideon found his enthusiasm lagging. There was still plenty to be done—formally inventorying and describing them; looking for signs of injury, pathology, and cause of death; and, when the partial long-bone formulas came—whenever the fog let up enough to allow the ferry to bring the mail, that is—calculating a stature range. By now, of course he was virtually certain that it would match whatever Villarreal's height had been.

The work—after the earlier excitement of finding the knife cuts, and then of pulling Edgar Villarreal out of the hat, so to speak—seemed pedestrian, even a little boring, so he was glad to take a break and run over to the museum a few blocks away to get the calipers. When he returned, the rumbling coming from his stomach prompted him to look at his watch. He was astonished to see that it was after one. Past time to go and meet Julie for lunch.

He yawned, stretched, and rotated his head to work the kinks out of his neck. Then he tidied the table, cleaned up in the tiny restroom, slipped into his jacket, and went out into the fog. He had gone half a block along Upper Garrison Lane when he stopped, turned on his heel, and retraced his steps back to the front of the police station.

With painstaking care, he made sure the effing door was good and shut.

THE first indication that something was wrong was the pack of vehicles in front of the castle entrance. The clunkers that Kozlov and Mr. Moreton used to get around town, along with the motorbike that Cheryl Pinckney had rented for the photographic expeditions on which she supposedly disappeared during the day, were stowed in a small lot at the back, usually leaving an open, vacant field of gravel in front. But today there were automobiles all over the place, parked every which way in the fog. Three of them Gideon didn't recognize, but the fourth was the unmistakable, chartreuse-striped police van. And now, on looking up at the castle, he saw a young, uniformed policeman—not Robb—looking impassively at him from the top of the stone steps that led onto the entrance bridge. Something was very wrong, something serious.

Gideon walked toward the constable. *This is where the term "heart-sinking sensation" comes from,* he thought, as something seemed to unplug in his chest, letting the contents spill down into his legs.

"What's going on, Constable?" he asked from the bottom of the steps.

"Oh, just police business, sir. Routine," the cop said. He was no more than twenty, with a long face pocked with acne. On his head was the ceremonial bucket helmet, not the more comfortable cap, and he looked extremely uneasy, or perhaps even distressed.

Gideon, more worried by the second, started to climb the steps toward him.

The policeman held up a hand. "Sorry, sir, no one's permitted in."

Gideon stopped halfway up. "But I live here. That is, I'm staying here. For the week."

The officer frowned. "Are you? I thought everyone was—" He undid a flap on his tunic and took out a sheet of paper. "Your name, sir?"

"Gideon Oliver."

He scanned the sheet. "Sorry, sir, you're not—"

"You're looking at a list of consortium Fellows. I'm not a Fellow. I'm a . . . I'm a spouse."

The officer shook his head. "I'm afraid—"

"Look," Gideon said, "Julie . . . Julene Oliver, who *is* on your list, is my wife. Can you at least tell me if she's all right?"

"I'm fine, Gideon!" Julie called, emerging under the "ER 1593" from the entry passage. "I thought I heard your voice."

"Julie, what's going on?"

"Let's take a walk. I'll tell you about it."

But to this the young cop objected as well. No one was permitted to leave the premises. Julie told him that she had already been interrogated and had Sergeant Clapper's authorization to go. This the officer checked by means of the two-way radio attached to his collar, after which permission to leave was granted and scrupulously recorded in his notebook.

Julie held off speaking until they had walked a few yards and turned left onto a path that was known as the Garrison Walk, a two-hour circular ramble that ran along the extensive coastal breastworks that had protected the castle from seaward attack during the Civil War. The walk was said to provide spectacular views of the neighboring islands, and they had intended to take it at some point during the week, but today they could barely see down to the rocky shoreline forty or fifty feet below.

"Joey's dead," she told him.

"Oh, is he?"

She threw him a quizzical look. "You don't seem very upset."

"No, of course I am. But, you know, I'd figured somebody had to be dead, with all this going on, especially after the way Clapper took off from the station. All I didn't know was who." What he didn't tell her was that his strongest feeling at the moment, almost his only emotion, unworthy though he knew it was, was a draining, overwhelming sense of relief. He was just glad it hadn't been Julie, that's all. His heart was still finding its way back up from his ankles.

Joey had been found that morning by Mrs. Bewley, the housekeeper, Julie explained. It looked as if he'd fallen into the passageway from the catwalk that ran around the building just under the eaves, where he liked to smoke a bedtime cigar and commune with the night skies.

According to Kyle Robb, with whom she'd chatted briefly, it had happened quite late last night. The catwalk and the passageway were under police seal. Like everyone else, Julie had been interviewed by Clapper: When had she last seen Joey? Where was she between—

"Clapper interrogated you himself? That must have been fun, considering the mood he's in. My hand still stings from getting whacked with the ruler."

"No, he was a lamb. He couldn't have been more considerate. We're now old friends. I'm on a first-name basis with him, too."

At Gideon's surprised expression, she smiled and explained. "Kyle told me what was going on. When Mr. Moreton called the police station to report what had happened—the first possible homicide in St. Mary's in decades, or maybe ever—Mike just assumed that headquarters would take it away from him and hand it to a detective team that would helicopter in from the mainland. That's the way the process is supposed to work. But when Kyle called Exeter—"

"They told him it was too foggy to get a helicopter out here, so Mike gets to run a possible murder investigation after all?"

"That's it."

"Which sent the ogre into remission and brought back the genial, amiable Sergeant Mike," Gideon said, nodding. "I see. Julie, it's after one. Would you rather go back into town and get some lunch somewhere? A pot of tea, maybe?"

"No!" She wrinkled her nose, a behavior he found annoying in everybody but his wife, in whom it was adorable. "I couldn't eat anything. Can we just keep walking?"

"You bet. I can't say I have much appetite either."

They walked without talking for a while, the unseen waters of St. Mary's Sound on their right, the barely seen outer walls of Star Castle disappearing into the fog behind them on their left. Jackets were zipped up against the moisture-laden breeze. Gideon lightly kneaded the back of Julie's neck until he felt the tense muscles relax and heard a small, grateful sigh, after which they continued hand-in-hand on the path.

"Gideon, I've been thinking. If it *was* murder, it pretty much had to be done by someone at the castle, right? One of us."

"Oh, I wouldn't go that far. Likely, yes, but hardly certain. This happened late, you said, when people would have been in their rooms for the night. I can easily imagine an outsider getting into the castle, up to the third floor, and out again without being seen."

Julie shook her head. "No. Mr. Moreton locked up after we all got in from the museum, which was about ten. He locks up every night. And Mrs. Bewley left after that, but the doors—the entry to the building, and the one in the outer walls—automatically lock after her when she leaves. There would have been no way in. I specifically asked about that."

"I didn't realize that," Gideon said. "You *have* been thinking, haven't you? I assume you mentioned this to Mike."

"Mike's the one who told me about it."

" 'One of us,' " Gideon echoed, thinking. "I didn't know Joey very well, but he seemed like a nice enough kid. Some pretty strong views, yes, and maybe too fond of the sauce, but basically harmless. It's hard to imagine any of these people wanting to do him in."

"Well, he did get on Donald's nerves quite a bit."

"Yes, sure, but . . . murder? Do you really think—"

"No. Well, I don't think so, who knows?" She hesitated. "But I do have a theory. I've been giving it some thought."

"What's your theory?"

"Now you're not going to laugh at me, are you? And you won't interrupt me and start arguing before I've finished?"

"Have you ever known me to?"

She laughed. "That doesn't even deserve an answer. And you're not going to tell me it's not a theory at all, that it's a hypothesis, or a speculation, or a—"

"I don't see how I'm going to be able to tell you *anything* unless you get around sometime to letting me know what it is."

"All right, then. Now I know this sounds a little convoluted, so just let me—"

"Julie—"

"Well, what if it *wasn't* Edgar that killed Pete Williams? No, don't interrupt. What if it was someone else? And what if Joey knew who that person *was*? Gideon, please, you promised. Just let me finish for once. And what if that person was afraid Joey might tell? Wouldn't that person—" She threw up her hands. "Okay, okay, I should have known you wouldn't be able to let me finish. What's wrong with it?"

"What's wrong is that the bones aren't Pete Williams's, they're Villarreal's."

At that she stopped in mid-stride to stare at him. "*Edgar!* But how can that be? Edgar was eaten by a bear! In Alaska!"

"Julie, I'm not sure how it can be, but it is. I'm ninety-nine percent positive. He wasn't eaten by a bear, he was stabbed to death—pretty viciously, too—and right now he's lying—what there is of him is lying—on a desk at the police station right here on St. Mary's. And I can guarantee that the remains haven't been through the innards of a bear or of anything else."

"You're saying the newspaper got it wrong?"

"I believe such things have been known to happen."

"You don't sound very surprised."

"I'm surprised that the bones on the beach are Villarreal's, yes; but, no, I'm not surprised that the people in Alaska got it wrong. When you're looking at tiny bits of bone that have been chewed up by a bear, gone through its digestive process, and come out the other end, it's easy to let your imagination run away with you and conclude they're human—especially if you have an unaccounted-for human being on your missing persons list. And the paper made it clear there was no physical anthropologist involved; just the local police surgeon, who almost certainly wouldn't have been trained to distinguish human from nonhuman." He shrugged. "So, yes, I had my doubts."

She nodded slowly, with a faint smile. "That's what that 'Hm' was, when I read you the story back in Penzance, wasn't it?"

"That's what it was," he said, smiling back. They began walking again.

"But why in the world would Edgar have come back to Saint Mary's?" she wondered. "*When* would he have come back?"

"Never. I don't think he ever left."

They had come to one of the several batteries along the path—a grouping of three black, well-preserved, seventeenth-century cannons, glistening with moisture and arranged in an arc to aim out to sea. Julie leaned against one of them, shaking her head. "But he resigned from the consortium after he left, remember? He sent Vasily a letter, a fax. From the States."

"No, *somebody* sent Vasily a fax from the States."

"That's so, I suppose. It could have been someone else."

"For that matter, do we really know that anybody sent Vasily a fax, or do we know only that he says someone sent one?"

"Well . . . I suppose . . ."

"As far as I know, no one's seen it, isn't that right?"

Julie frowned. "Gideon are you suggesting . . . you're not suggesting . . ."

"That Vasily's a murderer and faked the fax to cover himself? No, of course not. I'm only pointing out—"

"I mean, for all we know, Vasily still has the fax. In fact, he probably does."

"Which still wouldn't prove that Villarreal sent it. Look, all I'm saying is that the evidence for Villarreal's ever having left and gone back to the States, let alone getting chomped on by a bear, is not exactly overwhelming."

"That's so, yes." She gazed out into the fog. Below, unseen wavelets lapped at the rocky shore. "I'm trying to think of whether I actually saw him get on the ferry or not, at the end of the consortium. I know we all left the same day. We caught the ferry. I was on it with . . . well, let's see . . . Liz, and Rudy, and . . . come to think of it, that's all. Edgar and the others were going to catch the early morning plane, or the afternoon ferry, or something."

"Did you see him at all that day?"

She chewed on her lip, trying to remember. "I don't know. I don't think I did. I'm not sure."

"What about the day before?"

"The night before was when he gave that speech in town, where he got into the shouting match with Pete Williams, so he was definitely there then. After that, I don't remember." She pushed herself from the wet cannon, wiped her hands on a couple of Kleenexes to dry them, and stuffed the sodden clump in a pocket. They resumed walking.

"Okay," she said, "let's say you're right. Somebody here on St. Mary's killed Edgar. Two years later, somebody kills Joey. It's got to be the same somebody, wouldn't you think?"

"I'd say so. Unless we have two murderers running around the place, which is *really* low on the probability continuum."

"And the two murders—they just about have to be related."

Gideon nodded. "The Law of Interconnected Monkey Business."

This was a "law" posited only partly in jest by Gideon's old professor and all-around mentor, Abe Goldstein: When too many extraordinary things—too much monkey business—started happening to the same people, in the same context, you could count on there being some connection between them. And while "two" might not be very high on the "too many" scale, murders were off the charts on the "extraordinary" scale.

"Okay, then," Julie said, "what if you took what I said before and switched the names?"

"What you said before?"

"About why somebody would kill Joey. What if Joey knew who killed *Edgar*? And maybe he was keeping quiet these last two years, but now that the news was going to come out that the bones weren't Pete's after all—they were Edgar's—that changed things. And the person who killed him—killed Edgar, I mean—couldn't trust Joey to keep quiet, so he—"

"Uh-uh," Gideon said.

Julie, swept away with her reasoning, didn't hear him. "No, wait a minute, what about this as an idea? Maybe it wasn't murder at all, in Joey's case. Maybe it was suicide. Maybe *Joey* killed Edgar, and now that he knew it was going to come out, he killed himself."

"Uh-uh," Gideon said again.

"*Uh-uh?* Just plain uh-uh? Not even a 'maybe'? Not even a 'possibly'? At least an 'improbably'?"

"Nope, just plain uh-uh. Julie, maybe it was murder, maybe it was suicide, maybe it was an accident, but it couldn't have been because Edgar's murder was going to come out. Neither Joey nor anyone else could know that, because I didn't know it myself until this morning. And you, Mike, Kyle, and I are still the only people who do know. Last night, when Joey was killed, everybody—including me, including Joey—still thought the bones were probably Williams's."

"Oh," she said, deflated, "that's so, isn't it?"

"Not only that, but even if he did know, which he couldn't have, there was nothing to tie Joey—or anyone, for that matter—to Villarreal's murder, so why should he have been worried? I hadn't even come up with a cause of death yet. The only reason we knew it was foul play was the fact that the body was dismembered."

"That's true," she said thoughtfully. "You know, for all we know it wasn't a murder at all—I'm talking about Joey now, not Edgar. Maybe he fell off the catwalk while he was trying to light one of those awful cigars or something. He was pretty well sloshed, after all, and the railing isn't much above your knees. Maybe there's no big mystery here at all."

"I agree. That could very well be. But it still leaves Edgar. And *that* was no accident."

"No." She nodded soberly. "And unlike Joey, there's no shortage of people who had it in for him."

"No."

They walked on in gloomy silence for a while, and Gideon had no doubt that their thoughts were running along the same lines: compiling the long list of Star Castle residents whom Edgar Villarreal had antagonized—a list that would most assuredly have to be given to Clapper. There was, first and foremost, the sexual-predator angle. Liz Petra and Victor Waldo had had good reason to detest him, and maybe Donald did as well. He appeared not to care about Cheryl's blatant peccadilloes, but you never knew about something like that, especially with a seemingly bland guy like Donald. And what about Cheryl? Had she dumped Villarreal, or was it the other way around? And then there was Rudy, whose wilderness convictions had made an enemy of Villarreal and vice versa. And Kozlov. Hadn't Julie mentioned that he and Villarreal had grated upon one another?

Other than Mrs. Bewley and Mr. Moreton, neither of whom had been in Kozlov's employ at the time of the last consortium two years ago, that was pretty much everybody in the place; everybody who was still alive, anyway. The only one who hadn't shown any ill feelings toward Villarreal—who had, in fact, declared his admiration and even affection for him—was Joey. And Joey, like Villarreal, was dead.

After a few more steps she shivered. "Let's go back, I'm chilled through. 'Fog season,' brr. The people here must hate this time of year."

"Everyone," said Gideon with a smile, "except Mike Clapper."

* * *

DINNER at the castle was a sober affair, and quiet as well, inasmuch as Clapper had asked them not to talk about Joey's death for the time being. But it was clear, from the few comments that were made, and from the furtive, side-long glances shooting around the table, that they had all arrived at the same conclusions that Gideon and Julie had: Joey's murderer, if indeed Joey had been murdered, was sitting right there among them. It was also clear, from their generally dazed demeanor, that learning that the bones from the beach were those of the very definitely murdered Edgar Villarreal (Clapper had informed them) had hit them hard; an appalling double whammy. Already upset about Joey, they were all thoroughly stunned by the news about Edgar.

All but one.

EIGHTEEN

THE next morning Kozlov, true to form, announced it was back to work for the consortium, starting with the usual working breakfast, so Gideon walked down the hill and into Hugh Town for something to eat. By now he looked forward to a couple of those D-shaped Cornish breakfast pasties to start the day and would miss them when he got back home. Egg McMuffins were fine, but nothing like these supremely dense, tasty things that sank to your stomach like so much lead and continued to warm you for hours.

Late the previous afternoon he had met with Clapper for the distasteful purpose of telling him about the numerous antipathies that Villarreal had aroused among the consortium Fellows. Clapper, tired and preoccupied, had seemed unimpressed, but that was his affair. Gideon was simply glad to have the task behind him. Today he would be pleased to get back to his own element: bones.

When he came out of the café and turned toward the station he noticed that the fog had abated a bit. Not thinned, but shredded here and there, like torn curtains, so that there were sporadic glimpses of the sound and even the outer islands between thick pillars of whitish-gray. It was like the occasional, shadowed sight of earth you got looking down from an airliner through heavy, broken clouds. He found that being able to see more than a few feet, even intermittently, raised his spirits, so that when he opened the door of the station he was whistling.

Clapper, sitting in Robb's office, cradling a mug of coffee in one hand and holding a cigarette in the other, was looking happy, too, and much restored. "Constable, you made a damned mockery of the majesty and stateliness of Force!" he was bellowing at Robb, but he was laughing. Robb looked cheerfully mock-sheepish.

Clapper waved Gideon in cordially. "Ah, Gideon, a pleasure to see you. Now what do you suppose this fellow has done to so arouse my ire?" he asked, jerking a thumb at Robb. "Tell him, Constable."

"I'm not really sure, sir," Robb said to Gideon. "Near as I can tell, the sergeant is upset because I donned contaminant-restrictive headgear at the crime scene, as I was taught to do at—"

"Contaminant-restrictive headgear!" Clapper howled. "I'm sitting there minding my own business, interviewing Mrs. Bewley, and I turn around and glance out a window, and there in the passageway, I see a 'orrible sight—Constable Robb, this very Constable Robb, prowling about with a *shower cap*, a plastic bloody shower cap, on his head! Next thing, I expected to see him in a tatty bathrobe and bedroom slippers."

"Sarge, they told us at school—"

"And he had the effrontery to offer one to me as well!"

"Sarge, the reason—"

Clapper shushed him affably. "I know, lad, I know. I'm just having you on. You go ahead and do it if that's what they taught you. But please, not in my presence. Gideon, get yourself some coffee and come join us, why don't you? I met Mrs. Oliver yesterday. Delightful woman."

"She told me," Gideon said from the other cubicle, pouring coffee into the same mug he'd used the day before and wishing he'd remembered to rinse it. "She thought you were delightful, too. 'He was a lamb' were her exact words."

"A lamb," Robb said to the ceiling, "I bet that's a first."

"*Au contraire, mon ami,*" Clapper said, leaning expansively back in his chair, one thick, hairy forearm hooked over it, then switching to an atrocious French accent: "Eet ees zat I hear zis constantlee." For a guy with two death investigations on his plate—Joey Dillard's and Edgar Villarreal's—and a professional staff of exactly one, he was looking very much at his ease.

"I have something for you," he said as Gideon returned with his coffee. He waved a few sheets of paper. "Yesterday I put in a call to my fellow copper in Talkeetna, Alaska, and asked if he'd be kind enough to send over what they had on the death of Edgar Villarreal, the gentleman supposedly eaten, and subsequently deposited, by a bear a couple of years ago. Here it is. Not very much of a case file. Police report, police surgeon's report—both quite brief—and a photograph of the remains, none too clear. They scanned them into the computer and e-mailed them, and there they were, waiting for us this morning."

"Ah." Gideon dropped into the empty chair, put his mug on the desk, and took the printouts with considerable interest. The police report covered the same ground as the story in the *International Herald Tribune*: remains discovered in a bear den, identified as human by one Dr. Leslie Roach, consulting police surgeon, and assumed to be those of Edgar Villarreal, missing from his nearby base camp for the previous two years. The surgeon's report added little: "Forty bone fragments were recovered, the largest measuring approximately four centimeters and most less than five millimeters. A virtually complete second phalanx of a human thumb, measuring three centimeters, was found, as was a five-centimeter rib fragment. Other fragments were too small and splintered to be conclusively identified."

Gideon turned to the color photograph of the remains, which had been spread out on a table, first having apparently been cleaned. The picture was either fuzzy to begin with, or had been much degraded in the scanning process. But it was clear enough for his purposes. He placed his finger on one of the bones in the photo, the only complete one. "This thumb phalanx?" he said.

"Yes?" Clapper and Robb responded.

"It's from a sheep, maybe a goat."

"Goats have thumbs?" Robb asked.

Gideon couldn't help laughing. The thing was, Robb was so *earnest*. "No, but they have breast bones—sternums—and this is the manubrium, the top segment of a sternum. And this . . ." He indicated another bone in the picture. "And this would be the rib fragment he talked about. He's right enough about that, but it's way too flattened to be a human rib. It's from a quadruped too; probably the selfsame unfortunate sheep, would be my guess." With a gesture, he took in the entire photograph. "There's nothing else I can be sure of. This one might be part of a tail vertebra, but that's about it. Definitely nothing to suggest anything other than a quadruped, a bovid. Well, maybe a couple of little mole or gopher bones, or something like that, mixed in there too. Ferret, maybe. More than one meal here, I'd say. No reason to think any of it's human."

Clapper was expelling smoke from a cigarette and shaking his head. "You'd think a police surgeon would know the difference between a goat and a man."

"Well, you know," Gideon said, finding himself again defending the medical profession, "once he's out of school a physician never sees a bone all by itself, out of context—

which I do all the time. And there are no courses in medical school that teach comparative skeletal anatomy. Why would they?"

The same was true for dentists, Gideon knew. His own dentist, in whom he had complete confidence when it came to his own teeth, had once telephoned him in some distress to say he thought he'd found a human infant's mandible in a roadside ditch. It had turned out to be the mandible of a young dog. And when it came to police cases, another factor was at work as well. When the cops walk into your office all excited about the suspicious bone or tooth they've brought with them, there is always a subtle but substantial pressure on you, mostly self-induced, to tell them what they've told you *they* think it is.

"Anyway, I don't really think you can blame the guy," he finished.

Clapper didn't agree. "The Alaska State Police ought to get themselves another police surgeon, that's all I have to say. Or at least hire on a physical anthropologist when the occasion arises."

"No argument there." Gideon put down the photograph and picked up his mug. "How's the Dillard investigation going?"

Clapper responded with a concise summary. The work at the scene was done, as were the initial interrogations, but they knew little more than they'd known yesterday. Quite a lot of evidence had been collected and bagged at the scene and was awaiting a change in the weather that would permit it to be sent to the lab in Exeter. But whether or not they were dealing with a homicide they were having a hard time determining.

The matter was complicated, as Gideon would understand, by a number of factors. First, Joey had been in the habit of enjoying a late-evening smoke out on the catwalk, and all agreed that he had had more Pimm's Cup than was good for him at dinner (they expected a more exact finding on that from Dr. Gillie shortly). Was it possible that the deceased, his coordination muddled by drink, had accidentally fallen over the railing, which was, indeed, dangerously low? The possibility had to be allowed for. Moreover, the only injury Dr. Gillie had found in his on-the-scene examination, aside from some contusions and lacerations, had been the massive damage to Joey's head, and the problem with that kind of complex trauma, according to the doctor, was that it was next to impossible to determine whether it was entirely the result of a simple fall or might involve something more sinister, such as a blow or blows. It was hoped that the autopsy would shed some light on the cause of death, but—

"You know, I'm not so sure about that," Gideon murmured.

Clapper's eyebrows went up. "About . . . ?"

"About not being able to tell whether the head injuries came strictly from a fall, or something else was involved. I mean, I don't want to second-guess Dr. Gillie, and I never even saw Joey's body, so I may be all wet, but all the same, there are some criteria that can be used to differentiate between various kinds of blunt-force trauma—"

But Clapper's attention had wandered. "Well, yes, that's interesting. I'll put you in touch with Davey Gillie and maybe you can help him out there." He shot a look at his watch. "Kyle, are you ready to go?"

"Ready and eager, sir."

"We're off to the castle for another round of interviews," Clapper explained to Gideon. "Got some new questions for them today."

The phone cheeped. Robb picked it up. "Isles of Scilly Police Station, good morning," he said and quickly straightened up in his chair. "Yes, sir. I understand. Of course, sir." He covered the mouthpiece.

"Exeter," he said to Clapper.

Clapper made a disgusted noise. "What do they want?"

"They want to talk to you. It's Detective Chief Superintendent LeVine."

"Tell him I'll call him back."

"Um, Sarge, he sounds like he's not in the mood to wait. It's a conference call; they've got somebody else on too." He hesitated. "It's about Joey Dillard."

Clapper's big hands clamped on the arms of his chair as if he thought they were the necks of two detective chief superintendents. "Damn his eyes," he growled, pushing himself to his feet and stomping to his office, the door of which he slammed shut behind him.

"He'll be right with you, sir," Robb said brightly. He listened until he heard the phone in Clapper's office being picked up, then replaced the receiver. "This may be bad," he said.

"Why, what is it?"

"Well, the other person on the blower is the Force pathologist down at the hospital at Treliske. He does the postmortems for southern Cornwall. So I'm guessing he's going to be autopsying Dillard's body after all, which would seem to mean headquarters is going to scupper our investigation and take the case back themselves." He gestured with a tip of his head toward the window behind him. "The fog's dissipating pretty fast. They might be able to fly in their mainland detectives now."

"That's not going to make your boss very happy."

"It's not going to make me very happy either," Robb said. "Excuse me." He picked up the phone again. "Isles of Scilly Police Station, good morning. Oh, hello, Mrs. Hobgood. No, I'm afraid we haven't found Eloise yet. Yes, of course we're actively searching. No, of course we haven't given up hope, it hasn't even been a full day yet. We'll find her, you'll see. Don't we always? Oh, definitely, we'll let you know the moment we do. Don't you worry, now."

"Runaway kid?" Gideon asked when Robb turned to him again.

"Runaway duck. She keeps her as a pet. Won't use a leash. Loses her a couple of times a month. I'll swing by the wastewater treatment plant this afternoon. Eloise always turns up there to root around after a day or two. I'll pile her in the van and drive her home." He grinned ruefully. "What was that again about the majesty and stateliness of the Force?"

They hadn't been able to hear Clapper's voice from his office, but they had no trouble hearing the telephone slam into its cradle, and then the squeal of his chair rolling back. They looked at each other, the same question on their minds. When the door opened, who was going to come through it, Dr. Jekyll or Mr. Hyde?

It was Dr. Jekyll, smiling and complacent. "Well, that was interesting."

"They don't want the case back?" Robb blurted.

"'Want' and 'get' are two different things," Clapper said, returning to his chair and his coffee. "I told them to shove it. I'm the case investigator and I intend to continue being the case investigator, and if I need any of their bloody help I'll bloody well ask for it."

Robb's jaw dropped. "You told Detective Chief Superintendent LeVine to . . . to . . ."

"Look, lad," Clapper said kindly, "you have to understand the way these things work. I'm still a bit of a, shall we say, a legendary figure there, despite a few problems in my latter days. People are reluctant to get into a row with me, especially the detective chief superintendent. Teddy LeVine is fifteen years my junior in age and six years my junior in seniority. He's never made Officer of the Year, and he has no decorations for valor, and when I really assert myself—which I haven't done now for many a day—when I put my foot down, young Teddy is not the man to stand up to me. With a few face-saving mutterings about making sure to keep the computer log up to date, he withdrew from the fray. The case is mine. Ours."

From someone else it would have been hyperbole, but

Gideon had the impression Clapper was telling it as it was, without any self-inflating embellishments.

"Now the one thing I *can* use their assistance on is with the postmortem. Nothing against Davey Gillie, of course, but the man would be the first to admit that he's not forensically trained. Since Teddy has already arranged for an autopsy with the Force pathologist at Treliske, I've let that stand. A helicopter is on its way to pick up the body even as we speak. Kyle, you'll want to get hold of Davey right now and tell him to keep his bloody hands off the corpse."

Robb immediately got on the telephone while Clapper clasped his hands behind his head and leaned back in his chair, savoring his victory and the job ahead.

"Just in time, Sarge, they say the body's already on the autopsy table. Dr. Gillie's about to get started."

"Well, tell him to stop where he is and get the body bagged up. Have him send off whatever he's written up, too. Oh, and see that a copy of our report goes out to Treliske along with the body as well."

Clapper, content and serene, leaned back and re-clasped his hands, but suddenly sat up straight and smacked his forehead. "Gideon, I forgot, I've left the pathologist hanging on the blower. He asked to speak with you. You can take it in my office, line one, if he's still there."

"With me? About what?" Puzzled, Gideon got up.

"He didn't say. I happened to mention your being here, and he said would that be Dr. *Gideon* Oliver, the Skeleton Detective, and I said yes, and he said, may I speak with the gentleman, and there the matter stands."

In Clapper's office, Gideon leaned over the desk to punch line one and picked up the phone.

"This is Gideon Oliver. Sorry to keep you waiting."

"Not at all, not at all!" a bluff, jolly voice declared. "How *are* you, old friend?"

The voice was only vaguely familiar. "I'm sorry, I don't—"

"This is Wilson Merrill!" the voice cried, after which there was an expectant pause.

It took Gideon a second to make the connection, but when he did, it was with real pleasure. "Wilson!" he said. "How good to hear your voice. Do I understand that you're the Cornwall and Devon pathologist now?"

"Indeed, yes. My aged mother lives in Falmouth, and Lydia and I are happily settled here now. I left the Dorset Constabulary two years ago. We had some fun there, didn't we? Remember Inspector Bagshawe?"

Gideon remembered, all right. In the annals of successful police bogglement, the experience with Detective Inspector Bagshawe of the Dorset CID was at the top of his list. Gideon had been staying in the coastal village of Charmouth in connection with an archaeological dig nearby, and a rotted corpse had turned up in the bay. Merrill, who knew Gideon by reputation, had been responsible for the autopsy. He had asked Gideon to attend, which Gideon, who hated autopsies—especially on corpses well along the road to putrescence—had reluctantly done. As it turned out, there was so little soft tissue to work with that Merrill had simply turned the remains over to him to see what could be gotten from the skeleton. In less than an hour's time, Gideon had emerged from the autopsy room with his conclusions.

The unidentified body, he told Merrill and the supercilious (until then) Bagshawe, was that of a large motorcycle-rider in his mid-thirties who also, by the way, happened to be a left-handed baseball pitcher (not a cricket-bowler, a baseball pitcher!). Might that possibly be of some help in identifying him?

"Fun" is not something that is generally associated with forensic anthropology, but this was surely as close to fun as it ever got. Bagshawe's big, curving cherrywood pipe had actually fallen from his mouth and clattered to the table, scattering ash and tobacco shreds. And the delighted Merrill couldn't have been more pleased. He'd come near to embracing him.

"You bet I remember," a laughing Gideon said now. "Wilson, it's really nice of you to say hello. You know, I'm not exactly sure where Treliske is—"

"It's a neighborhood in Truro, really."

"Well, I don't really know where Truro is either, but—"

"Just up the road from Trelissick," Wilson told him unhelpfully.

"—but maybe we can get together before I leave. It'd be nice to—"

"I didn't want to speak to you merely to say hello, old man."

"You didn't?"

"No. I want to invite you to the postmortem! Lend a hand, don't you know."

He made it sound as if he'd just invited Gideon to a private reception at the White House. It was Gideon's experience that forensic pathologists in general were a happy, outgoing crew, but he had never met another one quite as exuberant as Wilson Merrill, or one who found so much challenge and fulfillment in the grisly work that took place on the slanted metal tables. But for the notoriously squeamish Gideon, watching a human body get debrained and disemboweled to conduct a postmortem had about as much allure as watching one get dismembered to conceal a murder; namely, zero. And "lending a hand" made it less than zero.

"To the postmortem?" Gideon said, trying for surprised delight. "Well, I really appreciate that, Wilson, and of course I'd *like* to come but, I'm not sure how I'd get there—"

"No problem there, Gideon! The helicopter should be arriving at St. Mary's any time now for the body. You could ride back here with it."

"Umm . . . well, I'd like to, of course, but I do have some things to do here—"

"Nonsense. You can spare a few hours. We'll have you back in St. Mary's by teatime."

"Oh. Well, actually . . ."

"I'll see you in an hour, then. It will be a treat to work with you again. We'll have a jolly time of it, you'll see!"

"I'm looking forward to it, Wilson," Gideon managed. It wasn't the first time he'd been overwhelmed by Wilson Merrill.

Or in this case, only partly overwhelmed. He had to admit that he was extremely interested in having a look at those "complex trauma" of Joey's skull to which Dr. Gillie had referred. It was the process of getting down to the skull that he wasn't looking forward to.

Back in Robb's cubicle, he was explaining what the call was about when a clatter overhead drew all three men's eyes to the window. A red helicopter was descending mantislike toward the open space of Holgate's Green. "Cornwall Air Ambulance," it said on the side.

"Your conveyance, I believe," said Clapper.

"Mine and Joey's," Gideon said.

NINETEEN

TRURO is a venerable cathedral and market town, but the Royal Cornwall Hospital at Treliske, on its western outskirts, is sleek, modern, and well-equipped, with its gleaming basement mortuary being no exception. The waiting room, mercifully unoccupied at the moment by any apprehensive, fearful relatives or friends, was living-room friendly, with plum-colored fabric on the walls, homey furniture, flowers, coffee-table picture books, and up-to-date magazines. Having announced himself to the receptionist, Gideon had finished an article on human cloning ("Another you—the next best thing to teleportation") in *New Scientist* and was starting one on a methane-spewing volcano that had been discovered on one of Saturn's moons, when his host came barreling through the door from the interior.

Wilson Merrill in the flesh, was, if anything, even heartier than he was on the telephone. A ruddy, stocky, country-squireish sort of man who radiated bluff good humor, he stuck out a blunt-fingered hand in greeting. "Well, well, it seems the Dynamic Duo is back in business again."

"It's good to see you, Wilson," Gideon said.

"Come on, old man, let's get you suited up."

"Oh, I don't think I need to put on scrubs," Gideon said. "I don't really expect to be doing anything—just observing." From as great a distance as I can get away with, he might have added.

Merrill laughed as merrily as if Gideon had told an amusing joke. "Nonsense," he said, taking him by the elbow and shuffling him along the corridor. "Gets a bit splashy in there sometimes. Wouldn't want to get anything nasty on that pretty shirt."

Merrill himself was wearing the green, oversized, hand-me-down (from the hospital upstairs) scrubs that were usual in mortuaries around the world, fronted by a plastic apron, and complete with oversize booties. Gideon had noted before this preference of pathologists for roomy scrubs. They needed them, too. Unlike surgeons (other than orthopedic surgeons) who work mostly in small spaces with delicate instruments: scalpel, forceps, probes, retractors—pathologists use implements that look as if they came from a carpenter's tool chest: hammers, chisels, saws, even pruning shears (for snipping through the ribs). A grizzled, old-school coroner Gideon knew claimed that he bought all his instruments at kitchen shops and hardware stores. "They're the same damn knives and things, just as good, but if it has 'autopsy' in front of it, they charge you an arm and a leg."

Five minutes later, in the locker room a few yards down the hall, Gideon was getting similarly outfitted in scrubs that must have been made for a professional wrestler. While he was swimming his way into them, Merrill used the time to browse through the file folder of materials that had come with Joey's body.

"Oh, dear," he said as Gideon wrapped the drawstring twice around his waist, "did you see what his blood alcohol level was?"

Gideon shook his head. "Pretty high, I imagine."

"That's putting it mildly. One hundred and fifty-two milligrams. Not surprising he fell off that catwalk. The wonder is that he was able to get out on it in the first place."

"You're inclined to go with the 'accident' theory, then?"

"Well, I wouldn't go quite as far as that. That's what we're here to try and determine, isn't it? But I must say it seems like a reasonable starting hypothesis. At that level of intoxication, one is anything but steady on one's stumps."

Gideon slipped into the booties—normal-sized ones—and the two men shuffled down the corridor to the autopsy room, Gideon stolidly, and Merrill practically skipping at his side.

"It's a pity you weren't here just two days ago," the pathologist told him. "We had an astonishing case, really incredible. This chap had committed suicide by turning on his table saw and jamming his head into it. Never seen anything like it. Cleaved his head in half right down the middle, neat as a pin, exactly through the longitudinal fissure, clear down to the vermis of the cerebellum, can you believe it? Like looking at a median sagittal section of the head in an anatomy text." He sighed. "Gone now, though. Had to release the body."

"Sorry I missed it," Gideon mumbled. "My bad luck."

Merrill brightened. "We have photographs, though."

"Oh, great. Maybe later if there's time."

"Here we are, then," Merrill said with transparent pride, pulling open the door to a spic-and-span, white-tiled autopsy room. *"Hic locus est ubi—"*

"—mortui viventes docent." Gideon finished for him. *This is the place where the dead teach the living.* A favorite motto of forensic labs. Gideon had it on a plaque on the wall of the anthropology department's bone room at the university.

The moment the door opened, the mildly unsettling smell of hospital antiseptic was displaced by the more unsettling, though more familiar, mixture of formaldehyde and tissue going bad, *l'arome de la morgue*. Inside, Joey's graying body lay faceup on the metal table, naked and pitifully vulnerable under glaring fluorescent light fixtures. Above the foot of the table hung the usual meat-market scale, shocking in its ordinariness, in which his internal organs would be weighed. A tall, somber, long-limbed Indian man, the diener—the autopsy assistant—was finishing up his tasks of preparing the body and the instruments, and taking the preliminary measurements and photographs.

"We are all ready, Doctor," he said on seeing Merrill.

"Hello, Rajiv. X-rays?"

"Yes, Doctor. The physician from St. Mary's sent them." Rajiv nodded toward the wall-mounted viewing box, to which four X-ray plates had been clipped. Merrill walked to the box and, leaning over, peered briefly at the indistinct images. "Fractured spinous processes on these upper thoracic vertebrae, you see?" he said, pointing. "Some damage to the sacroiliac region as well. Both perfectly consistent with a fall onto his back, wouldn't you say?"

Gideon nodded and placed a finger on a photograph of the left arm. "And I think the olecranon is broken, too; that'd go along with it as well."

"Yes, I believe you're right. The cranial photos are ambiguous, though, but then who can read a cranial X-ray? There's damage to the head, all right, inside and out, but hard to tell exactly what kind." Merrill straightened up, his eyes alight and already straying toward the saws and knives that Rajiv had set up on a small rolling table. "May as well have a look at the real thing, shall we?"

"May as well," Gideon said forlornly.

"Well, let's cover him up, Rajiv," Merrill said.

"Cover him up?"

"For decency's sake."

"Decency's sake?"

"Yes, we'll start at the top—"

The top? Gideon said to himself.

Rajiv didn't disappoint him. "The top?"

"Yes, the top. Dr. Oliver will be most interested in the skull, I believe, so let's begin there. In the meantime, let's drape him from the neck down, why don't we?"

Rajiv was obviously dubious about the correctness of this—pathologists generally began with the trunk; the famous Y-incision—but he did as he was told without even a murmured "Drape him?", pulling a sheet neatly, even tenderly, up over Joey's body. Clearly, understanding that Gideon had known Joey, Merrill had had this done out of sensitivity for his feelings, and Gideon very much appreciated it. It was, for whatever reason, easier—less of a violation, less defiling—to open up Joey's head with the rest of him covered up.

Rajiv handed both men plastic "bouffant-style" operating room caps, which they slipped on over their hair. Gideon was grateful that Clapper wasn't there to see him.

"You didn't want gloves, did you?" asked Merrill, who was partial to doing his dissecting bare-handed. "When I'm working with tissue, I find the sense of touch in my bare hands extremely sensitive," he had once told Gideon—who much preferred gloves, and for exactly the same reason.

"Gloves?" Gideon said now, as if they were the furthest thought from his mind. "No, of course not." With luck, he wouldn't have to touch anything.

Many pathologists had their dieners do the gross cutting—the Y-incision, and the ear-to-ear over-the-top-of-the-head incision to get at the skull—but not Merrill, of course. He preferred to do it all himself, so once Rajiv had placed a support block under the back of Joey's head and turned on the hanging microphone to record their observations, the diener stepped away from the table, awaiting further instructions.

"Well, let's see what we have," Merrill said happily. Gideon half expected him to rub his hands together, but with his arms remaining folded, he peered long and hard at Joey's head. "What do you think?"

Until that moment, Gideon hadn't looked directly at Joey's face, but now he did. It helped, he found, that Joey didn't look much like Joey anymore. In addition to the puffiness and distortion that went with death from cranial blunt-force trauma, on his face had blossomed a pair of bilateral periorbital hematomas—spectacular, purplish, shiny black eyes, which were known in the trade as "raccoon eyes," and for good reason. Huge and round, blackening both his upper and lower eyelids, swelling them closed, and as dark as stage makeup, they made it look as if he were wearing a strange, pale face mask with black holes cut out for the eyes. His hair, so colorless and fine to begin with, had been rinsed by Rajiv under the faucet at one end of the autopsy table and was still damp, so that it seemed limper and sadder than ever. High on the back of his head, about two inches up from the part of the scalp overlying what anthropologists called "lambda"—the Y-shaped juncture where the two parietals meet the occipital bone—a circular area three or four inches in diameter had been shaved, the better to show a gaping, star-shaped laceration where his scalp had split open.

"You're the pathologist," Gideon answered. "What do you think?"

"I think we're looking at a pretty obvious case of blunt-force trauma to the posterior parietal region, which, of course, goes along with the injuries on the radiograph." He added a few observations for the microphone and pressed gently against Joey's cheeks and temples. "No indications of superficial damage around the eyes, and the craniofacial skeleton seems undamaged. I expect we'll find that the orbital hematomas are not distinct injuries, but a result of the parietal trauma, the force having been transmitted by the brain."

Gideon nodded. "Contrecoup."

"Contrecoup," Merrill agreed.

They were talking about one of the most intriguing and least understood aspects of damage to the human skull and brain: the distinction between coup and contrecoup injuries. Generally speaking, when a moving object hit a stationary head—a blow with a hammer, say—the injury to the brain was going to be directly under the impact point. Whack a man hard enough on the occipital bone at the back of the head, and it will almost always be the occipital lobe of the brain that gets pulped. That was a "coup" injury. But when things were reversed, when a moving head hit a stationary object—in a fall, for example—the brain injury was likely to be at the *opposite* pole of the brain. Let a man fall off a catwalk onto stone paving and land on that same, rearward occipital bone, for example, and it would be the *frontal* lobe of the brain that got mashed into red jelly: a "contrecoup" injury.

Why this should be had puzzled scientists for centuries. In 1766 the Royal Academy of Surgeons in Paris had offered a prize for a definitive explanation of contrecoup. They didn't get one then, and they still didn't have one that satisfied everybody. Gideon, no expert on the brain, was willing to accept the common theory that, in a fall, the skull is traveling faster than the brain that is cradled inside it, so that when the back of the head hits the ground the brain continues to move, subjecting it to a piling-up of impact forces at the front.

Whether that was really the way it worked or not, contrecoup injuries were a fact, and he agreed with Merrill that they were looking at one now.

"Well!" exclaimed Merrill, and now he really did rub his hands together. "Let's get on with it!" He stuck out a hand, into which Rajiv slapped the scalpel that he had waiting. Gideon moved a discreet step back. Rajiv, who was already wearing surgical gloves, now pulled up the mask that had been loosely tied around his neck.

Merrill, maskless and gloveless—contrary to both forensic and hygienic protocol—was a quick, sure worker, with no wasted movement. One hand, on Joey's forehead, steadied his head against the block, while the other placed the scalpel blade behind the left ear. A moment's pause to align the blade to the path that was to be followed, and the scalpel was deftly whipped over the top of the head, well in front of the scalp wound, and around to the back of the other ear: the standard coronal mastoid incision to expose the skull. With Joey dead so long, there was very little blood, but all the same Gideon's stomach contracted, almost as if he could feel the blade slicing through his own scalp. This was at least the twentieth autopsy at which he'd been present, and before them he'd dissected two corpses in gross anatomy in graduate school, yet it was always the same. Would he never get used to them?

Probably not, but at least he no longer scandalized the autopsy staff by throwing up in the nearest sink, which he'd done the first time, in the San Francisco city morgue, a place he'd never again had the nerve to show his face.

With the cut made, the scalp was now essentially divided into two flaps. The rear one was pulled back and the front one vigorously tugged forward and down over Joey's face, hair side down, depersonalizing him yet a little more and helping Gideon toward thinking of what he was looking at simply as a cranium, and not as the cranium of the nice kid he'd had dinner with the night before last. The yellowish, blood-flecked skull, its delicate, meandering coronal and sagittal sutures faintly visible, was now exposed from the ears up, and Gideon, took a step toward it for a closer look, interest overcoming aversion.

"Depressed fracture," he said.

"Yes, that's a bit of a surprise, isn't it?"

Gideon agreed that it was.

The thing was, coup and contrecoup injuries weren't the only way in which stationary heads that got in the way of moving objects usually differed from moving heads that ran into stationary objects. The skull fracture that was most likely to result from a fall was what is known as a linear fracture—or in common parlance, a crack—that might be anything from a single, relatively straight fissure, to a spiral network, to a maze of large and small cracks that broke the skull into a hundred pieces. A depressed fracture, on the other hand, was one in which the bone directly under the impact point was partially or fully separated from the rest of the skull and driven in, toward the brain, much as a hammer, striking a block of foam, wouldn't crack it in half, but would leave a sunken imprint of itself in the block. And, naturally enough, such "imprints" were most likely to be the result of blows with instruments—hammers, rocks, ashtrays, or anything else that came to hand in a murderous moment. One didn't often find depressed fractures in falls onto flat surfaces.

One did, however, occasionally find them in falls directly onto edged or pointed objects.

Which is what Merrill concluded had happened. "His head must have struck something when he fell—something in addition to the paving, I mean. Would there have been any relatively small objects lying on the ground that his head might have hit? Rubble, rocks . . . ?"

"I never did see the body in place, so I don't know exactly where it landed," Gideon said, "but yes, there was a lot of stuff lying around in the passageway: tools, construction material, pottery shards—"

"Well, there it is, then. It might have been anything: a rock, or . . ." He paused, seeing Gideon's scrutiny growing more intense. "I say! You can probably tell what it was from the shape of the wound, can't you?" he asked eagerly. Merrill was something of a fan of Gideon's, and had been from the first, having earlier read several of his papers in the *Journal of Forensic Sciences* and some of the more sensational articles in the general media about his work with skeletal remains. And so he tended to expect more than Gideon could always deliver.

"Well, sure, sometimes you can," Gideon said, shaking his head, "but this one? I don't know, it's not a very well-defined imprint. Doesn't look like anything to me at this point. No, I wasn't looking at the depressed part, I was looking at the fracture pattern around it, trying to make out . . ."

His voice faded away, as it frequently did when he was studying bones or thinking about them. And there was something about this one that intrigued him. Sometimes the impacting force of whatever had caused the depressed fracture stressed the surrounding bone enough to create a network of radiating cracks around the depression, and that was what had apparently happened with Joey. The depressed fracture itself was an irregular disk of bone, no more than an inch across, and driven only a couple of millimeters below the rest of the skull, but it lay in a spiderweb of cracks that ran jaggedly off in every direction, over much of the skullcap; the calvarium, as it was known. But unless he was mistaken . . .

Merrill had waited politely for a minute while Gideon stood unmoving, then for a second minute, and then exchanged a what-in-the-world-is-the-man-doing look with Rajiv, who shrugged.

Merrill coughed gently. "I say, Gideon, I'd certainly like to see what the situation is inside the braincase. I have to remove the calvarium anyway. Why don't I just separate it and give it to you to examine at your leisure while I scoop out the brain, don't you know?"

Pathologists, Gideon had noticed, were often in a hurry

to get through the skeletal architecture, feeling that the "real" information was going to come from the internal organs and structures. Anthropologists, naturally enough, saw it the other way around.

In any case, Merrill's offer suited Gideon just fine, and he was quick to agree. "You'll make sure you don't cut through any of the fracture lines, though?"

Merrill sighed and looked at him.

"Sorry, sorry," Gideon mumbled.

Merrill held out his hand, into which Rajiv plunked most pathologists' instrument of choice for skullcap removal: the Stryker saw, a vibrating saw with a small, semicircular blade that oscillated in a narrow arc of about twenty degrees. This limited action ensured that the blade would not cut through to any soft tissue, "such as," Merrill had laughingly told him last time, "the pathologist's hand."

Gideon stepped back again, keeping well clear of the mist of bone tissue that the saw threw up as it circled the outside of the brain case, deeply scoring it. Once that was done, the saw was replaced by a small hammer and a narrow chisel, and then by a miniature pry bar, with which the top part of the skull was delicately pried away from the bottom. For the first time, Gideon closed his eyes, preferring not to watch. If he could have gotten away with it, he would have stuck his fingers in his ears as well, to avoid the sucking sound that came when the top of a skull was pulled off.

When he opened them, the rounded calvarium was on the table near Joey's head, interior side down, and a concerned Merrill was frowning at him.

"Is anything wrong?"

"Uh, wrong? No, I just had something in my eye. It's okay now."

"Good. Would you like me to scrape the dura off, so you can have a look at the underside as well?"

The dura—the dura mater—was the outermost layer of

the brain coverings—the meninges—and when the brain
was removed it remained behind, stuck to the inside of
the skull, making it impossible to see the skull's interior
surface.

"No, don't," Gideon said. "The calvarium's really frag-
mented. I'm afraid the dura is all that's holding it together.
Anyway, it's the outside I'm interested in."

"Yes," said Merrill, "mm, ha, look at that. Well, now.
My word." He was now as absorbed by Joey's naked, glistening brain as Gideon had been by the skull, and why not,
Gideon thought. Who was he to shake his head in amazement at someone who got enthusiastic about prodding with
a finger—an ungloved finger—into a bloody brain? There
were plenty of people who had a hard time seeing what it
was about bones that so fascinated *him*.

"Wilson?" Gideon said. "Would there be someplace I
could go with this?"

The question was met with raised eyebrows. "You don't
want to stay on for the rest of the autopsy? But we've
hardly begun."

"Oh, well, yes of course I do, I'd love to, but I only have
a limited time, unfortunately. I do need to get back, so I'd
better get on with looking over these fractures. And, really,
I'm afraid I'll be underfoot here. You don't have that much
room. And it would be better if I could examine it someplace quiet, maybe sitting down somewhere."

It was overkill for a simple request, and Gideon feared
that Merrill might read it for what it was—a lame attempt
to get the hell out of the autopsy room—but all he could
make out on the pathologist's face were disappointment
and surprise, both of which were manfully overcome.

"Certainly," he said. "Rajiv, take Dr. Oliver to the specimen room. He can use the table there."

Placing the calvarium on a towel, Rajiv led Gideon a
couple of doors down the hall to a tiny room that stank
even more of formaldehyde, and with good reason. The

shelves that ran around three of the walls were loaded with specimen jars filled with various organs in cloudy formalin, some floating, some sunk to the bottom, some hanging on strings. But specimens in jars, well-separated as they were from their owners' bodies, didn't bother Gideon, and he had no trouble concentrating on the cracked, ivory-colored dome in front of him.

Without a word, Rajiv smilingly handed him a set of gloves, and Gideon smiled his gratitude in return.

"Well, Joey," he said softly, as Rajiv pulled the door shut behind him, "let's see what you have to tell me."

At that, he smiled. Maybe Julie was right. Maybe he *did* talk to bones.

In a way, it was worse than that, because this particular one was talking back to him.

TWENTY

CLAPPER yawned and stretched. It had been a long afternoon and little had come of it. He was feeling grungy and depleted. Grumpy, too; not wanting to violate Kozlov's no-smoking policy, he'd had but one fag since noon, when he'd run outside for a quick break; half a fag, actually. He reassured himself by touching his breast pocket to make certain they were still there. He was on his last interview of the day; in twenty minutes he'd be leaving and lighting up in the fresh air.

"Mrs. Bewley," he called into the kitchen, "if we could have a fresh pot of tea, love, that would be grand."

This being the third pot he'd requested, she was ready for him, and in she bustled with the pot, several cups, and the associated paraphernalia. She set them down on the table as quickly as she could, cleared the earlier service away, and hurried back to the kitchen as if worried that the sergeant might clap the cuffs on her if she stood still long enough to give him the chance.

Clapper poured himself a cup, added milk, sipped the

fortifying liquid gratefully, and closed his eyes. With the consortium proceeding upstairs in the Victorian lounge, he was conducting his second day of interviews in the Star Castle dining room, a big, irregularly shaped (everything in this old place was irregularly shaped) space walled with the unplastered, unpainted, rough-cut granite blocks that made up the castle's exterior. He was sitting at a linen-covered table before an ancient, soot-blackened stone fireplace, with a cavalier sword and a musket leaning against it on either side, and a rusty old saber hanging from the mantel. Above the table was a medieval-style chandelier made from a hammered ring of black metal and fitted with candle-shaped bulbs, and on the walls were metal sconces, also with bulbs shaped like candles. He had been told that the room had been the original sixteenth-century officers' mess, and he had no trouble believing it. If not for the electric bulbs, he thought, he might have been back in the fifteen hundreds right now.

Not his cup of tea, Clapper thought—he had little interest in the past—but certainly highly atmospheric. A good place for deeds sinister and foul.

At the sound of footsteps he opened his eyes to see Vasily Kozlov, who had left the table a few minutes ago, come bouncing back in, fresh and sprightly in his sandals, shorts, and crisp, bright T-shirt, and brandishing a sheet of paper.

"Got it right here!" he declared, sitting back down. "Ah, tea!" He dropped four sugar cubes into a cup, poured hot tea over them, stirred, and swallowed half a cupful.

"You found the fax, then," Clapper observed.

"Sure, right in file." Kozlov slid it over to him.

Clapper aligned the sheet and read:

To: Vasily Kozlov
Fax: 1720 422343
Sender: Edgar Villarreal

Vasily:

It will come as no surprise to you that my stay in St. Mary's was not the most pleasant or enlightening time I have ever had. I have no intention of wasting another week of my life two years from now, so I hereby withdraw from the seminar (or consortium, or Three Stooges convention, or whatever the hell you call it).

Obviously, this means I will not receive the $50,000 stipend, and frankly, my dear, I don't give a shit.

Edgar Villarreal

"I'm beginning to see why he wasn't the best-loved man in the world," Clapper mused aloud, placing the fax on the table.

"He not such good fellow," Kozlov agreed.

The body of the message was computer-printed, and the logo above it said "The Mail Cache, 3705 Arctic Boulevard, Anchorage, AK." The time stamp at the top said "06/08/03, 14:47" and gave the shop's fax number. That was everything. Clapper hadn't expected much to come of it, and he'd been right. If Kozlov had come back saying that he was unable to find it, that it was inexplicably lost, well, that might have been something to think about; but here it was. And it proved nothing, disproved nothing. Gideon was perfectly right: anyone could have sent it.

"May I keep this?" Clapper asked.

"Of course."

"Did you reply?"

Kozlov shrugged. "For why?"

"I understand. And you never heard from him again?"

A shake of the white, wild-haired head. "Never."

Clapper sipped at his tea but found the cup empty. He removed the cozy from the pot, offered to serve Kozlov, who declined, and poured himself a fresh cup with milk.

"Well, then, Mr. Kozlov, let's go on to something else. Another question or two and we'll be done." He pulled his notepad around to write on it. On the open page he'd already drawn a diagram of the guest room layout on the second floor. "I'd like to know who was staying in which room."

"Sure." He raised his eyes to the beamed ceiling and began to count off on his fingers. "In Sir Henry Vane Room is Lizzie. In John Biddle Room is Victor. In Duke of Hamilton Room is Julene and husband. In—"

Clapper crossed out the names he'd already written and put down his mechanical pencil. "No, those are the rooms they're staying in this year. I meant two years ago. Where did they all stay then?"

"Oh, where they was staying *then*," Kozlov said. "Let me think." He thought. He shrugged. "Who knows?"

"You don't remember?"

"Nope."

"What about you? Were you living on the floor above then, too?"

"Sure, this where I live."

"But as for the attendees, you have no record of where they were?"

"For why I shall keep such records as this?"

"Mr. Moreton, would he know?"

"No. He was working for me since this year only."

Clapper slipped the notepad and pencil into his pocket, already tasting the Gold Bond he'd be lighting up inside of two minutes, already feeling the cool, corky filter-end against his tongue.

"Well, not to worry," he said, "we'll ferret it out."

"AH, back, are you?" Merrill said brightly, glancing up from what had once been Joey Dillard but now looked like a gutted deer carcass. His scrubs bore the unappetizing effects of his work. (Gideon's were as spotless as when he'd put them on.)

"Well, it's pretty much as we thought," the pathologist

said, cheerfully wiping his hands on a towel provided by Rajiv. "Let me show you exactly what we found."

Which he did. First, the shattered orbital roofs, now visible from above with the skullcap gone and the dura stripped from the base of Joey's emptied cranium. "The result of contrecoup forces, no possible doubt about it."

"Looks like it," Gideon agreed. As they'd thought, it had been these fractures that had emptied blood into the orbital sockets and caused the massive black eyes.

Then, to a specimen jar on the nearby counter in which Joey's brain was already suspended in formalin to solidify the tissue (the natural consistency of the human brain, as one of Gideon's early anatomy professors had accurately but unfortunately pointed out, wasn't all that different from that of Jell-O) so that it could later be sectioned.

"As you can plainly see," Merrill said, "the frontal lobe shows the effects of those same forces. Massive trauma. Pulped right up to and beyond the anterior ascending rami of the lateral cerebral fissures. But in the back, we find that the direct impact of whatever caused the depressed fracture also resulted in severe, if less extensive, coup damage, the contused area involving the left superior parietal lobule and extending partway into the occipital lobe. So we have both contrecoup *and* coup injuries resulting from the same event. Not usual, but hardly unheard of. The result of brain 'bounce-back,' generally speaking, but not, I believe, in this case."

He cleared his throat, a long process heralding the coming of the windup. "My working conclusion is as follows: death from massive trauma to the brain resulting from a fall onto the back of the head, complicated by the intrusion of a relatively sharp object that had been lying on the paving— a wayward stone would be as good a guess as any. That's all clear enough, isn't it? Shall I take it out of the jar?"

Gideon's answer was quick. "No, thank you, not necessary."

Truth be told, he was having a hard time telling which

end of the brain in the jar was the front and which was the back, let alone remembering what or where the anterior ascending ramus of the lateral cerebral fissure was. This, he thought, was a good lesson to him. All week he had been explaining away the ignorance of physicians in regard to bones, and although he had gone out of his way to be charitable, in his heart he'd been feeling mightily superior. Well, now he knew that what was true for them was true for him: even the most qualified experts knew only so much. They knew what they were familiar with, what interested them, what they worked with day to day. And to Gideon, who hadn't held a human brain in his hands since graduate school, and who hoped never to do it again, that most definitely did not include the soft and squishy organs of the human interior.

But if Merrill said the brain injuries were thus and so, and covered such and such a surface area, he was certainly willing to accept it. What he was not willing to accept was the pathologist's conclusion.

"I don't think so, Wilson."

Merrill scowled. "Don't think what?"

"I don't think that's the way it happened."

There were a few—a very few—forensic pathologists who enjoyed having their minds boggled, and their hypotheses overturned, and Wilson Merrill was one of them. Apparently, Gideon had lived up to expectations, and he was delighted. "I *knew* you'd say that! I was *hoping* you'd say that! Rajiv, didn't I tell you he'd say that? All right, tell me, what have I gotten wrong?"

Gideon gestured at the skullcap, which he'd placed, still on its towel, exterior side up, on a corner of the instrument table. "There are two separate injuries here, not one."

"Two?" Intrigued, Merrill peered down at it. "Good Lord, with all that disruption, how can you possibly tell? It all looks like one big mess to me."

"No, if you look carefully, you can see two separate

loci. There's the depressed fracture, of course, here on the left parietal."

"Yes, naturally. I see that."

"And here, across the sagittal suture, on the right parietal, about three inches away, is another, separate point of impact with its own set of fracture lines. You see how the bone here broke up in a rough pattern of concentric circles: one, two, three rings"—he traced their shapes with his ballpoint—"in the center of which would be the impact point. And then there are all these linear fractures radiating every which way out of the rings, which is what complicates things."

"By George, yes, I do see," Merrill said. He mused, frowning. "*Two* impact points. Two separate traumatic incidents. Well, then . . . well, then . . ." He looked up into the fluorescent lights for inspiration. "Might he not have somehow struck his head on that broken pipe on the way down—that would be the depressed fracture—and then struck it again when he hit the flat pavement below? Is that what happened, do you think?"

"No."

"No," Merrill echoed. "I didn't think so. You believe, then, that he was struck and then fell. That this is a homicide after all. A murder."

"I believe it's a murder, all right, but it was the other way around."

"The other way around," Merrill repeated, enchanted. "Whatever can that mean, I wonder."

"First he fell," Gideon said. "Then he was struck."

"And you know this . . . how?"

"Look at the cracks," Gideon said. "Look at the way they intersect."

Merrill looked, then jerked his head. "What about the cracks?" he asked, but a bit testily. He'd had his fill of befuddlement, Gideon thought, and was impatient to be enlightened.

"The cracks from the injury on the right, the one with the concentric pattern, go every which way, until they peter out on their own.

"Yes, yes, as you said before."

"But the cracks radiating from the depressed fracture . . ." He paused, wanting to give Merrill a chance to work it out himself, and the pathologist came through with flying colors.

"—are arrested wherever they run into a crack coming from the other fracture!" he cried. "They never continue across them. Of course! A crack can't cross another crack; the energy is dissipated. That means that the other fracture was there first. The depressed fracture came afterward!"

Gideon nodded, as pleased as Merrill was. "Right. He fell from the catwalk—was pushed, would be a pretty good guess at this point—and whoever pushed him came down, found him still alive, or at least thought that he might be, and smashed him in the head again to make sure the job was done."

Merrill nodded, suddenly solemn. "Do you know, I've always hated blunt-force homicides," he said thoughtfully. "A gun, a knife, will kill quickly, but blows—they usually take more than one, sometimes many, many more than one, demonstrating, to me, at least, a horrible, brutal tenacity in the human psyche that I don't like thinking about."

"But in this case there was only the one blow."

"Yes, only one, but imagine what it was like. Young Joey Dillard, lying on the stone, helpless, terribly injured, his head already shattered, and the killer . . . the killer cold-bloodedly . . ."

"I too hate these things," Rajiv declared with feeling.

"I'm not too crazy about them myself," said Gideon, doing his best to block out the picture that Merrill had conjured up for him.

TWENTY-ONE

DESPITE Merrill's promise, he did not arrive back by teatime. It was 5:50 P.M. by the time the helicopter set him down on Holgate's Green, and he immediately telephoned Clapper's private number to bring him up to date on the autopsy, but it was Anna at the answering service that picked up, and she had a message waiting for him.

"Hello, love, the sergeant's just gone out for dinner with his lady-friend, but he said if you get back by six or six-thirty, why don't you come and join him, and bring your wife, if you like? They've gone to the Atlantic Inn. Do you know where it is, love, or do you require directions?"

Gideon did not require directions. He had passed it several times on his way to his morning pasties and coffee at the Kavorna Café: a pleasant-looking old hotel and pub on the main street, right at the foot of the pier. He put in a call to Julie, who was at the nightly cocktail hour in the castle dungeon—it had been canceled the night before on account of Joey's death, but Kozlov had now reinstituted it—and passed along the invitation.

"I'd *love* to!" she exclaimed. "Aren't you dying to find out what Mike's 'lady-friend' is like?"

"What his lady-friend is like? Yes, sure. I suppose so. Sure."

"Men," Julie grumbled.

AS it turned out, however, Clapper's choice of lady-friend surprised—and, on reflection, pleased—both of them. It was, of all people, the bangled, gabby Madeleine Goodfellow, director of the museum, and they heard her before they saw her. She and Clapper were at a table on a little, white-washed terrace in back, looking out over a picture-postcard view of beached fishing boats resting all askew on the sand at low tide, and her jolly cackle of a laugh easily penetrated the buzz of conversation in the restaurant, the click of balls at the pool table, and the whirring of the slot machines.

"It's Madeleine!" Julie said, delighted. "How wonderful! She's just what he needs. She'll be so good for him."

"And I suspect he'll be pretty good for her, too. He's a pretty solid guy, Julie, underneath it all."

Over dinners of oxtail soup, roast beef, and Yorkshire pudding, Gideon explained what he and Merrill had come up with, keeping the more grisly autopsy details to himself in deference to Julie's and Madeleine's sensibilities. Still, the conclusion was clear enough to all: Joey had been thrown from the catwalk (probably) and then bludgeoned (certainly) while he lay on the ground. Murdered.

Sobered, they talked about the two killings for a while, throwing around conjectures—obviously, Clapper had been keeping Madeleine abreast—but by the time dinner was finished, and the men were into their second pints (ginger beer for Clapper) and the women into their second half-pints, they livened up and conversation turned to other matters. Clapper and Madeleine were to be married in the fall and would live, not above the police station, but in a nineteenth-century house on Tresco that had been in Madeleine's family since the 1930s and was now being restored. They would have a view over the famous old Abbey Gardens and out across the Sound toward St. Mary's, from which they would be a mere ten minutes by boat. Gideon and Julie were enthusiastically invited to the wedding and enthusiastically accepted. They clinked glasses—Madeleine's bangles jingled—and talked on and on, until after eleven.

All in all, it was a welcome break from the events of the last few days, and Julie and Gideon were utterly relaxed as they walked back up Garrison Hill to the castle, hand in hand.

"Well, one mystery is solved anyway," Julie said.

"What would that be?"

"Remember when you showed up at the museum reception the other night, straight from the police station, and you were surprised that Madeleine already knew about the bones from the beach?"

Gideon nodded.

"I think I can make a pretty good guess who she heard it from."

"You just might be on to something," Gideon said.

WHEN he awakened the next morning, Gideon was sorely in need of a break. The session at the morgue had taken more out of him than he'd realized, and he wondered once again at Merrill's ability to seemingly draw strength from his gruesome work. He'd suggested to Julie that she might want to play hooky for just one morning and join him, but while she'd obviously been drawn to the idea, she felt that she owed it to Kozlov and the others to be there.

"What's the morning's topic?" Gideon had asked.

"Victor's presenting his paper on . . ." She'd looked at her copy of the program, open on the bed. "'. . . a three-tiered social-constructivist ecological paradigm derived from monistic-subjectivist epistemology, relativist ontology, and genuinely hermeneutic methodology.' God help me."

Gideon stared open-mouthed at her for a moment. "Oh, well, you sure wouldn't want to miss that. Damn, sure wish I could be there."

So he was on his own, which suited him on this particular morning. After breakfast at the Kavorna Café (he'd been coming long enough for the waitress to ask if he wanted "the usual," which he did), he decided to take advantage of the pleasant weather and see some of the island's Neolithic sites.

On a whim he'd inquired about bicycles at the Kavorna and been directed to Buccabu Bike Hire on the Strand. Once there he'd somewhat shamefacedly asked for the least-complicated, easiest-to-operate bicycle they had (it had been a while since he'd been on one).

The clerk smiled knowledgeably. "Know just what you want, mate, got it right here," he'd said, rolling out a one-speed, heavy-bodied Hampton Cruiser with wide tires, coaster brakes, and upright handlebars.

"Will that do you, mate? Just like you had when you were a kid, eh?"

Indeed, it was closer to his old Schwinn than he'd believed possible. "Just what I wanted."

Armed with directions from the shop, he had cycled, only a little unevenly, up Telegraph Road, stopping at the Porthmellon store to pick up a picnic lunch, and then onto a dirt road until he found Bant's Carn and Innisidgen Graves, two well-preserved Bronze Age entrance graves—open, rectangular, half-buried chambers situated at the tops of impossibly green hills, constructed of giant granite slabs, and roofed by huge capstones. With no other visitors at either place, he enjoyed pottering around for a while, but once he'd gone in and out of the chambers, and marveled at the size of the building stones, and wondered at how they'd gotten the massive capstones up there, there wasn't much to do. The graves were empty, of course, having long ago been excavated, and the explanatory plaques, while informative, quickly wore thin in entertainment value. (". . . a substantial mound revetted by a kerb of coursed walling and a partially infilled central chamber of trapezoidal form . . .")

Still, the outing renewed him, body and spirit, and it was in a relaxed and contented frame of mind that he had his lunch of Stilton cheese, hard salami, and French bread sitting atop the Bant's Carn capstone and looking out over the moor toward the islands of Tresco and Bryher.

Half an hour later, having returned the bike, he stopped in at the police station, where he found Clapper and Robb eating sandwiches at Robb's desk, and about to return to Star Castle to continue their poking about.

"There you are, Gideon. Sit down, just the man I wanted to see," Clapper said genially, chewing away on an archetypal English sandwich of soft white bread (crustless and thin as a dime), cucumber, and egg salad, his feet up on the desk and his ankles crossed. "Just how sure are you that those bones in the next room are really Edgar Villarreal's?"

Gideon shrugged. "Pretty sure. Everything points to him. Of course, I've been wrong before—"

"No, not since yesterday, when you were pretty sure it was Pete Williams. Let's not have any false modesty."

"Now wait a minute, Mike, that's not fair. You know I—"

"Easy, easy," Clapper said, laughing, "just having you on a bit, no harm intended. But what do you make of this?" He wiped his fingers and scrabbled unsuccessfully among the papers on the desk until Robb came up with the one he wanted. "You read it to him, lad, it's your work, after all." He went back to his sandwich, talking around the bites. "And very well done, too."

Robb swallowed what he had in his mouth, dabbed his lips with a napkin, and read: "According to Skybus records, Mr. Edgar Villarreal, who had previously booked his ticket to Bristol, did indeed fly from St. Mary's to Bristol on Flight 400, at 8:00 A.M., on 7 June 2003, the final day of the last consortium. It is uncertain how or exactly when he returned to the United States, but on 8 June, at 3:22 P.M., he paid the parking fee for his car, a four-wheel-drive Toyota SUV, at the South Terminal Long-Term Lot at Anchorage International Airport, and exited. It was understood by an estranged sister, Maria Beasley, that he was going straight to his base camp ninety miles east of Anchorage, but she did not personally speak with him. When he failed to return home to Willow, Alaska, at the beginning of August, police were notified. On 4 August, local police visiting his camp found it deserted. The vehicle was not located. Further investigation produced no—"

"All right, Constable, that'll do. What do you think about all this, Gideon?"

"I think it doesn't prove anything at all. Anyone could have taken that flight in Villarreal's name, or picked up his SUV and dumped it somewhere. Why *wasn't* it found at the camp? Did the bear eat that, too?"

"A good question," Clapper said, nodding.

"But the one place where he'd *had* to have been who he said he was, would have been the flight from England to the States, where he'd need to show a passport. And apparently there's no record of his having done that."

"There isn't," Robb said. "I was able to computer-search the manifests of every flight from the UK to the United States from 5:00 P.M. on the seventh of June to noon on the eighth. The name of every person who was at the consortium shows up—except Villarreal's"

Gideon spread his hands. "Well, there you go. Somebody went to a lot of trouble to build a paper trail that 'proved' he was alive. But the one thing he couldn't do was to get Villarreal's name on an international flight." He gestured at the scatter of bones on the table in the cubicle across the hall. "So I'm still betting that's him right there."

Clapper finished his sandwich and stood up. "And I'm agreeing with you," he said. "That's the way I see it, too."

"I'd like to do some more work on the bones this afternoon. Maybe I can come up with something else for you."

"Very good. Kyle and I are off to the castle to irritate the residents a bit more. You can have the station to yourself if you want it."

He did; he had plenty to do. There was a formal inventory and description of the bones to be prepared, and then a careful, bone-by-bone analysis (the tables he'd been waiting for had arrived), with the results written up into a report that Clapper could use later on. And he needed to prepare something for Merrill as well, setting out on paper his autopsy-room conclusions and a rationale to accompany them. Accepting Clapper's invitation to use his office and computer, he first wrote and printed up his findings for Merrill, then took some coffee, prepared earlier by Robb, into the cubicle where the bones were and prepared to get to work on them.

He did so with an unaccustomed sense of guilt, one that had been nagging at him for a couple of days, but which he'd managed to keep more or less at bay. The fact was, in almost every way, his handling of the skeletal analysis so far had been far short of the professionalism he demanded of his students. He'd acted like a raw grad student himself, running off in whatever new direction grabbed his interest. First he'd rushed to find evidence of dismembering; then he'd tried to see if the bones could have been Pete Williams's. Then he'd gotten all caught up in the fruit-picker syndrome and the admittedly thrilling identification of the remains as Villarreal's. And then . . . then he'd lost interest and dropped it; the exciting part was over, and what remained was a lot of measuring, counting, and describing.

Understandable enough in a first-year student, but that just wasn't the way it was done. This was a science, not

some magic act in which you went around pulling one rabbit after another out of the hat to the amazement and stupefaction of all concerned. There was a methodology, an
order to be followed, and the very first, most elementary
steps—laying out *all* the bones, not just the interesting
ones, in their anatomical position and inventorying them—
had yet to be taken. He had made no record of the number
of fragments he had or exactly what they were, because he
didn't yet know himself—after three days with them right
there in front of him on the table. *I'm getting careless,* he
thought gloomily. No, not careless, cavalier. Rules were for
lesser people, students and such, and not for him.

Well, he'd put an end to that line of thinking right now.

Some of the bones were still in their sacks. He got them
all out onto the table, and then by way of penance, started
with the ones that gave him the most trouble when it came
to distinguishing between them and determining right from
left: the thirty-five hand and foot bones. Without a text or a
comparative skeleton it wasn't easy. There was a public library just down the street, and chances were they had an atlas of anatomy he could have used, but what kind of
penance would that have been? Sorting the maddening little bones was frustrating, but because it didn't require anything like coherent thought—it was basically a matter of
comparing bone to bone, nodule to nodule, foramen to
foramen—it untethered and relaxed his mind, allowing it
to float off on its own.

And it was while he was in this drifting, hovering state
that the repugnant thought that had been niggling away at the
borders of his mind broke through his defenses and entered.
Julie had suggested that Joey could have been killed because
he knew who had murdered Villarreal, and the killer had silenced him before he could tell anyone. And Gideon had rejected it because Joey's death had come when everyone still
thought the remains were Pete Williams's, and how could
anyone predict that he, Gideon, would identify them as Vil

larreal's the next day? But now . . . now he realized that there was indeed someone who might have foreseen just that.

A crime of passion, Clapper had called it, and most assuredly it was. But crimes of passion were hardly limited to sexual jealousies, let alone resentments over academic disputes or prima donna status. There were other possible causes. And while the specific cause he was thinking about now was as improbable as it was repugnant, it had to be looked into. If nothing else, it was the only thing—the only thing he'd thought of so far—that might conceivably explain Joey's murder.

The skeletal inventorying had waited this long; it could wait a little longer. He put down the left cuneiform bone he'd been holding in one hand and the ballpoint he'd had in the other, and went to Robb's computer but didn't have the password to access the Internet. Instead, he locked up the station and walked a block down Garrison Lane to the little public library—the Scillies' one and only—where he plunked down five pounds for an hour's Internet access at one of the two computers. He brought up the ProQuest search engine, typed in "Selway-Bitterroot AND Villarreal AND grizzly OR grizzlies," clicked to sort the results by date, and waited while seventy-five references scrolled down the page. The last one, the oldest, was the one he wanted, and he brought it up.

CANADIAN COUPLE KILLED, PARTIALLY EATEN BY GRIZZLY

Bill Giles
The Associated Press

Selway-Bitterroot Wilderness, MT—In a horrific incident at Lost Horse Creek campground, on the Idaho–Montana border about forty miles southwest of Missoula . . .

TWENTY-TWO

WHEN the Fellows of the Consortium of the Scillies reconvened after a late lunch, they were surprised to find Sergeant Clapper awaiting them in the Victorian lounge, seated on the piano bench, his back to the upright piano.

"I'll take but a minute of your valuable time," he said convivially, as they placed themselves on the red, overstuffed chairs. "I wanted to inform you that the premises of Star Castle will be examined again this afternoon. Is that all right with you, Mr. Kozlov?"

"Me? Sure. What I got to hide? Just don't break nothing."

"Very well, then—"

Donald Pinckney's forefinger went up. "Do you mean you'll be searching *our* rooms again, Sergeant?"

"Yes, I do."

"*Again?*" Rudy Walker said. "You've already gone through all our things once."

"Yes. It's not that pleasant to have someone pawing through your personal things, you know," Donald said. "I mean, well, my wife doesn't appreciate having some stranger . . ."

Clapper's eyebrows drew together. "I don't expect anyone will be interfering with your wife's personal things at this time. Or yours, either."

"Oh, I see" Donald said, quick to show that he wasn't objecting, not really. "It's just a sort of general search, then. For clues and things."

"Exactly."

"Oh, well, that's all right, then."

Not with Victor Waldo. "Look, I understand this is Vasily's house, but as his guests, don't we have some rights to privacy? I ask as a matter of principle."

Clapper waited to see if there were other protestations. When none came, he said: "Yes, sir, of course you have rights, and those rights have been observed." He held out a folded sheaf of papers. "I have here a search warrant authorized by the magistrate in St. Mary's this morning, applicable to all rooms in the house, including those occupied by guests. You're welcome to examine it."

"No, of course not, there's no need for that."

"Don't you have to have specific cause in order to get a search warrant?" Liz Petra asked. "I know we do in the States."

"Yes, we certainly do."

He could see that Liz and several others were on the edge of demanding to know his cause, but no one had the nerve to ask. He waited a moment longer and then said, "I must request that no one enter his or her room again until the room has been examined."

"Oh, brother," Liz grumbled. "That's really a pain."

"It should be much quicker than yesterday's search," Clapper assured her. "I expect we'll be done by dinner. Oh, and should any of you wish to be present in your room during the execution of the warrant, you may do. Anybody?"

Nobody took him up, although for a moment Liz and Victor seemed close to it.

"Very well, then—" he began again, and again he was interrupted. This time it was by Robb, who came in to tell him that the crime-scene examiner that he had requested from Exeter had arrived and would like to begin as soon as was convenient.

"Well, then," Clapper said with evident enthusiasm, placing his hands on his thighs and pushing himself up, "shall we get on with it?" He tipped an invisible hat to the attendees. "Do enjoy your afternoon."

THE librarian at the reference desk, a disciplinarian of the old school, looked up sharply and with a pencil to her lips sternly motioned to silence the large American gentleman at the computer.

"Ah, no," he had murmured.

ANYONE seeing Gideon Oliver trudging up Garrison Hill toward Star Castle might have wondered if his feet were bothering him. Indeed, he was literally dragging them, scuffling along with his shoulders hunched and his hands in his pockets, unhappy to know what he now knew, reluctant to do what he now knew had to be done.

As he walked under the carved "ER 1593" he heard voices and clinking—cups on saucers, forks on plates— from above. He looked at his watch: three-thirty. The members of the consortium were starting their afternoon tea on the lawn atop the ramparts. He climbed the stone steps to find them just arranging themselves in plastic lawn chairs, most of them balancing cups and saucers in their hands or on their thighs, and some managing to deal with a pastry as well. Behind them, Mr. Moreton, very proper in tie and coat, manned the bar, which was set up with tea and coffee things.

Julie lit up and waved when she saw him. "Hi, sweetheart, come on over." She was sitting in a little group with Liz and Kozlov. Near them Victor, Rudy, and Donald formed another conversational clump, along with Mike Clapper, who was demurely sipping his tea—pinky extended—while sitting atop one of a pair of stubby, seventeenth-century cannons set out on the lawn. A little further away in a group of their own, Cheryl Pinckney, not off tooling around on her motorcycle for once, was working her feline, high-cheekboned magic on Robb and was having some success, judging from his rigid, uneasy posture and his bright pink face.

Gideon pulled up a chair beside Julie and sat down heavily.

"Not having anything?" Liz asked.

"Have some tea!" Kozlov amiably commanded.

"No, thanks, I really don't want anything."

Julie's brow wrinkled. She brought her head closer to his and lowered her voice. "Is something wrong?"

"No, not wrong," he whispered. "Not exactly. I have to talk to Mike, that's all. There's—"

"So, Sergeant," Kozlov boomed, bringing the other conversations to a halt, "the searching shall have been finished?"

"Oh, yes, it's done," Clapper said pleasantly. "We won't have to bother you lot any more."

"And you find what you looking for?"

Clapper smiled. "I believe we did, yes, as a matter of fact."

What do you know, he's figured it out, too, Gideon thought. He hoped it was true, because it meant that it wasn't going to be up to him, Gideon, to rat on anyone after all, a duty he was dreading. His stiff shoulders relaxed a bit. He began thinking that a cup of tea might be a good thing.

"Good, good," Kozlov said, "you make progress."

"Oh, yes," Clapper boomed genially on, his voice carrying well on the soft, warm air, "we should have it all sorted out pretty soon now. I have to clear up a few minor areas of inconsistency, that's all."

"Inconsistency?" Donald asked after a few seconds of silence that was very definitely pregnant. "Are you referring to our interviews with you?"

"Yes, as a matter of fact. Minor things, really, but—"

"Well, this would be a good time to resolve them, wouldn't it?" Rudy asked. "We're all here."

"Oh, I don't like to intrude on this splendid tea."

Like hell you don't, Gideon thought.

"Is okay, is good, is interesting," Kozlov said. "What kind inconsistency?"

"Well, all right, then. It's a simple matter of room assignments at the first consortium two years ago." Hatless but otherwise in his casual summer uniform of white short-sleeved shirt and blue trousers, Clapper looked crisp and robust. He lifted the flap of his breast pocket, took out his mechanical pencil and notepad, licked the point of the pencil, and pretended to study the diagram he'd drawn earlier.

"Now let me see . . . Mister Waldo, you stated that you and Mrs. Waldo were in the Sir Henry Vane Room. . . ."

Waldo colored slightly at the mention of his wife, but nodded. "That's correct."

"Mrs. Oliver, you were in the Sir John Wildman Room; and Ms. Petra, I believe you said you were staying in the Duke of Hamilton Room. Mr. Walker, the John Bastwick Room."

Nod, nod, nod.

"Very good. To continue—"

"Wait a minute," Donald said. "I'm pretty sure Cheryl and I were in the John Bastwick Room." He frowned. "Weren't we? Isn't that what I told you?"

"That is what you told me," Clapper said, pretending to scrutinize his drawing again, and then raising his head to level his gaze at Donald, "and therein lies the source of my confusion. I rather doubt that the three of you were lodged together."

"Of course we weren't," Rudy said primly. "Donald, if

I'm not mistaken, you two were in the John *Biddle* Room."

"The hell we were," Cheryl said, turning her attention from Robb. "We were in the John Bastwick Room. Joey was next to us in the Marianus Napper Room, and you were on the other side of him, in the John Biddle Room, down at the end of the hall."

"That's right," Liz said. "I remember, too."

"So do I," Julie said. "Definitely."

"Was I?" Rudy shrugged. "That's not what I remember, but maybe I was. Too many Johns around here, I guess."

"Actually, Mr. Walker," Clapper said gravely, setting his tea down on the lawn and rising from the cannon, never taking his eyes from Rudy, "it's quite a significant point, I'm afraid."

Rudy wasn't laughing anymore *"What's* a significant point? What the hell difference does it make which room I was in? What's this all about? What are you trying to do?"

Clapper just kept gazing at him, as did the others now. The silence on the ramparts was profound. There was no sound but the soughing of the breeze.

"What's going on here?" Rudy blurted, looking now at Robb, who had gotten up and was slowly approaching him. "What's the difference? I forgot my room, that's all. I didn't kill anyone, you know, I just—"

"Yeah, you did," Gideon said. He hadn't meant to; it had just popped out. And he'd said if softly, mostly to himself, but in the silence everyone heard it.

"Yeah," echoed Clapper with what he must have thought was an American twang, "you did." He glanced at Robb. "Constable?"

Robb placed himself directly in front of Rudy, face to face, and stood tall. "Rudolph James Walker, you are under arrest for the murder of Edgar Villarreal. You do not have to say anything, but it may harm your defense if you do not mention when questioned something which you later rely on in Court. Anything you do say . . ."

TWENTY-THREE

GIDEON spent the following two hours at the police station, first talking briefly with Clapper and then, at his request, making out a deposition on Robb's computer. Meanwhile, three or four yards away, behind the closed door of the interview room, Rudy went through the lengthy English booking process. When the door opened for Robb to bring in coffee and sandwiches, Gideon got his first look at Rudy since the arrest. He was seated behind one of the two tables, gray-faced and rigid, and Gideon thought at first that they'd put him in some kind of white prison uniform, but then realized it was a paper suit. Did they think he was a suicide risk, then, dressing him in paper to be sure he had nothing that could be used for a ligature?

My amusing, irreverent old buddy in a paper suit to keep him from killing himself. Gideon shivered. Their eyes met, and Rudy sent him a smile, but it was like getting a smile from a corpse. When the door closed Gideon still seemed to see it, like a Cheshire-cat afterimage, and it sent what felt like a jet of ice-cold water up his spine and deep into his skull.

That's it, he thought. *Time for me to get out of here.* There was plenty left to be done—he had yet to properly inventory and record the bones—but there was no reason it couldn't wait until tomorrow. He printed up the deposition, signed it, gave it to Robb, and told him he'd be back the next day to finish up. Then he walked up the hill to the castle, trying to sort out his feelings. Contributing to the conviction of a two-time murderer; that was good. Helping put one of his oldest friends—at a difficult time in his life, his dearest friend—away for the rest of his life, not so good.

He found Julie on a bench at the top of the path, just outside the castle walls, staring out to sea and looking as pensive and down in the dumps as he was.

"Hi, sweetheart," she said vacantly as he sat down beside her. "What's happening at the station? Is Rudy admitting anything?"

"Don't ask me. I was all by myself writing my deposition. Rudy was in the next room being interrogated. Nobody told me anything." He took her hand. "What about you, Julie, how are you holding up? This has been a hell of a conference."

"Oh, I'm all right, I guess. I'm out here because I just couldn't bear to be in there"—a tilt of her head toward the walls looming behind her—"with them anymore. Isn't there someplace we can go to get away from them, and from the castle, and everything else, just for a while?"

He thought for a moment. "I think so, yes. Only a few miles away, but out of sight anyway, and far removed in time, if not in place."

"That sounds mysterious."

He stood and pulled her to her feet as well. "Come on."

They borrowed Kozlov's boxy, ancient Hillman Minx ("Not forget. Drive on wrong side.") and drove north to

Bant's Carn, one of the Bronze Age grave mounds he'd been at earlier in the day. As before, the hilltop site was deserted. When they climbed up onto the grave's monumental capstone and sat, legs hanging over the edge, they had it all to themselves: the ancient site itself, the rolling green and purple countryside that fell away from it, the sunset view of sea and islands, the fresh marine breeze with its trace of heather and gorse. They had stopped at Porthmellon for a bag of Maltesers, and it lay open now between them. Julie slowly rolled a malted milk ball around her mouth (she was a sucker, he was a chewer), already looking more relaxed, and for a few minutes, and a few malted milk balls, they sat in tranquil silence.

"This is good," she said, waving a hand to show that she was talking about the setting and not the Malteser she was working on. After another few moments, she said, "So, are you going to tell me what made you so sure it was Rudy? Were you and Mike working together?"

"No. I was surprised when Mike accused him. I still don't know what his reasoning was." He pulled his legs up under him and sat cross-legged. "But speaking for myself, I think the idea was in my head for a couple of days, although it didn't really hit me until this afternoon." He hunched his shoulders. "I guess I didn't want to face it. Actually, it started with something you said after they found Joey's body."

"Something *I* said?"

"That's right." She had wondered, he reminded her, if it was possible that Joey might have known what had really happened to Edgar, but, for whatever reason, had kept his silence as long as no one else knew. But once it became evident that Gideon was on his way to identifying the bones as Edgar's, Joey's continued existence became a huge risk to the murderer. So—

"And you said?" said Julie.

"Excuse me?"

"When I came up with this brilliant idea, which eventually solved the case, apparently. You said . . . ?"

Gideon chewed on a mouthful of chocolate and malt. "Well, I don't know, the chances are, I said it was a little unlikely, because of course it was."

She shook her head. "No, sir, you said it was *impossible.*"

"Well—"

"You said, 'uh-uh,' plain and clear. Not 'maybe,' not 'possibly,' not 'unlikely,' just plain 'uh-uh.' Period. And I quote."

"Okay, maybe I was a little, um, emphatic," Gideon admitted, "because—"

"A *little*!"

"—because at the time I thought: How could anyone possibly know I was going to identify the bones as Edgar's, when I didn't know myself? But it *was* a good idea, Julie, and it stuck with me, even if I didn't have the brains to realize it. Then today it all came together."

"What came together?" She had lain back on the flat rock and was watching the low, cottony clouds scud by. He lay back to join her, his hands folded on his abdomen.

"Okay, what it was that struck me today, while I was working with the remains at the station, was that there *was* one person who knew I was going to figure out it was Edgar before I knew it myself. And that was Rudy. He was the one guy with a background in physical anthro, and he was as familiar with that fruit-picker paper as I was, because our old major prof made it the centerpiece of one of the seminars."

"All right, but I'm not following you," Julie said. "How could he know who it was before you did? That is—"

"Because he *already* knew who it was—"

"Of course. Obviously, since he was the one who killed him. But what I meant was, how could he be so sure *you* were going to figure it out? How could he even know you had the right bones to do it?"

"That's easy. I told him. I told everyone. At the museum

reception, remember? I said Robb had come back with the scapulas, among other things, and I was going to be examining them the next day. Smart, huh?"

"Oh, well, how could you know?" She sighed and closed her eyes. She was getting sleepy.

"Anyway, to be on the safe side, Rudy had to assume that I wasn't about to miss all those specialized characteristics, or fail to put them together with the supinator crest and the squatting facets, and come up with fruit picker, loud and clear. And from there it wasn't exactly a giant step to determining it was Villarreal."

"Okay, that make sense. But it doesn't exactly prove he murdered Joey."

"Not prove; suggest. But it was more than enough to start me on a different tack, following up on something else that'd been niggling away at me. So I went to the library to do some checking. You remember Mary Borba?"

Her eyes remained closed, but her brows drew together. "Mary Borba . . . yes . . . weren't we just talking about her? Oh, I remember, wasn't she the girl eaten by the bear in Montana? She and her husband? You were the one who remembered their name."

"That's the one. But there was something else I thought I remembered about the name, so I got on the Web and looked up what I could find about the incident. And I was right. Her name was Mary Walker Borba."

"Mary Walker Borba," she repeated sleepily. Then her eyes popped open and she pushed herself onto her elbows. "Walker! Was she related to Rudy?"

"She—"

"Oh, my God!" Julie sat all the way up, her black eyes intent. "When you were asking him about his daughter . . . you said 'Mary.' Was she . . . was she . . ."

"Yes."

"But are you sure? Mary Walker's not exactly an unusual name. There must be—"

"No." He sat up beside her, shaking his head. "First of all, the original article mentioned that her father was an ecologist, and then some of the later ones identified him by name, and by the school he was teaching at in Canada. No, that was her, the sweet little five-year-old I remembered from Wisconsin."

"How terrible."

"Obviously, it completely changed the way he thought about the world. Six months later was when that piece in the *Atlantic* came out, where he pretty much said the hell with the animals, the important thing is to make wilderness safe for human beings. And as for Villarreal, remember, he was the one who'd pushed them into bringing the grizzlies back in the first place. Rudy would have seen him as responsible for her death."

"Well, he was, really. In a way." She reached absently toward the Malteser bag, but changed her mind and brought her hand back. With her arms wrapped around her knees she stared out across St. Mary's Sound, toward Tresco and Bryher, which were quickly turning golden as the evening came on. The windows of unseen houses, caught by the lowering sun, winked at them. "And then Edgar was so callous about the killings, even back then. What was it he said?"

"He said they were 'unfortunate.'"

"'Unfortunate,'" Julie echoed, shaking her head.

"And then, later, at the talk at Methodist Hall, according to what Liz and Joey told us, he said it was their own fault, that the Borbas were stupid people. He said—"

"He said the only thing he regretted was the killing of the bear. Oh, God, can you imagine the way Rudy felt? Gideon, do you think he came here planning to kill him?"

"I doubt it. I don't think he would have made a public show of how much he disliked him if he was planning to do him in. No, I'm guessing that he'd been simmering for years, and those last remarks of Villarreal's just sent him over the edge. It's hard to blame him. For going over the edge, I mean."

"But why would he have come back this year? Don't you think he would have stayed as far away from St. Mary's as he could?"

"Well, first of all, he thought he was completely safe. Even the police believed Villarreal had been eaten by a bear, months later. Second, there's that $50,000."

"Mm." The glitter from the windows had died out now. The islands were wrapped in evening haze. The sun had sunk below the horizon, and the bright blue water now had dull streaks of mauve spreading across it. "And you think Joey actually knew about it? Why wouldn't he have said something before?"

"I have no idea. But whatever he knew, it got him killed, too. By Rudy."

She nodded. "The Theory of Interconnected Monkey Business does not lie."

"That's pretty much it," he said, smiling. "Not exactly courtroom-ready, but maybe Mike knows more about that end of it. At this point, I have no idea what he knows or doesn't know. I don't even have a clue as to what made *him* decide it was Rudy."

"Well, you can ask him in half an hour. Madeleine called just before you showed up. Mike expects to have things wrapped up for the day by nine, and we're invited up to his apartment for a late supper."

"Let's head back then. I'd like to clean up first."

Julie peeked into the Malteser bag. "One . . . two . . . there are five left. How do we split 'em?"

He smiled. "I'm sure we'll work it out on the way."

"I get to hold the bag," she said.

TWENTY-FOUR

"AS a matter of fact," an animated Clapper said, gesturing with his fork as he talked around a mouthful of fried eggs, "what finally did the trick was something *you* said the other day."

They were at the dining table in Clapper's dowdy, comfortable, furnished apartment above the police station, enjoying bacon and eggs on thick, chipped, white china that had no doubt come with the furnishings. Earlier, Madeleine, showing a hitherto unsuspected domestic side, had bustled cheerfully about the minuscule kitchen humming Cherubino's arias from *The Marriage of Figaro* in a surprisingly sweet little voice, and had produced four perfect little mushroom-and-cheese omelets, each with a halved grilled tomato and two strips of bacon alongside it. And toast and tea for good measure. All in under ten minutes.

Clapper had spent what must have been an exhausting five hours booking Rudy—a more thorough and extensive process than it was in the States—wading through the related paperwork, and communicating back and forth with headquarters. Now, with the day's reports filed and the log filled out, and with Rudy locked up in one of the two holding cells downstairs (Robb and one of the volunteers were spending the night there), he was as fresh and talkative as Gideon had yet seen him, the words tumbling out of him like quarters out of a slot machine.

Gideon looked up from sawing through a strip of thick English bacon. "Something I said? And what was that?"

"Do you remember when we were on the beach at Halangy Point, and you were going on about the finer points of dismemberment? About how much blood you get cutting off the arms and legs, and carrying them about, and so on, and how it was usually done in a bathtub?"

"I remember."

"Charming, the mealtime conversations one has in the company of this sort of person," Madeleine Goodfellow said flutily.

"Better get used to it," Julie said. "That's my advice."

"And you were saying how difficult it is to get rid of every trace of blood?" Clapper went on.

"Yes, sure, even ten years later, even if the surfaces are washed down. Luminol will pick up blood at one part per fifteen million."

"Fascinating," Madeleine said. "Do tell us more." They had finished their meals and she was refilling their teacups.

Gideon thought for a moment. "With spectrophotometric analysis of the ammoniac residue, you can even tell how old a bloodstain is, how about that?"

"Fascinating," Madeleine said.

"The trick is not to ask them questions," Julie told her.

"The thing of it is," said Clapper, "once we established that the remains were Villarreal's, and then when Dillard's subsequent death made it clear that everything was linked to the goings-on at the castle, I rang up headquarters and asked for a crime-scene examiner with bloodstain expertise. He arrived this afternoon."

"And that's what the room search was all about?" Julie asked. "He was checking our bathrooms, looking for blood? And he found it in Rudy's—that is, in the room Rudy was staying in last time, the John Biddle Room?"

"Yes, in the grout above the tub, and between the tiles behind the wash basin, and in the crevices at the base of the walls. And not only in the bathroom, but in the bedroom as well, between the floorboards. I can't say I was surprised. I had my suspicions, as we coppers are wont to say."

"Really?" Gideon asked. "You suspected Rudy all along?"

"There wouldn't be another couple of eggs lurking in the pantry somewhere, would there?" asked Clapper plaintively, knife and fork clasped upright in his hands, their bases resting on the table. Oliver Twist again. "And a rasher or two of bacon?"

"Of course there are, my dear," said Madeleine, jumping up, bangles jangling. "Would anyone else care for more?"

Gideon and Julie declined, and Clapper continued. "Not all along, no. But since yesterday I've been virtually certain of it, only I had no evidence. Now, with the blood-stains, I do."

"But what made you think it was him yesterday?" Julie asked.

"Superior police work, my girl," said Clapper jovially. "Learning that the fax to Mr. Kozlov—ostensibly from Mr. Villarreal—originated in Anchorage on the eighth of June, and knowing that the previous consortium had ended one day earlier, I had Kyle run a search for the name of any consortium fellow that might have arrived at Anchorage International Airport on either of those two days. And what do you know, up popped the name of one Rudolph Walker, who had flown from Toronto on the morning of the eighth, having flown to Toronto from London the day before. He stayed five hours, long enough, I should say, to send the fax and to pick up Mr. Villarreal's car and dispose of it somewhere, then catch a 3:00 P.M. flight back to Toronto. That made it close enough to a virtual certainty to satisfy me. And the bloodstains in the room cinched it. So we nicked him."

"Well done, Mike," Gideon said.

"Hear, hear," Madeleine said in the kitchen.

"The blood will go off to a laboratory for DNA analysis, and along with all that you've come up with, Gideon, I should say we'll have a pretty strong case, whether Mr. Walker decides to cooperate or not."

"He hasn't confessed, then?" Julie asked.

"No, and I haven't asked him to. It's early days yet. He's entitled to a legal adviser, you see, and he's demanded one. The problem is that there aren't any solicitors on the island, not a one. I offered him the opportunity to have telephone advice from Penzance, or London, or any place he liked, but he said that wasn't good enough and refused."

"You can't really blame him," said Gideon. "It wouldn't be the same as having a lawyer at your side."

"I don't blame him. In his place, I would have done the same. In any event, he's gotten hold of an experienced solicitor from Truro, but the gentleman isn't available until tomorrow afternoon, so I've put the meat of the interrogation off until then. I want to be very sure I have all my procedural ducks in a row."

Madeleine returned with Clapper's bacon and eggs and put them before him.

"Ah, thank you, love," he said, immediately setting to.

"And what about Joey's murder?" Gideon asked. "Do you have anything to go on that connects Rudy to that? Anything solid?"

"Not yet," Clapper said placidly. "Nothing more than conjecture, but then we've only just begun, you know. Don't even have the autopsy report yet. I'm anxious to see that."

Madeleine seized on the lull in conversation to change

the subject. "What happens to you two now?" she asked Gideon and Julie from the kitchen. "I assume the rest of the consortium has been called off."

"That's because you don't know Vasily," Julie said. "No, we have one more day to go tomorrow, and he's already informed us that he expects us—"

"Those of you still left," said Gideon.

"—to be there. Vasily Kozlov's not the man to have his schedule upset by a murder or two." She accepted another cup of tea from Madeleine. "Thank you. And then on Monday we catch the 1:00 P.M. ferry for Penzance, and the train to London. We fly from Heathrow that night."

"Perhaps we can have dinner tomorrow night?" Madeleine suggested. "Something heartier than eggs and bacon?"

"Absolutely," said Gideon. "Our treat."

"And then we'll see you in October for our"—charmingly, she blushed—"wedding?" Although she was fifty, Gideon knew, this would be her first marriage, so blushes were in order.

"I suspect we'll see them, or Gideon, at any rate, before then," Clapper said. "We'll need him to give evidence at trial."

Having by now put away the last of his second helping, Clapper finally set down his knife and fork. "That was splendid, love," he said to Madeleine, who beamed back at him, then went so far as to dab at a bit of egg beside his mouth with the corner of her own napkin.

"Oh, don't fuss so, woman," he griped, but it was obvious that he was loving it; that they both were loving it. Madeleine kept on digging until the egg came away, while Clapper's happy eyes, raised helplessly to the ceiling, said: *What can I do? The woman is mad about me!*

TWENTY-FIVE

"I love a woman in a uniform," Gideon said, watching Julie come down the steps in her tan shirt and snug olive trousers.

"Lucky break for me," she said, leaning over for a quick kiss, then sitting across from him on the bench at the other side of the picnic table. "I'm starving. What did you get?"

Once or twice a week, depending on schedules and weather, they met for an alfresco lunch on the back lawn of the Olympic National Park's administrative headquarters just outside of Port Angeles, where a picnic table for the staff had been set up in a sunny clearing in a grove of fir trees. Gideon usually brought the food, and today it was fish and chips with Diet Pepsis, from the Landings restaurant down at the ferry dock.

"Great!" Julie said, unwrapping her portion. "This should get me through the afternoon. Is this haddock?"

"Cod. Guess what. Rudy's admitted murdering both of them."

"Yeah, I bet. Are you going to be using your tartar sauce?"

He handed her his packet. "No, really. I got a call from Mike Clapper this morning. Rudy's changing his plea to guilty. On the advice of his barrister."

"You're serious. What brought this about?"

"The marvels of modern science. The DNA results came in on Friday, and when Rudy's barrister saw them, he did an about-face on the innocent plea they had going."

There were two sets of findings, he explained. First, DNA extracted from the blood in Rudy's room matched not only the bones from the beach, but also made a convincing match with a sample from Villarreal's sister, thus establishing beyond any conceivable doubt that a) the bones *were* Villarreal's, and b) the dried blood in Walker's bathroom came from Villarreal as well.

But that had been expected; they'd been preparing for that. What had really turned things around was a second analysis that had been done on traces of blood and tissue found lodged in the links of Rudy's metal watchband.

"They found blood in his watchband?" Julie said. "I didn't know that."

"Neither did I. Neither did Mike, who's pretty much out of the loop at this point."

"That's incredible—that it would still be there after two years."

"No, this wasn't Villarreal's; this was fresh."

A ketchup-dabbed French fry on the way to her lips slowed. "Joey's?"

"Yup. Blood and scalp tissue, both identified as Joey's, based on comparisons with tissue from his mother."

"Wow."

"Wow is right. That did it, as far as the barrister was concerned. Can you imagine trying to convince a jury that these were *not* bits of Joey's head that got dislodged while

Walker was bashing it in with a rock?" He grimaced and peered doubtfully at the piece of fish he'd just broken off. "I think I got a little too graphic for my own good there."

"Much," Julie agreed. "So, did he say what made him kill Joey?"

"Yes, it's all down on paper now, signed and sealed."

"Had he known about Edgar's murder, was that it?"

"Yes," Gideon said, "and no."

He returned to his lunch and continued. Joey had been staying, Julie would remember, in the Marianus Napper Room, which was next to Rudy's room, the John Biddle Room, which was at the end of the hall. Late on the last night of the first consortium, after the squabble with Pete Williams at Methodist Hall and the nightly poker game, according to Rudy, a still-seething Villarreal had banged on Rudy's door, sick of being needled by him all week, and determined to get down to the source of it. Or perhaps he had just needed to vent some more after the Methodist Hall incident, or to argue some more. Whichever it was, their voices were soon raised and Joey, trying to sleep in the next room, had thumped on the wall and told them to keep it down.

They had, but it had done nothing to stem their feelings. Villarreal, of course, couldn't have had any idea of the real reason for Rudy's hatred, or of its passionate depth, or of the danger in which he had placed himself. After it had gone on for twenty minutes or so, and Villarreal had talked one time too many about how people attacked by animals in the wild had nothing but their own stupidity to blame, Rudy had had more than he could stand. He—

"In other words, he's saying that he didn't *plan* to kill him? It just sort of came on him?"

"Yes."

"Do you believe him?"

"I do. At that point he excused himself, went down to the kitchen for a knife—"

" '*Excused* himself'? Strolled downstairs for a knife? How believable is that?"

"Oh, I can imagine Rudy doing it. He's pretty good at not showing his feelings when he doesn't want to. Besides, it doesn't make sense for him to make up something like that. His barrister never would have let him say it if it wasn't true, because it shows premeditation. He may not have planned to kill him in the first place, but if you walk down two flights with the intention of getting a weapon and then walk back up and use it, you can hardly claim you hadn't thought about what you were doing."

"True." She finished her first piece of fish and went on to the second. "Go on."

"Well, he came back upstairs with the biggest kitchen knife he could find, slit Villarreal's throat after first telling him who he was and why he was doing it, and then couldn't stop stabbing him, he says."

Julie looked at her last half dozen fries and decided against them. "I don't know why, but I don't quite have the appetite I thought I did."

"Same here. What do you say we take a walk? The sun's getting hot anyway."

Between the back lawn and the Park Service maintenance yard a few hundred yards away was a shade-dappled path that curved through a bit of Pacific Northwest primeval landscape: fragrant wild blackberries and huckleberries in profusion, ferns, salal, vine maple, Oregon grape, and high above everything the cool, green canopy of the firs.

"Ah, this is better," Gideon said, as they entered. "Smells wonderful in here. So, do you want to hear more?"

"Yes. But no need for additional graphic detail, if that's all right."

"That suits me. Okay, once it was over, he goes back downstairs to the toolshed out back for a hacksaw and a supply of garbage bags, and he spends the rest of the night . . . well, doing what had to be done. Then he takes Kozlov's

car—the key was on a rack in the office—up to Halangy
Point and a couple of other places—he doesn't remember
them all—and buries everything in five or six locations. That
leaves him time to get back, clean up the room and himself,
and catch the ferry with you and Liz in the morning."

She shook her head. "I'm trying to remember if anything seemed different about him in the morning. I really
can't say I noticed anything."

"No, of course not. If people acted different after they
killed someone, the cops would have an easy job of it."

"What about Joey, though? Wasn't Rudy worried about
his having heard?"

"No, not then, because what had he heard? The murder
had been virtually silent, according to Rudy, so all Joey
knew was that they'd argued, which was nothing new."

"And no one knew Edgar was dead at the time," Julie
said, "and when they finally did find out, they thought he'd
disappeared from his camp in Alaska."

"Right. But once enough of the skeleton turned up for
me to come up with the fruit-picker connection, Rudy
knew that was the end of that. It was only a question of
time until the police were all over Star Castle, interrogating
everybody in sight. 'When was the last time you saw Villarreal?' 'Where were you on the night of . . . ?' And so on."

She nodded slowly. "And Joey would have been sure to
say he heard him arguing with Rudy late that last night,
and Rudy couldn't risk their starting to look into that."

"That's it."

A waist-high, moss-covered, fallen trunk blocked their
way and they walked along it until it was narrow enough to
clamber over and return to the path.

"But how could he be sure that Joey was the only one
who heard?" Julie asked. "What about whoever was on the
other side of his . . . oh, that's right, the John Biddle Room.
It was at the end of the hall. No other neighbors. And nobody across the way."

"Right. Only Joey, poor unlucky Joey. He had no idea Rudy'd murdered Villarreal. He didn't know there'd been a murder at all. He died not knowing what he was being killed for."

They walked on for a while without talking, until Julie said: "Gideon, this all must be pretty awful for you, what with Rudy being such an old friend."

"Well, it was at first, I guess, but now I've separated them into two different Rudy's. The one I knew, my old pal Rudy—before Fran died, before Mary was killed—wasn't a murderer. But he doesn't exist anymore."

"But in a way," she offered after a few more steps, "it's not hard to understand how he felt, how terrible it must have been for him to listen to Edgar going on and on the way he did, so smug, so self-righteous. I'm not excusing murder, of course, but, well, in a way, he brought it on himself, didn't he?"

"Maybe," Gideon said softly. "But Joey didn't."

"No." She looked at her watch. "Time for me to get back."

"Me, too, I guess."

All the same, they walked another minute or two until they came to the abrupt end of the path, the chain-link, barbed wire–topped fence that surrounded the maintenance yard and the equipment sheds.

"I do have a question, though," Julie said as they turned back.

"Mm?"

"If Rudy was smart enough to know you'd figure out the bones were Edgar's, why did he kill Joey the way he did? Why wasn't he smart enough to know you'd be able to tell from his skull that it wasn't just a fall, that he'd been murdered?"

Gideon considered the question, then responded with a shrug and the faintest of smiles. "I guess he should have gotten that Ph.D."